Dragonfly

CARRIE SPARKS MCCLAIN

Happy Reading!

Carrie S. McClain

ISBN: 1495215768
ISBN-13: 978-1495215766

Book cover design by Bryan Hufalar – bhphotoart.com
Author's photo by Erin Cassell – photography.erincassell.com

This is a work of fiction. Names, characters, places, and events other than those in the public domain are the product of the author's imagination. Any resemblance to actual persons, living or dead, businesses, or events is entirely coincidental.

To my husband, Clark, the first person to ever call me a writer.
I love you!

ACKNOWLEDGMENTS

My baby girl: I love you more than life. You make each day a bright and shining adventure.

My mother and father: You have often questioned my crazy ideas and wondered where they may lead, but you let me give it a try anyway and learn from my experiences as well as my mistakes. Thank you for letting me fly, and giving me a safety net just in case I should ever fall.

Former WPD Sgt. Jody Westbrooks: Thank you for your willingness to answer my crazy questions at all hours of the day and night, and for talking me through scene after scene. You have been a gem and I'm so glad we have found our friendship once again. Be good to Jessica, always, and enjoy your life together in paradise!

My "First Read" team (Kathryn Crownover, Lori Greer, and Lori Crownover): You have been my support system through the many rough drafts of this book and the continued encouragement I have needed to believe in myself and this dream. I cannot thank you enough!

My editor extraordinaire, Pam Byerly: As truly afraid as I was to have you read, critique, and correct my work, I would not have trusted it to anyone else. You are amazing!

My cover designer, Bryan Hufalar: Your creativity brought so many random ideas to life in a remarkable piece of art and captured my thoughts for the book beautifully. Thank you for your patience.

To the many other family members and friends who have supported this project and given me feedback to help guide me through a new beginning, I sincerely thank you. I have enjoyed every minute.

"True love cannot be found where it truly does not exist,
Nor can it be hidden where it truly does."
- Anonymous

Prologue

The heat of the Tennessee sun barreled down on the teenage face of Aubrey Todd as she rode shotgun with the top down in her aunt's BMW. As they drove over the bridge that crossed Majestic Lake, she breathed deeply the scent of fishy water and fresh cut grass. It was the essence of summertime for her and she wanted the memory to last. She had been able to spend six weeks with her aunt this summer, basking in the opportunity to get away from her parents and their rules for the short amount of time, but the summer was drawing to an end and so was her annual visit to Walker.

Tonight would be her last night in the small country town for this summer and she intended to make it a memorable one by spending the evening with her best friend of almost ten years. As her Aunt Jane pulled the car into the dusty gravel parking lot of the ball field, Aubrey could hear the chants of the onlookers for the next player up to bat. When she was away from home, Aubrey missed the conveniences of the big city shopping malls and eateries; however, she enjoyed small town life at times like these. She gathered her cell phone and the money that her aunt had given her for any snacks or outings after the game and rammed them deep into the pocket of her khaki shorts not to lose them. She heard her golden bangle bracelets jingle a tune as she pulled her hand back out of the pocket and examined the car for anything else she might need to include in the additional compartments of her wardrobe. Finally satisfied that she had everything she would need, she opened the car door and stepped out one tan leg at a time hoping there might be a male onlooker to notice. If she had nothing else, she had her aunt's beauty and loved to turn the boys' heads although her interest in them was not a high priority. This was a notion taken directly from the Jane Todd handbook of life.

Jane was the type of lady who put her career and her family first in her life. All of the other things would have to take their place in line and nothing else was considered important enough to demand her attention. Aubrey had shared in that view. She had been raised by a loving affectionate set of parents, but followed in her aunt's footsteps when it came to goals and her future. Even now at sixteen she didn't see herself married and having a family until she was well into her thirties. She would take a different path from her parents, maybe go on to college and find a job that would allow her to climb the career ladder. She knew she wanted to be near the action of life and to enjoy every minute of it.

"Thanks for the ride, Aunt Jane. Macie will give me a ride home," she said while getting out of the shiny silver foreign car. "We shouldn't be too late."

"Just be careful sweetheart," her aunt said in a smooth tone. "I'll see you in the morning."

"Have a good night," she shut the door then immediately turned around and held up her pointer finger to signal her aunt to wait a moment. "I love you."

"I love you, too, my darling. Have fun!" her aunt smiled with grace and charm. She was beautiful when she smiled, Aubrey thought, as her aunt slowly drove through the gravel parking lot to not disturb the children walking to their games.

Aubrey turned to glance through the sea of young faces running and laughing and adults chatting as they carried folding chairs and snacks. She was looking for that familiar person she held dear, the face of her summertime companion.

"Macie!" she said as she crossed the parking lot raising a hand to wave. "I made it."

"Hi, I'm so glad you are here," Macie embraced her friend with relief on her face.

"So, what is it we have to do?"

"We have to keep the records and the scoreboard for the next softball game. It's Melissa's team and they are paying us four dollars each and all the drinks and burgers we want from the concession stand." Macie took the arm of the content teenager in front of her and turned her in the direction of the colorful jersey clad children.

"That sounds good to me," Aubrey said as they walked toward the cinder block tower behind home plate.

"Go up ahead to the viewer's box and I'll pick up the log book from the concession stand," Macie said.

Aubrey stopped dead in her tracks and turned her head to face her friend, "You didn't tell me he was going to be here."

Macie stared past the kids and the softball gear and saw two handsome teenage boys standing at the edge of the bleachers to the left of the tower. "I didn't know. He must be here with Trey," Macie encouraged her to continue walking to the concession stand by giving her a slight nudge. "Trey's little sister, April, is on the opposite team. Hi, I'm Macie Sanders," she said to the lady at the concessions window, "and I need the log book for the next game."

"Sure, hon. You want a couple of Cokes to take up with you?" asked the bleached blond wife of the ball park owner while she desperately chewed her gum smacking her lips as she blew an occasional bubble. She resembled a waitress from Mel's diner, only with less eye shadow and taller bangs, if that could be possible.

"That would be great, thank you," Macie replied.

She returned with two small paper cups sporting the Coca-Cola logo filled with the dark brown fizzy drink, ice cold, and delicious. She pulled the log book out from under the counter and slapped it down with a pop that startled the group of small boys standing in the circle next to them, "Just find the next blank page and fill it in. The coaches should be up with their line-ups soon."

"Thanks," Macie and Aubrey took the drinks then turned to walk away hoping to avoid the egotistical young men that had caught their eyes earlier.

"Just don't look at him and maybe he won't realize we are here," Aubrey began to walk toward the tower faster than before. Macie followed rolling her eyes.

"Yeah, I think it is too late for that. They are heading this way," she replied.

"Wait up, Sweeney. Decide to get out from behind your books and be seen in public," Jason McNally teased as he jogged to catch up with them stretching his thin t-shirt across well-defined chest muscles.

"What do you want Jason?" Aubrey asked in hostile reply.

"Come on. I just thought I would come over and say "Hello." Is that a crime in this town now?" he chuckled as his rustic blue-green eyes beamed with juvenile charm.

"Macie and I are here to work so I don't have time for your crap," Aubrey said with a sneer on her face turning in an attempt to walk away from him.

"I bet I could put you to work and it would be a lot more fun," Jason narrowed his eyes as she turned back around to face him with disgust. He smirked before giving her a devious wink.

"I'm not impressed and I doubt that anything with you would be much fun," she replied with sarcasm dripping in her voice.

"Try me," he offered.

She leaned forward and looked up into his eyes. "Never!" she said and simply walked away.

Macie shifted her weight from one hip to the other and pursed her lips as she shook her head, "You're never going to break her Jason. Haven't you figured that out?"

"One of these days she's gonna want me. She just better hope that I care when that day rolls around," he said smiling and staring at her as she strutted to the staircase of the viewer's box.

"Whatever. Trey, tell April I said good luck in the game," she said.

"Same to Melissa," Trey replied as Macie turned to join Aubrey.

"That girl is so sexy, Trey. It's too bad her attitude sucks," Jason told his best friend as his vision followed the tucks under her round cheeks that wiggled when she walked.

"Man, you ever think that you bring it on yourself," Trey informed him. "Maybe she just doesn't like you because it's you."

Jason started to laugh and punched Trey in the arm, "Come on, let's go check out some easier babes that appreciate the attention."

***

"Can't you even try to get along with him?" Macie requested of Aubrey as they climbed the concrete stairs.

"Why? He doesn't try to get along with me. His purpose in life during the summer is to pick on me and make me miserable. I'm not going to help him do it," she stomped on each step releasing her frustration.

"Fine. We'll just continue the way we always have. Jason can insult you, you can get mad, he will make some snide remark, and then you will refuse to talk to him until he insults you again and we will start the process all over," as they reached the top of the stairs, Macie made her way over and slammed the book down on the barn wood makeshift table in front of the open window overlooking home plate.

"Now, I'm going to get it from you?" Aubrey accused walking over to the window and examining the freshly drawn lines in the dirt connecting three of the four white padded squares in the shape of a diamond.

"No, it's just been such a pattern for so many summers. I wish you got along better because I've become really good friends with Trey and they are always together. When you are in town, it makes it hard for me to spend any time with Trey," Macie admitted.

"Well, I'll be gone soon and you can have your time with him," she said sitting in the chair to the right of the log book, taking in the smell of the dust as it rolled up from the catcher's squatting position.

"You know I wouldn't trade time with anyone for the time I get with you. Just forget it," Macie said shaking her head. "I should have known better than to try to get a truce between you and Jason McNally," Macie decided to give up the fight and she sat in the seat next to Aubrey. "You feel like a little spin around town after the game?"

"Yeah, that sounds good. How about a drive to Sonic for a suicide slush and then we can head back to Aunt Jane's. We can stay up late and listen to the David Dean radio show. There should still be about an hour and a half left before he signs off for the night," Aubrey suggested.

"It's a date," Macie opened up the log book to the next empty page and heard footsteps scratching up the back of the tower. She turned to find one of the coaches with a small piece of paper in his hand. It was time to play ball.

After nine innings including a home run by April Cashion, Trey's sister, the Eaglettes celebrated a victory over the Ladybugs with a 6-5 score. Melissa and her team had given it a forceful try, but in the end there was a hole in the left field that couldn't be filled when it needed to be and the opposing team discovered a way to use it to their advantage. The girls on each team lined up in front of their dugouts and drifted toward each other with hands outstretched to give a slap and the congratulatory words "Good game" before reuniting with their coaches and discussing the valiant efforts given on the field. With heads hanging, the Ladybugs left the field hearing the encouragement of those in the stands who supported them as the Eaglettes heard the chants of proud admirers from their side of the stands. Both teams would then leave this game behind and begin a strategy for the next game in a week.

Macie and Aubrey made their way back down from the block tower with caution as they wondered who they might find at the bottom of the stairs. Aubrey shed a sigh of relief when she reached the bottom and there were no unwanted boys waiting on them. They dropped off the log book at the concession stand and brushed the dust from their shorts as they made their way to Macie's car.

"Are you packed?" Macie asked as they dropped into the front seats of her midnight blue Impala.

"For the most part, I have everything together, but you can help me finish tonight," Aubrey hated packing to leave Walker. After spending six weeks at her aunt's home she was settled and felt as if she were uprooting herself in order to leave.

"I'll help, but I won't like it. I wish you could stay a little longer. Your visit was so early this year. There is still a lot of time left before school starts," Macie relayed the information as if she hadn't already told Aubrey numerous times during her stay.

"I've got to get back this year. Mom is doing some work on the house and she insists that I be there to help, but I'll call and write," Aubrey replied.

"I know," Macie pulled into the Sonic Drive-In where she was greeted by classmates and acquaintances from the ball park. Aubrey was very reserved with who she made friends with in Walker. It was a way to protect herself when she had to leave at the end of the summer. Macie was the exception, but there were a few others that she had gotten to know over the years. They were always friendly to her when she was with Macie and it became just enough to satisfy her sense of belonging during her stay.

The girls pulled out onto the main boulevard where they followed the teenage trail from Sonic up to the square and then back down to circle the drive-in again. After about an hour of honking horns and hellos, they decided they were ready to turn in for the night and spend every last moment they could together enjoying a little girl time.

As they drove north of town past the practice fields at the lake and out of the city limits Macie noticed headlights that looked familiar, "I think we have company."

"What?" Aubrey leaned forward and turned all the way around to gaze at the car behind them. "Is that Trey and Jason?" she squinted to see past the headlights through the windshield, and struggled to make out the forms in the shadows of the front seat. "I think it is."

"What are they doing?" Macie asked noticing the car was gaining momentum.

"I believe they are trying to catch up with us. Speed up. We can't let them pass," Aubrey coached her.

Macie put her foot down and the car jetted forward in response. Before she realized it, they were blazing down the back country road toward the lake house at 70 miles an hour. She took curves going dangerously fast, but the girls were determined not to let these arrogant mischief makers catch up.

On the straight away of highway 290, only five miles from Dragonfly, Macie gunned the car up to 80 and Trey matched her gutsy move. He pulled up beside them on the wrong side of the broken yellow line and all they could view were the muscular butt cheeks of Jason McNally and the bottom edge of a dark shadow running down his left rib cage as he pulled his shirt up and glanced over his left shoulder eager to see their reaction. Appalled and scared to death at the speed of the chase, Macie finally took her foot off the gas and let the car ease down to a reasonable speed. The boys flew by in the Camero easing on the brakes as they approached the turn onto the road that lead to Jane Todd's lake house. Trey turned left into the driveway and watched in his rear view mirror as Macie turned in behind him. Before Aubrey could unfasten her seat belt and get out of the car, Jason was already at her door opening it for her and putting his hand out to impersonate a gentleman helping her from the vehicle. She smacked at his hand and proceeded to exit the vehicle slamming the door behind her.

"I believe there's a full moon out tonight, Sweeney," Jason said with a tantalizing grin on his face.

"Are you crazy? We could have wrecked," she pushed him back with the palms of her hands on his chiseled chest and her brows furrowed with disgust at the childish actions.

"You scared me to death driving like that, Trey," Macie took her shot slamming the back of her hand into his shoulder.

"Don't act like you know how to drive then," Jason's attention was directed toward Macie as Aubrey raised her open palm. Jason grabbed Aubrey's right wrist in defense before she could hit him. He read in her face that she wanted to badly.

"You are ridiculous Jason. What are you trying to do?" she said as she jerked back her hand losing balance for a moment and stumbling to stay on her feet. She gasped for air to settle her nerves as the rustle of the leaves on the trees surrounding the lake played a late night lullaby high above them.

"I'm trying to get you to loosen up a bit," a serious look floated across his face.

"You sure like playing games don't you," her fear changed to fury as she raised her voice.

"I'm not playing anything," he replied.

"That's it. I didn't want to see your naked backside and I don't want you here. Leave!" she snapped at him.

"Come on down to the lake and you can see a lot more than my backside," he gave her a devious smirk as he had earlier at the ball park and walked toward her reaching out for her waist, pulling her closer to him so he could feel her rapid heartbeat against him.

"In your dreams," she shoved at him loosening his hands from her body. "Get away from me and leave me alone."

"Aww, come on Sweeney. You know you would love it," she turned to walk away from him and then shifted back around for one last shot at his over-zealous ego.

"I'm glad I'll be leaving tomorrow Jason McNally and I swear I'm never coming back," she said.

"You'll be back next summer. You just can't resist," he said as he motioned up and down his body. "Besides you can tell everyone you are messing around with a high school graduate next summer and impress all your city friends."

"Not only can I resist it, but I loathe it," hatred began to fill her hazel eyes. "I'll be back in the city where the boys aren't so ridiculously stupid," the words slipped through her clenched teeth like water through a sieve. "Let's go in Macie, I can't even stand to look at this pathetic excuse of a person anymore."

Aubrey turned and began to walk to the house as Jason reached for her. He wrapped his arm around her waist and drew her back with a bear hug until their bodies lay flat against each other. He bent down slightly to let his breath tickle the skin behind her ear and softly whispered, "Someone must have broken your teenage heart, Sweeney, to make you so pissed all the time." He could not let her have the last word.

"Jason, no one has ever been good enough to interest my teenage heart especially a loser like you. Goodnight, Trey," she nodded her head to Trey and disentangled herself from Jason's arms. She then turned to Jason and mumbled, "useless human being."

She set her path toward the house signaling to Macie and then moving to the front door leaving it propped open as she walked in.

"You just never learn, do you Jason." Macie shook her head slowly. She would now get to hear Aubrey call him every name in the book for the rest of her night.

Chapter One

557 Lakeshore Drive, the home of Jane Elizabeth Todd. Aubrey shook her head slowly from side to side in disbelief that she was now standing at the front door of her Aunt Jane's lake house. She stared for at least fifteen minutes at the worn navy blue door with slightly chipped paint around the bottom edge from the comings and goings of her aunt's loved ones and dear friends. The color popped against the medium gray shaker shingle siding on the house. The pewter antique door knocker was centered in the middle of the door, and just above it, shining with silver lettering on a dark grey background, written in a classic script was a single word, *Dragonfly*. Her aunt had always felt that the lake house was the center of her soul and from it she could soar like a dragonfly across the lake to any adventure, from which she would always return home.

Aunt Jane's keys felt lost in Aubrey's trembling hand. With her heart pounding double time in her chest and her breath at half the capacity leaving her gasping from one minute to the next, she wondered how she could even enter this precious palace of memories that had molded her life as a child. It was time. She had to go in. Aubrey took one more deep breath, a step forward, then a step back, and another deep breath. She knew this would be the hardest part, but she had no idea it would be this hard. Suddenly, she felt something comforting, like a gentle hand on her back sending her forward, letting her know it would be all right. With a slight breeze pushing the midday warmth across the porch, she could almost hear the rhythmic voice of her Aunt Jane whispering. One last deep breath, she closed her eyes, took a step forward, opened her eyes again and raised the key to the door knob. She took the knob into her left hand and matched the key to the jagged hole in the center of the knob.

She walked carefully over the threshold and stepped back into her sixteenth year of life, the last summer she had spent at Dragonfly. The house was beautiful, complete with the smell of the lake water that the day's pleasure boaters had churned up just down the path of plank steps. Aubrey's eyes opened a little wider looking immediately to the floor tile in the foyer. She slowly moved her head to the left to see up the white painted baseboards to the soft sage green walls fitted with black picture frames. Within the frames were family photos, including a black and white picture of her in her high school graduation gown hugging her aunt. They both sported large smiles on their faces for her accomplishments. She felt the burn of tears as they trickled down her cheeks. Fumbling through her purse, she found one last tissue in the packet. She would need more tissues to manage her way through this daunting chore. She glanced back around to the sage wall to her right to see through damp eyes, pictures of her parents as well. Looking up, she again, as she had so many times before, admired the bead board vaulted ceilings as the foyer opened into the window clad living room. It gave the most amazing view out to the wooded backyard and the lake below.

As she looked around to find a home for her keys and cell phone, Aubrey noticed a small wooden bowl on the cherry finished sofa table in the center of the living room settled against the back of the beige microfiber couch. She sat her things down and drew her fingers around the edge of the bowl, curious about the small rectangles of paper that lay inside. She dipped her hand into the bowl to find a mix of business cards. She pulled them out one by one and read the names on the front, Jones Yard Services, Bill Jones, Owner, Water Works Plumbing, for all your plumbing needs, Gray and Hedge Refrigeration, Heating and Air. Each card was for a service person to help with home upkeep and repair. These must have been her Aunt's trusted associates that serviced her astounding home. She placed all of the cards back into the bowl. She might need them in case there were any damages to repair or to make any changes to the home to help it sell quickly in the market.

Aubrey continued through the house to the left to view the kitchen. Her aunt loved to cook so there should be all the necessary gadgets and kitchen tools she would need during her stay, but she would have to go to the grocery to stock up on food. To begin she would need to clean out the old things, so she opened a couple of cabinet doors to get an idea of where she would need to start. She then turned around to open the refrigerator. There was milk and other perishable foods on the shelves. She closed the door and moved her eyes across the kitchen to see the mail lying on the counter's edge. Aunt Jane had begun that day like any other. She had no idea her life would be cut so short.

Aubrey's father had told her that Jane had been on her way to meet a prospective client in the neighboring county when the accident occurred. Traveling was often the case for the small town realtor. Aunt Jane had been on a two lane highway that wound toward a local college when a young man, driving in the wrong lane and speeding, turned the curve and hit her head on. He had been drinking heavily the night before and apparently still retained his lack of reflexes due to the hangover. *"Who is drunk at ten o'clock in the morning,"* she had thought.

Aubrey continued on from room to room touching memories while an ache built in her chest. Her eyes moved from ceiling to floor in each space. It had not changed. Maybe her aunt had moved a chair, added a picture, or even painted a wall but the basics had not changed in all these years. She could see it all in her mind as if she were still sixteen years old. It flashed through her heart as if the ten years had not gone by and she could almost see her aunt's shadow moving through the hallway.

She suddenly felt dizzy and blinked her eyes, but it did not still the motion that stirred around her. Aubrey watched the room as it started to spin, and things began to look darker. She sensed nausea welling up inside the pit of her stomach and suddenly knew she had to get out of the house. She ran for the sliding glass door at the back of the living room that led outside to the back porch. Gasping for breath as she made her way outside, she clung to the railing and closed her eyes. She breathed large amounts of the crisp clean air deep into her lungs.

"Not Aunt Jane!" Aubrey whispered as she turned her back to the view of Majestic Lake. Sliding down to sit on the wooden deck, she pulled her knees to her chest and let her face fall into her hands. This could not be happening. Her Aunt Jane was gone, forever.

Aubrey had found herself picking up the phone often to call her aunt and tell her about some strange, stressful or happy thing that had happened in her life. She could see her aunt's smile every morning in the mirror while she was getting dressed staring back at her, telling her that it was a bright new day and everything would be all right. She was always told how much like her aunt she had become.

Jane had been her rock during the struggles in her life. She was the strength for all her challenges and the platform for her to use to reach her goals. Aubrey wanted to be just like her aunt from the time she was a young girl. She had even gone into the same profession selling real estate in Memphis and had gained notoriety at an alarming speed for her youthful years.

She was always good at keeping secrets too, especially for Aubrey. She could talk to her aunt about anything from boys to sex to concerts and it never got back to her parents. There was even the time Aubrey had snuck out of the house to see Aerosmith in concert at the Amphitheater and Jane had never breathed a word, just asked her how the concert was and if the boy she went with showed her a good time. The tales of the past circled over and over in Aubrey's mind, reliving what her aunt stood for and represented in her life.

Aunt Jane never made excuses for the things she did or the way she did them. Aubrey loved her for that. Her father's only sibling, Jane made it all right to be independent and free. Now Aubrey felt lost without her.

After a few aching moments her anxiety began to subside and

she realized she was looking out over the lake as she heard a boat speed by in the distance. She opened her eyes and saw the trees that over shadowed the sleeping backyard swaying in the early evening breeze. It was the calm to her storm only a few moments earlier.

As she gathered herself back together from her breakdown, Aubrey heard the phone ring inside. She rushed back in wondering who could be trying to reach her. She had told Bradley Stark and the evil twit, Chelsea, who had excitedly agreed to help with her client load, that she would be unavailable for at least two days until she was settled. The lack of sympathy from her co-workers had not come as a surprise. They were such simple minded people, never understanding that there could be complex emotional situations creeping into their midst. The real estate business often made your heart cold. As an agent, it was her job to close the sale, and that was all. It had even made Aubrey a little shallow over the past few years. They could not comprehend that she felt something deeper than a southwest canyon and her chest ached for relief.

Bradley Stark, her broker, would begin his morning ritual with a bathroom break that would continue through the employee kitchen where he would open the refrigerator and glance to see if some misguided person had put food on the shelf with no name on it. Anyone who had ever brought in their lunch knew to add a name to the surface of their prize or it became fair game to anyone looking for a morning snack. It only took a time or two of losing your food to recall that all the remaining scrumptious findings had something in common, a name written in bold black letters. After this venture, Bradley would slip out the back door and around the storage unit where the three year old and older closed files were kept and give in to a secret dirty habit of smoking Swisher Sweet faux cigars favored with cherry tobacco. This little treasure was not a fully mature cigar, but looked more like a cigarette with the hopes of one day growing up to become a real stogy. They gave off an oddly sweet smell in the breeze and although Bradley thought no one knew of his little obsession, the truth was all the agents were aware and they did not care.

That fateful morning, he had strolled back by Aubrey's office, pleased with his smoke break and noticed her head down on her desk. Although not truly interested in what was happening in her world, Bradley did think enough of her to ask in his condescending way if something was wrong.

"You tired or just hung over? Ha, ha!" he had said laughing slightly as if he were making a sly remark, but only he thought it was funny.

"My dad just called and my aunt was in a terrible accident. She passed away. Brad, I'm going to need a little time off for the funeral." she had told him.

"Don't you have a closing on the Highland property in Collierville this week?" he had given her just the cold-hearted reaction she had expected. "Well, I guess Chelsea can go over to Trader's Title and watch over the closing. You take a few days for yourself and let me know how everything goes." Bradley turned to leave and then stopped in the doorway. He turned back around to add, "Yeah, sorry about your aunt too." She tilted her head in dismissal of his careless words and picked up the phone to make arrangements to have untrustworthy co-workers cover her clients for the next week before she dialed each client to reschedule her showings or pass them along to another agent for the appointment.

Her thoughts of the office were interrupted when she heard the phone chime again. She picked up the pace to reach the small black rectangle before it shifted to voice mail.

"Hello," she answered to the person on the other end of the line with haste and curtness in her voice.

"Hello sweetheart, it's Mom," she could hear her mother's precious voice through the phone and immediately relaxed her defenses.

"Hi, Mom. Is everything all right?" she was so thankful to hear her mother. Her emotions were so unstable at the moment, she needed to hear someone familiar.

"Of course dear," her mother replied. "Daddy just wanted me to call and be sure that you made it."

"Yeah, I arrived about an hour ago," she looked around the house as she was moving through the living room.

"So, what does it look like? Is it still in good shape? It has been a few years since Daddy and I made a trip up that way, but I'm sure, knowing Jane, it is as stunning as ever," her mother inquired.

"It looks just like it always has, beautiful and decorated like Aunt Jane," Aubrey answered brushing a fingertip through the dust that had settled on the table top. She would need to find cleaning supplies and her aunt undoubtedly had some in the hall closet in a caddy where she had always stored them.

"Are you sure you are all right, dear?" she asked knowing her daughter's dread before she left to make the trip to the lake house had given her a great deal of anxiety.

"I will be. It's just hard seeing it all again. It's bringing back a lot of memories," Aubrey told her mother as she stood in the middle of the living room and made a complete circle around the room taking it in inch by ever loving inch. She let herself be transformed to her past to soak in the sounds, the smells, the loves of this place, then closed her eyes as if to seal them inside herself.

"I know this seems strange, but honey you should let yourself have all the memories your mind can hold. It will be the very thing you can always keep that will remind you of how far you have come and the person you are meant to be," her mother told her as if she could see Aubrey's motions taking it all in.

"Thanks Mom. I needed to hear that," she smiled as she opened her eyes.

"Now, if you get afraid in that big house or just a little lonely you can call us. We are just across town. Ms. Ross gave us a good deal on this B&B room and she said she can fit you in too, but I'm sure little Macie will be a more comforting choice," her mother reminded her.

"I'll be fine. I'm going to settle in, maybe catch a quick nap, and then change for the visitation," she reassured her mother. "I'll see you soon."

"I love you!" she said almost in a whisper.

"I love you too, Mom. Thank you again for calling. You always know just what to say," Aubrey said gratefully.

"That is what mothers do, dear. Now go get some rest," she replied.

"I will, I promise," Aubrey hit the red and black button on her cell to disconnect the phone call, and then turned to reconnect to her past.

As she hung up the phone she noticed out the glass window

panes that large drops of rain were beginning to fall. Normally she would be thankful for the late summer shower because it made the colors of the fall leaves more vibrant and beautiful when they changed in the month to come. However, today it just made her sad and suddenly lonely.

Chapter Two

Aubrey pulled into the parking lot of the Walker Funeral Home and Memorial Gardens around 1 p.m. with a pounding headache and hunger pains in her stomach that were demanding her attention. Driving through the parking lot, she circled around the right side of the building to gauge the direction of the general flow of traffic and to search for a parking place. Looking for a white car that resembled her father's Buick, she found both local car tags as well as those from Memphis and even other states. There was no doubt she would be introduced to old friends and companions of both her parents and her aunt. She found her destination for the next few hours and gazed in the mirror for one last look at herself. More than anything she wanted to look acceptable for her aunt's sake. She had taken extra care applying her eye makeup in order to cover the dark circles under them, and she certainly wanted to disguise any redness she may have gathered when a hint of reality struck her as she drove through the city and realized she was coming to the service for her aunt's death. It was then she had her most recent breakdown and tears had burned her eyes leaving red streaks down her cheeks. She had pulled over to the side of the road to release the hurt and regain her composure. They couldn't see her like that. She balanced her cosmetic case carefully on her knee as she reapplied her lipstick one final time. It was not the best impression she had intended to make, but it would have to do.

The memorial to her aunt was exceptional. The room was draped in white tulle and glowed with soft pink lighting. There were flowers overflowing at the front of the room. Her father had stated that everything had been taken care of as far as the arrangements. If she knew her aunt, it had been carefully planned out, and she had made all her provisions years prior to her death. She had most likely pre-paid the funeral and burial plot, picked out the music for her service, and even decided on her final resting bed. It was exquisite just as Aubrey knew it would be. Visitors crowded the pews and formed a line that reached around the room. It poured into the vestibule where newcomers signed the register. It was always terrible that tragedy brought family back together more than the family reunions, and this was the worst tragedy Aubrey could have imagined. She pushed her way through the crowd nodding her head and accepting hugs along the way as she passed through the onlookers. She made her way to the front to find her father and mother standing next to the closed casket. With red wet eyes, they accepted the condolences of friends, family and acquaintances. Aubrey's father saw her approaching through the crowd and waved her to the front to take her position next to him.

"This is my little Aubrey. Hasn't she grown? Aubrey, do you remember your great-aunt Millie?" her dad asked as he held the hand of a classically dressed lady in her 80s.

"I'm sorry but it has been a long time. It is good to see you, although I wish it were under better circumstances," Aubrey replied.

"I remember when you were just a tiny thing running around your mom's and dad's porch when we were there for a cookout. What was that, about twenty something years ago? I sure am going to miss sweet Jane. She never had the chance to get married and have any children of her own," Millie told Aubrey in a somber voice as if there were something wrong with not being married and tied down with a herd of curtain climbers.

"Well, I intend to continue in her footsteps," leaning forward and whispering she continued, "I think marriage is highly overrated in today's society. It's much more fun to play the field with all the handsome single men that are available. Thank you again for coming, Aunt Millie. Dad, can I speak to you for a moment?" She led her father away from the woman she now wanted to refer to as an old hag to give him a hug and steal a few private moments with him. Great-aunt Millie with a shocked look on her face moved on to visit with her mother.

He had not been amused at her words to her great-aunt, "Aubrey, you can't say things like that."

"I just hate it that people like her are going to take the time to come to this funeral home to give words of encouragement and sympathy one moment and then criticize the next," she said. "How are you daddy?"

"I'm about as good as I can get, baby. I'm glad you made it with no problems. There is going to be a family viewing in the morning an hour before the funeral to say one last goodbye," he informed her.

"I'll pass on that, Daddy. I know in my heart that she is gone. I want my last vision of her to be a pleasant, healthy, and happy one. I hope you understand," she pleaded.

"I do, baby. I think that is why she arranged for a closed casket," he mused.

Aubrey recalled the comment her aunt had made once as their family sat around her mother's dining room table after a hefty homegrown meal. She laughed as she told her sister-in-law how she didn't want everyone and their dog staring at her lifeless body after she was gone. It was just a terrible morbid thought and she wasn't going to have it. She would have a closed casket and no one was to ever come looking to see if it were really her in there. Aubrey smiled as she remembered the story.

"Well, come stand with me and mom so you can meet people. There will be a lot of folks that want to see how you have turned out, and try to be nice sweetheart. They don't mean any ill will to you or Jane, so don't be so easily offended," her dad requested.

"I'll do my best," she smiled.

***

The next day Aubrey managed to come to the funeral home early for the family visitation. She sat in the pew by herself in her black mourning dress and the precious pearls she had worn to occupy her fingers during the service as the rest of the family went behind the closed curtain to view and cry over her aunt. It was a southern tradition to take a last look at the body before the other guests arrived for the funeral and when it was finished eight men would take a handle of the box and lead the procession into a long black car to escort her to her final destination. Aubrey mentally prepared herself for the show as she waited. One by one the viewers came back out and shifted to the side door to gather their composure. When there were no other family members to walk through, Aubrey gave a quick glance around and stood up. She moved slowly to the front and gently swept the curtain back to enter the viewing room alone. She stood in silence shifting her head to see from one end to the other of the casket holding her aunt.

She reached out a hand to lay it on the silver casket in front of her. It was the same shiny color as the BMW her aunt drove the last summer she came for a visit. It made her heart ease, if only a little. She felt a hand slide down her back and wrap around her waist. She didn't even have to look to know who it belonged to but turned her head anyway to give Macie a smile.

The positive in such a negative situation was that she would have her best friend by her side through her heartache. She had only seen Macie Sanders on her terms in the past ten years and the times had been few and far between. On average they were able to meet for a visit two or three times a year and normally in Nashville to catch up. They made a point to call a couple of times a week to have a few laughs and plan the next outing. Macie had majored in finance at Belmont University only to return to work at a local bank in Walker, but like Aubrey she had not married. They were truly soul sisters and also like Aubrey it had broken Macie's heart that Jane was no longer going to be in her life. She had grown to love Jane as an aunt because of Aubrey's devotion.

Aubrey didn't say a word as she dropped her head onto Macie's shoulder letting the top of her head make contact with Macie's cheek.

"I'm going to miss her so much," she said, trying so hard not to let the tears flow yet again.

"I know. I am too," Macie replied.

"She gave me a life. I don't know who I would have become without her."

"A beautiful person, but maybe a little less fun," they both let a small giggle slip from their curved lips.

"If it hadn't been for her, I wouldn't have you," Aubrey couldn't hold it in any longer and tears began to stream down her cheeks. She straightened up and turned to look back at the casket. Nothing else needed to be said. They understood each other too much to need words to show the emotions they felt. Macie wrapped her arms around her best friend and held her close until she stopped shivering. Loosening the tight embrace they both gave a soft kiss to their fingertips and touched Aunt Jane's casket in love and thanks for all she had done to bring them together.

"I love you, my darling," Aubrey said softly to her aunt. "Goodbye."

***

After a beautifully moving service with an exquisite speaker and numerous sympathy wishes, Aubrey was ready to return to Memphis. She had become overwhelmed by the events and was feeling the urge to get away, back to work, back to something that would take her mind off of the emptiness she was experiencing. This trip might have been a release from her hectic city life, but it had only proven to add to her distress. She walked out into the vestibule and toward the double doors that lead to the cars lined up at the front of the funeral home.

"Ms. Todd," she heard a voice behind her soft and gruff, as if he had a cold.

Aubrey turned around to see Mr. Bernard Shipley, her aunt's attorney. He was a rather heavy set man standing at about six-feet tall, with a round sweet face that matched his round belly. He had always been a kind person to her aunt. She recalled seeing him around town as a young girl when she went to the grocery store or clothes shopping with her Aunt Jane. As with many of the citizens of Walker, he always spoke, tipping his head in a graceful bow as he passed.

"Yes, sir," Aubrey replied.

"I don't know if you remember me, but…"

She interrupted, "Yes, of course, Mr. Shipley, I remember you well. It is good to see you again. Thank you for coming."

"Yes ma'am. I'm very sorry for the loss of Miss Jane. We are going to miss her in town. She was such a good lady," he said.

"Thank you, she will be missed by us all," she added.

"I needed to let you know about something before you head back home, Ms. Todd. I hate to talk about business at these times, but you have been requested to attend the reading of Miss Jane's will," he said.

"Her will?" Aubrey questioned. "I can't imagine why I would need to be present for the reading of her will. Can't you just call me when I get back to Memphis? I'm afraid I really need to be getting back. Surely you can simply mail me anything that she leaves to me, or better yet, you can send it with my parents. I believe they plan to stay for a few days to help clear up any business matters," she said clasping her hands tightly together in front of her as she gave him a generous look that allowed her eyes to sparkle and her smile to glow. "My aunt was a very organized person and I think that probably rings true with how she wanted her things dispersed. I assumed much of her wealth would go to her church and her favorite charity organizations. I'm sure my parents can bring whatever it is back to Jackson and I'll pick it up when I get the chance."

Mr. Shipley stood with his cocoa suit jacket unbuttoned and pushed back to his sides while his hands twitched in his matching pants pockets. He wrinkled his forehead until a rather confused look settled on his face. "Well, Ms. Todd, I believe you really need to be at the reading. I think you will find it much more interesting than something your parents can bring home to you."

"Well, it's just that I had planned on returning tomorrow morning. I have a house closing on Thursday. I would like to get back in time," she said.

"Ms. Todd, since you are mentioned in the will you really need to be there," he said in a pleading voice.

She could not imagine what her Aunt Jane had given her that would require her to appear at the reading of her will. But she had to admit that it was sparking her curiosity.

"Well, Mr. Shipley, I guess I will be there," she replied.

"All right, I'll see you at 8 tomorrow morning then, Ms. Todd" he tipped his head, smiled one last time and turned to walk away.

***

After a simple breakfast of coffee and a protein bar that she had bought at a convenience store on her way to Walker, Aubrey dried her damp hair and slipped into something a little more professional for her morning in the office of Shipley, Brock and Staples. A little black dress with a white floral design in the material sporting three quarter sleeves would be warm enough for the morning breeze and thin enough for later when the southern sun would warm up the spring day. She pulled her auburn hair back into a wavy ponytail to give a laid back casual look. She would hate to give Mr. Shipley the idea that she was a cold and brutal business woman. After layering a long, beaded necklace with a medium length silver chain, she slid into her high heel pumps. She took her car keys and cell phone and slipped them into the side pocket of her briefcase and walked out the door of her hotel room to solve the mystery that had her lying awake wondering for a good bit of the night.

Walking into Mr. Shipley's office was like walking into an abstract art gallery. It was a mixed media of classic décor and convenient items. As she glided through the glass door, she found the typical water cooler to the left, candy dispensers to the right, and an open room the size of a small conference room large enough to contain a number of cubicles if needed. Instead of cubicles though it contained numerous wooden chairs padded with mauve fabric both on the bottoms and backs. There were side tables harboring business, womens, and sports magazines. Only one desk toward the back left corner was in the entire room, and behind the desk sat a very lovely lady in her late 40s, a few streaks of gray in her dark brown hair, dressed in a seasonal pastel yellow pantsuit reminiscent of an Easter egg. She was typing away on her computer while answering the occasional phone call with a kind voice of confidence as if she had been working this job for a long time.

"Excuse me," Aubrey said as she walked carefully up to the lady's desk. "My name is Aubrey Todd and I'm here to see Mr. Shipley."

"Yes ma'am, Ms. Todd. Let me see if he is available at the moment," the petite woman said.

She quickly picked up the phone and dialed two numbers which were followed by a beep.

"Mr. Shipley," she called out.

"Yes, Maxine." Aubrey overheard him say.

"There is a Ms. Aubrey Todd here to see you," she asked.

"Yes, Maxine," he said. "Please ask Ms. Todd to give me just a moment."

"Yes, sir," she looked up from the phone, "Ms. Todd, if you will, please have a seat and Mr. Shipley will be with you in a moment."

"Thank you," Aubrey replied.

She sat down in what seemed to be a red padded folding chair which, although comfortable for the most part, did not go with the Tuscan scenery hanging in acrylic on the wall behind it. After only a short time, Mr. Shipley walked through a solid wooden door to the side of the receptionist's desk and greeted Aubrey graciously.

"Ms. Todd, the others are back in the conference room. Please come and join us," he said guiding her toward a similar wooden door in the back of the room. Aubrey followed him into a large room with an oval walnut table surrounded by family, a man she recognized as the preacher who conducted Jane's service the day before and two other unfamiliar couples in rolling black hard back chairs. She suddenly felt very uncomfortable.

"Just have a seat, Ms. Todd, and we will get started," Aubrey sat down as requested in a seat next to her mother. "Now, we are all present for the reading of the will of one Ms. Jane Elizabeth Todd. I have been her attorney for a number of years now and am familiar with her last wishes as it pertains to this will. There is a lot of lawyer mumbo jumbo so I can give you the easy version if you like instead of reading it verbatim." He looked to her dad for approval. As Jane's closest living relative, Andrew Todd turned to his wife Marie then faced back to Mr. Shipley nodding his head. "Then let's continue. Jane left instructions for everyone here today.

To the church she left ten-thousand dollars in cash to be used for the evangelism of the youth and family program. She also left ten-thousand to the Christian academy in trust of the board of directors to be used to start a scholarship fund at the school. To the humane society of Walker she left five-thousand dollars in cash to be used for operations and adoptions. To the American Cancer Association and the American Diabetes Association she left each five-thousand dollars to be used for research so that maybe one day there will be a cure for the diseases that took her parents away too soon.

To each of her remaining living aunts and uncles she left three-thousand dollars in cash and for each of those aunts and uncles who have passed she left the three-thousand in cash to be split evenly between their children, her cousins. To her darling niece and namesake, Aubrey Elizabeth Todd, she leaves one-hundred-thousand dollars in trust, her beloved lake house and the contents therein," Aubrey gasped causing everyone to look at her. "Is everything all right, Ms. Todd?" Mr. Shipley asked.

"Uhh, yes sir. I'm sorry, please continue," she quickly replied.

"She leaves all other investments, cash, and possessions to her dear brother and beneficiary, Andrew Jacob Todd. She felt confident that he would use discretion with the estate so that it may benefit his family and others. This concludes the majority of the disbursement of the Todd estate. Other much smaller amounts will be given to the needy organizations she was particularly fond of and believed would use the money wisely. Does anyone have any questions?" Mr. Shipley concluded. Aubrey wanted to blurt out *"Why did she leave me the house?"* but thought of the gift she had been given.

***

Aubrey struggled through the door of her apartment overloaded with her keys, purse, and the imitation dinner she had picked up at a fast food joint on the way home. With her luggage in tow and her mail clenched between her teeth, she tossed her keys on the table next to the door and closed it with her foot. As she walked in the dimly lit living room, she began losing her grace of walking in heels. She loosened the rest from her shoulders and let it fall to the floor. She checked her answering machine for messages, only to find the normal political surveys and telemarketers. Crossing the room she still had the events of Walker on her mind. It had been a five hour drive with only one idea circling in her head, why Dragonfly, why her?

Through the solid glass window in her apartment living area, Aubrey looked out over the city with its tall gray steel buildings and bug-sized economy cars surrounded by buses enveloped in the foggy haze of the humidity. She could almost hear the sound of the blues from Beale Street and smell the exhaust of the hustle and bustle of the busy night life. This was her city. This was her home. What would she do with a lake house in Walker? The estate would spend time in probate waiting on Aunt Jane's life insurance to pay out and settle any debt she owed, though it was sure to be very little. After everything was distributed, Mr. Shipley would call to inform her that she could take ownership of the house and its internal possessions. She would have to make the dreaded trip back to sort through the contents. She wondered what she might find and how hard it would be to dispose of her aunt's things if she made the choice to do so. It was a lot to think about and would no-doubt cross her mind numerous times before she packed her things and returned to the country roads hours away. But tonight she needed to put it to rest and find some sleep for her weary soul. Walking through her apartment like a zombie, Aubrey turned out the lights one by one and fell into bed asking God to help her make it through the following days with the grace and stability of her Aunt Jane.

Chapter Three

Aubrey stood at the kitchen sink looking out the open window onto the lake, listening to the chirp of the morning birds singing like a Beethoven melody. She hadn't slept well, tossing and turning to every noise that swept through the lake house that night. Honestly, she had not slept well since her father called with the news of her aunt's death, but being in Aunt Jane's house for the first time since her death two months earlier had made the situation almost unbearable. Her dreams were getting more ferocious and anxious as each day passed. She held her aunt's memory not only in her heart, but in her mind and it was haunting her. She felt that it all must have to do with her not knowing what she was going to do with the house, or the many lovely things that were in it. Aunt Jane had not left any instructions about the care of her belongings, just that she wanted Aubrey to have the house and everything in it. The words in her will stated "Aubrey will know what to do with it." If only she had as much faith in herself to know how to handle this most important situation.

She knew she wasn't strong enough to start going through all the bits and pieces of her aunt's life and sorting them into piles of *Keep*, *Toss*, and *Sell*. She needed a clear head and a calm demeanor before she could even begin the task, although her time off from work was only two weeks. Now that she was here, she was realizing her wounds had not healed at all, but if she expected to return to Memphis and her life in a timely manner, she would just have to suck it up and get started immediately.

The lake whispered to her from the breeze that skipped up the pathway and across the sweet odor of the redwood planks that were laid out in a pattern to form the deck. Maybe the work could wait until tomorrow. She wanted to enjoy a day of being lazy and taking her mother's advice. She would spend her first full day basking in her memories. Well, there it was. The first thing she had been able to think through since she had arrived at Dragonfly.

Aubrey decided to head down to the dock to find the sense of peace she had as a child; the place where she could be alone, find her freedom, and meditate on her life, although, she believed the last time she went to the dock for peace it was to meditate over a boy. She almost giggled out loud with the thought. The water would rock in and out of the slough, splashing white foam onto the rocks along the lake's edge. Fish would hear the boats pass by slowly as they cruised through the main waterway and think that it was feeding time. Then they would one by one take their chances by lifting their slick bodies out of the water and pass back through the current revealing their greediness for food to the nearby fishermen. As a child Aubrey would sit out on the dock for hours sunbathing and thinking of the cute boy she had passed by in town, or wondering what was going on back at home, maybe dreading the day she would have to leave this haven. She read many books under the large oak tree that ended the pathway from the house to the dock. Aunt Jane even let her drag a comfy old folding chair down to the tree one summer, but most of the time she would just bring an old quilt to place on the ground in the shade of the tree. She thought that would be the best choice for today. There were still some old quilts in the guest room closet bright with named patterns and ornate colors of blue, pink, yellow, and green. She would be sure to find one that didn't look to be handmade, since those were much more valuable and she would hate to stain it on the cold dew kissed ground of the morning. After determining the perfect accompaniment, she would grab the latest Mary Kay Andrews novel and head to the lake, but only after her coffee and maybe a piece of toast with the strawberry jam she had purchased in town. Aubrey was excited to discover it had been made locally in the Mennonite community at the edge of town and sold in one of the downtown markets.

Before she was even able to gather her belongings for her outdoor adventure, Aubrey had been interrupted. Phone call after phone call came and Aubrey didn't find herself leaving the house to enjoy the shade tree until much later in the day. It was almost 3 o'clock when she could finally set the phone down and promise herself not to pick it up again until she had found time to think. Of course Mr. Shipley had called concerning the will and questioning her about the transfer of the deed, and the possibility of an estate sale. She assured him that she would be by his office tomorrow to clear up anything concerning the will and inheritance. Once news of her arrival to take possession of the house had spread through town, her pending decisions concerning Dragonfly had certainly become the hot topic of town gossip. With that brought calls from a couple of the local antique dealers asking for a preview of some of the items she intended to let go in the so-called sale she had not committed to yet. Following that were the local real estate agents interested in listing the house, and the newspaper asking for some information for a tribute article about the gifts her aunt had left to the charities. She was beginning to feel the power of the small town pressure. There were of course the nosy neighbors that heard she was in town and wanted to let her know they were "here if she needed them." Then to polish off the early afternoon, the hospital had called concerning some paperwork about Aunt Jane's ambulance ride to the hospital when she had her tragic car wreck, something she truly knew nothing about and thought it best that they discuss with Mr. Shipley. All in all, it had been an exhausting day and she hadn't even left the house. It had become a necessity for her to find some time to relax.

Even though it was September, the afternoons were still fairly warm in the South, so she decided to take advantage and slipped into a white button up twill shirt that would allow some air to flow through it as she rolled the sleeves up to her elbows. She left off her top undergarment to enjoy the freedom from the binding restriction of an underwire. To that she added a ragged pair of cut off jean shorts. Normally she wore something more modest in public, but many of the people in Aunt Jane's neighborhood were older and didn't come down to the lake this time of year. It was very unlikely that she would run into anyone. Aubrey grabbed an aluminum bottle filled with fresh filtered water from the refrigerator, a pair of new Chanel sunglasses she had purchased as a splurge for the trip, her two-year-old worn out sandals, and the machine stitched quilt that she had found in the closet of the back bedroom. She opened the back door that lead out onto the deck as the phone rang. She turned to look simply from habit, turned back around, and then continued to walk through the door and into the sunshine. As she heard the answering machine pick up she began to walk down the earth tone stairs to her youth.

She didn't recall there being so many steps to the dock when she was a girl. She would practically skip to the lake as a youngster and never found herself out of breath, but today was very different. She counted as she walked step by lonely step and came up with eighty-seven wooden planks with a handrail down the left side reminding her that her dear Aunt was the only one in the family that was left-handed. Once at the bottom, she stood in amazement at the beauty of the lake this time of year. The banks of the slough were filled with trees of every shape, tall and short, wide and thin, colored with a few red and yellow leaves just beginning to change for the fall season; still mostly green, but some slightly brown from the dry heat of the summer in the South. She took a deep breath filling her lungs with the soul of the fishy green-brown lake water as it chimed gently against the edge. Aubrey felt for the first time in a long time like she was in someone else's skin, someone who was guiding her footsteps home and it made her smile involuntarily.

She had spent the good part of an hour watching the ripples in the lake and counting the boats as they skimmed across the water. Then she turned to her novel for a getaway into the imaginary world that the author so gracefully and delicately described. Aubrey could envision the details of the characters, their body type, hair color, and clothing. She could see the beach house, the love interest, the surroundings and the mystery of the plot being laid out as she read word after word. This was her peace, what she had been searching for, and it came back to her so elegantly. As her eyes wandered from the pages, she saw something in the brush under the trees that belonged to the property next door. She wondered why she had not noticed it when she first arrived at the dock, but since it seemed that no one was around and since she just wanted to use it for a short time, Aubrey decided to help herself to an early evening ride in the small V-bottom fiberglass boat. Her eyes became heavy as she lay back against the hull and let the gentle waters slap against the sides of the boat wisping her off to a relaxing dreamland.

Chapter Four

"Mmmm" Aubrey could hear a voice from the bank of the lake, but she was still lost in the wonders of her cleared mind and had no idea what the person was saying. It couldn't be of any importance to her anyway she thought. She wanted to continue to bask in the silence and tranquility she was feeling by floating in the slough of the lake. She was away from the stress of buyers and sellers, away from old relationships, and finally beginning to see things clearly when her reason for being in Walker came to her, why give up those few minutes of freedom.

"Mmmm" she heard it again. What was so important that this person just couldn't go away?

She slowly opened her eyes, but chose not to rise up hoping that the person would decide to leave and she could drift back into her state of relaxation.

"...from the Walker Police Department. Ma'am, are you all right?" a man's voice became clear and for some reason it seemed familiar.

Aubrey jerked up from her position to look around and find the gruff male voice and where it might be coming from, only to feel herself off balance in the bottom of the boat. Suddenly, her arms reached out for anything to steady herself, but found nothing as she rotated around the edge of the boat and into the lake water with an ungraceful splash. She fought to discover which way was up. Without much of a breath underwater, she reached for the slight gleam of dusk and imagined herself shooting out of the water like a beautiful mermaid in an 80s movie, although it probably looked more to the gentleman like a bass shooting out of the water after being grappled by the treble hook of a fisherman's crank bait.

She quickly jerked her head around looking for the owner of the deep voice, but the lake water still wouldn't let her see clearly enough to know who had been asking the questions. She gathered her senses and realized which direction led to the bank, and began to swim toward the gentleman who seemed so genuinely concerned about her. She wondered how he even knew she was in the boat on the lake.

Making her way to the shore, she replayed the story in her head. She thought it best to have the simplest explanation possible, just a quick story that would get right to the point.

Coming out of the chilly early fall water of Majestic Lake, she saw the man dressed in nice clothes. She dragged herself out of the water as he introduced himself as a police officer. Blinking her eyes profusely, she looked down to try and see that she was not stepping on anything that might remain in her foot for the duration of her visit. Then she straightened up to look him in the eyes with a slight playful grin of her face. She felt her kind smile falter into a furious glare as rage from years past filtered through her water soaked bones. She was standing wet and cold in a white shirt, and realizing such, she quickly crossed her arms.

Aubrey had raised her hazel eyes to see a young man standing before her that took her breath away. His tan skin gleamed in the orange glow of the setting sun as he stood over her at a good 6'3" with strong arms that could take the life from someone if necessary. As soon as she caught the gleam in his eyes she knew it was him, the boy that had taunted her as a child, pulled her hair when he saw her in town, called her a nickname whenever she walked by. His face had changed with age, but she remembered those eyes, the blue green color of his beloved lake and dark hair that lay in beautiful waves even in a midsummer rain storm. But the one thing that always caught the sweet girls' attention in town was the slight dimple in his right cheek as he smiled, a cunning "I have you all figured out" grin. That was the smile that Aubrey couldn't stand, a look that he would give every time he played pranks on her over the years.

From the first summer she came to Walker when he had decided to pull her pigtails, to the last summer she visited Aunt Jane and he found a number for a boy she was fond of back home and decided it was his place to call and tell him things about her that he found amusing, she had despised the very thought of him. And now he was towering down over her.

Aunt Jane had always told her that the true reason for his immature actions were because deep down he liked her, but it certainly did not feel that way at the time. And now here he was, standing right in front of her. Only this time he was a stunning man with a muscular build and a tailored looked. He obviously spent time on the lake, and his voice was much deeper and sterner than she had recalled. He was standing before her in a rugged pair of jeans that hugged his leg muscles in all the right places and a black polo shirt that clung to his chest as the wind blew toward him.

"What are you doing here?" she asked in what she was sure was a monstrous tone.

"The station got a call from old man Carter that there was a dead lady floating in his canoe in the Center Grove community. I was just coming off duty, but I was passing this way so I told them I would swing by and check it out. I had no idea it was you. I didn't even know you were in town." he explained.

He worked for the Walker Police Department?

"Well, I am here and I'm just fine as you can see. There was no need to call the police," she stomped up to the quilt where her book was lying and grabbed them both, shaking out the quilt and using it as a make shift wrap.

"What were you doing out there? A tribute to Alfred Lord Tennyson?" he asked.

"I decided to borrow the boat to take a little drift on the water and became lost in peaceful thought. I guess I just fell asleep," she stated as she began up the plank steps to return to the back deck of Dragonfly.

He began to follow her taking the first few steps two at a time to catch up.

"So, I'm sorry to hear about Miss Jane. There are a lot of folks that are going to miss her around here," he said to try to regain her attention.

It was a kind gesture so she decided to ease down her guard for a moment.

"Thank you. I'm going to miss her too, terribly," she continued with the quick pace up the steps.

"So, I hear you are the new owner of Dragonfly. Do you have any idea what you are going to do with it? Are you thinking of moving down here?" his questions were starting to get on her nerves already.

"I can't imagine that I would. I have my life in Memphis. I'm just taking it a day at a time," she answered and walked on to the porch tossing the quilt onto the patio chair that rested close to the back door.

She turned around to see him coming up from the last step onto the deck. He looked at her with that same smirk on his lightly stubbled face that she remembered.

"Well, isn't it a little ironic that you have become a police officer?" Standing in front of the door she returned his smirk as if to tell him that it was ridiculous for someone like him to end up in such a noble profession.

"Actually, I've made the rank of detective. Since it is a small town I help out in any area where they need me," he replied with a slight shrug of his shoulders and crook of his neck.

Forgetting the reason she had crossed her arms to begin with, she raised her left hand to brush back a strand of hair, letting the other arm fall to rest at her side.

"You had better get on inside and change out of those wet clothes," he said with a sultry grin. "I can see that you are, um, pretty cold."

She suddenly recalled that her arms were no longer covering the now see through shirt she was wearing and he was soaking in quite a view of her peaked nipples. She quickly returned her arms to their folded position and gave a huff in his direction before opening the door and stomping into the house.

He followed her into the house closing the door behind him.

"Hey, wait a minute. Slow down." Hearing the words from him made her shiver more than the cold from her wet clothes. "Oh, come on Sweeney, I didn't mean anything by it," he chimed, following behind her through the great room of the lake house.

She stopped in her tracks and slowly turned around. No one had called her Sweeney in ten years, in fact only Jason had ever called her that. He always seemed proud of coming up with that one, as if there were any other way of making fun of the last name *Todd.*

"I thank you for your concern, Jason McNally, but as you can see I am just fine and am no longer in need of your assistance." *Not that I ever was in need of your assistance*, she thought.

"You have got to be kidding me, Sweeney…Aubrey," he tried to correct his boyish game.

She walked across the great room and took the handle to the front door in her hand. It no longer mattered if he got a clear view of her through her wet white shirt, she just wanted him gone. She gently turned the knob and opened the front door, and glancing back at Jason she motioned with her head that he had now overstayed his welcome. She wished for him to leave.

"Don't worry Mr. McNally, if I decide to open a barber shop you will the first one in the chair. I assure you."

"Are you threatening a police officer, Ms. Todd? That is a felony you know," he reminded her in a more assertive tone.

"Not a threat, Mr. McNally, but a promise if you continue to bother me during my stay in Walker. I do thank you for your time, please leave now," she demanded sternly.

Jason bowed his head as if to admit defeat and started toward the door. Stopping just short, directly in front of her, he turned his head toward her, gave her one last long look from her face to her chest and back up, and leaned over to stare directly into her eyes only a few inches from her lips.

"I look forward to seeing you around town…Sweeney." His smile was so devious and so familiar from her younger days. As he strutted out the door and down the stairs to his masculine jet black 4x4 Chevy pick-up, Aubrey narrowed her eyes in fury. How could such a frustrating boy become such a brilliantly breathtaking man?

Chapter Five

The next morning Aubrey awoke to find a chilly, foggy morning typical of fall weather on the lake as the clouds drifted over the water. The night had not been kind to her with thoughts of the illusive Jason McNally drifting through her dreams leaving her unsettled. He was not someone she wanted to think about, so why was it that the vision of him as he was leaving Dragonfly had wafted through her mind and made her body shiver as it had in the cool breeze after falling into the lake. It was certainly time to get out of bed and begin her day before her mind wandered off again. Her center had been shaken by his presence at Dragonfly, but her priority had to be getting everything taken care of so she could get back to her life in Memphis. She did not want to lose her status in the housing market, as difficult as it had been recently to make a mark due to the decline of the economy. Aubrey could not afford to lose her clients, especially over someone like Jason. She would simply push him out of her thoughts by keeping herself busy.

After spending an hour at Mr. Shipley's office discussing her future home plans and fighting off the offer of another cup of coffee presented by his always well dressed and attentive assistant, Maxine, Aubrey went by the Dollar Store to pick up some organizing supplies. It was time that she faced her greatest fear. She had been in the house for three days and had yet to begin the search through the remains of her aunt's life. That was always the most difficult part of losing someone. There would be memories to sort and papers to file. She would most likely pick out a few treasured things to keep and give some to different members of the family and her aunt's friends. Maybe the best thing to do would be to let them have their pick before she turned the remainder of the items over to an auction as Mr. Shipley had suggested.

She wanted to start in the main rooms of the house and work her way to the back leaving her aunt's room for last. Aubrey had decided that the easiest route of storage for the things she did not intend to keep would be the garage. She would just move those things out of her way and set it up in rows so the others would easily be able to scan the items and choose the things they might like to have as keepsakes. The small detached storage unit to the left of the garage would be ideal to keep the donations from the house. Aubrey could simply load them up when it was all over and take them to a local charity. Finally she had a stellar plan to begin work.

Her University of Memphis t-shirt and an old pair of cut-offs would be her work uniform as she struggled through cabinets, boxes, and drawers. She turned on the radio hoping that the continuous music of Taylor Swift, Kenny Chesney, The Zac Brown Band and others might blur her thoughts as she mulled over photo books and dug through old birthday greeting cards. Although Jane was not what you would consider a packrat, she did keep mementos that she felt were important. Many of the furniture pieces were exquisite, and Aubrey did not see a reason to part with them just yet. The antique cherry secretary from the living room would make an especially beautiful addition to her Memphis apartment. The other pieces fit the décor of the house and would make it easier to sell, so it might be in the best interest of the realtor for her to leave them in the house for now. She could always sell them later if she decided not to take them with her.

After searching through the kitchen cabinets and drawers, the desk, office closet, and the coat closet in the entryway, she felt she had accomplished enough to break for lunch. The more thought she gave to the process the more she believed she would take

Macie up on her offer to help and lend support. As hard as she tried to ward them off, she was finding it harder and harder to fight off the tears with each area of the house she strived to disassemble. She would need her friend and maybe a stiff drink to help her continue. With a plate loaded with a ham and turkey on wheat, a side of South Carolina tangy bar-b-que chips, and an apple in hand she fumbled for the phone and stepped out onto the back deck to check in with her childhood friend. She sat in the Adirondack chair, put her lunch on the side table and began to dial Macie's number.

"Hello" Macie answered with a smile you could visualize even over the phone.

"Hey, Macie! Do you have a minute?" she asked.

"Sure, sweetie. How are things going?" Macie replied.

"Well, I have managed to get through the living room, kitchen and office this morning. It helps that Aunt Jane was so organized," Aubrey looked out over the lake in the mid-day sun as the birds sang their songs in the trees overhead.

"You don't sound very sure of yourself," Macie could hear sadness in her voice and knew that the task of cleaning was weighing heavy on her friend.

"I feel like I've hit a brick wall," Aubrey admitted to her companion. "I'm getting into the more personal things now and it is becoming upsetting for me."

"Is there anything that I can do?" Macie questioned.

"You can come give me a hand," Aubrey used a pleading tone. "Do you have time to lend a little emotional support to a friend?"

"I think I can break free for a while to give you a hand, or a shoulder."

"I just don't think I can do it alone and I don't know who else to call. I don't want to put any of this on mom and dad," Aubrey felt relief that Macie would be joining her.

"And you shouldn't have to," Macie said as she continued her work. "I know this has been a tough time for you and for them."

"I could really use a friend," Aubrey said in a whisper.

"And you will have one. Is around two o'clock all right? I can finish the project I'm working on and be over mid-afternoon. That should still give us plenty of time to work," Macie looked down at her watch calculating the time until it was 2 o'clock in her mind.

"Yes, that will be perfect," Aubrey was grateful. "Whenever you can find the time."

"I'll be there as quickly as I can. Just hang in there," Macie suddenly became concerned. "Have you had lunch?"

"Yeah, I'm working on a sandwich right now," Aubrey told her as she took a bite.

"As long as you are eating something," Macie scolded her, knowing she had not been eating as she should, because she had noticed a weight loss since seeing her at the funeral a few months ago.

"I'm not going to starve myself, Macie. For the most part, I'm past the deep grief of what has happened," Aubrey assured her. "I've had these last few months in Memphis to deal with that. It's just the lingering memories that are leaving me shattered."

"I want to be sure that you are taking care of yourself," Macie told her.

"I am. I promise," Aubrey said.

"I'll see you soon."

"I'll be here, and Macie," Aubrey stopped in mid-sentence.

"Yeah?" Macie asked.

"Thank you."

"For what?"

"For just being you, and being what I need when I need it," Aubrey's voice trembled as the words slipped from her lips.

"You're welcome," Macie hung up the phone and returned to her job while Aubrey set the phone receiver down on the deck to finish her lunch.

***

Aubrey heard the rat-a-tat-tat on the door making a rhythm like the snare drum of a Van Morrison song. It was 2:15 and Macie was late, something she would never habitually be, so there must have been a delay in her travels. She opened the door sporting a sad expression although internally glad to see her friend.

"Hey, come on in," Aubrey said inviting Macie through the front door and motioning her on into the living room.

Giving her dear friend a sympathetic glance Macie greeted her with concern, "It's good to see you."

"Just drop your things anywhere and you can help me with the next plan of attack," Aubrey turned toward the hallway to the back of the house. "Ready to get started?"

"Sure," Macie replied, "but I would kind of like a minute to say hello and have a hug."

"Of course, I guess my mind has blinders on right now. How are things at the bank?" Aubrey asked.

"They are fine. I talked to my boss late last week and let him know that I might need a few hours off this week. I had a feeling you might need my help."

"You know me so well, don't you?" Aubrey was grateful that Macie was willing to look out for her.

"Aubrey, anyone in your situation going through this could use a helping hand. We have missed out on a lot by living so far apart, so I guess I want to be here for you now," Macie became serious and sentimental. "As much as I wish having this house would change your mind about moving to Walker, I'm sure it is not going to so I will take advantage of the time I have with you. For what it is worth, I really think you should keep the house so you can visit, but that's my opinion and that's all I'm going to say about it."

"I love you, Macie, and your candid views," she gave her dear partner in crime a crooked smile and a tight squeeze.

"Since you said that, I'm also going to tell you that you are looking a little pale this morning, and are those bags under your eyes?" Macie took a closer look at her face. "How are you sleeping?"

She didn't want to burden Macie with tales of the strange dreams she had envisioned for months about her aunt, nor was she ready to tell her the true reason for being so tired today. It still bothered her that Jason McNally's cunning smile was stuck in her head and his voice rang in her ears like the chime of the church bells on wedding day.

"Everything's fine," she beamed knowing that her friend would not believe the answer, but maybe it would buy her some time until she was ready to spill her real issues.

Macie tilted her head and narrowed her eyes with suspicion then replied, "Well, let's get to work then."

"Sure, we can work on the guest room," she said, happy to be moving away from the subject. "There is a whole closet full of stuff to go through."

"Do you have boxes for the things you are going to keep? Trash bags for the things you aren't?" Macie asked.

"Trash bags, yeah, in the corner," Aubrey replied in a melancholy tone while pointing to an orange box of white Hefty kitchen bags in the corner of the guest room.

"You are going to have to throw some things out," Macie shook her head like a mother consoling her child.

"I know. It's just difficult," Aubrey gave as an excuse. "I'm so confused on what to do with some of her things."

"Well, if you think you might need it then we can put it in a box and go through those again in more detail when you are ready," Macie reasoned. "Things that are truly trash will go in the bags."

"That is the very reason I needed you here, to tell me what to do to get through this. Let's face it, I have no spine right now and no organizational skills," Aubrey laughed slightly to try to find a more positive mood as she sat down on the edge of the guest bed.

"I don't know that you have ever had organizational skills," Macie joined in the humor sitting across from her in a reading chair that was added to the room for décor.

"Macie, I can't seem to wrap my head around why she gave me this place."

"It's pretty simple to me," Macie took Aubrey by the hands and forced her to look hard and listen to her words. "She wanted you to have the happiness that she had in this place. She loved this house," they both looked around the room finding the answer to the question was right in front of them both.

"I guess you are right," Aubrey agreed.

"Onto cleaning," Macie stood up ready to start. "We have a lot of work to do."

They started in the dresser drawers, the nightstand, and the chest of drawers then moved on to the largest chore of the closet. They sorted through old tax records and paperwork, found an ancient bread machine that had never been used, and fumbled through off season clothes and shoes. Aubrey discovered a green hat box in the back and sitting in the floor Indian style she opened it to view the contents.

"Hey, Macie look at this," she called out above the noise of rustling papers and discolored birthday cards.

"What is it?" Macie asked stopping her motions of sorting through a drawer and making her way toward Aubrey in the floor.

"It's old pictures from when we were kids. Look, here is one of us with our faces painted."

"I remember that," Macie recalled smiling. "We were artists making our grand creations until we got paint on our cheeks, then we just decided to paint our whole faces instead. It took forever for Jane to get that off of us."

"There are tons of pictures in here," Aubrey said amazed at the photos in the box. "Look at this one of us in the lake, and there's Trey jumping off the dock in the background. Remember that summer?"

"Wasn't that the one when Trey cut his foot on that piece of glass in the bottom of the lake and had to have stitches?" Macie asked.

"Oh, yeah, he was so mad. He couldn't go swimming with us for three weeks," Aubrey glared at the photo going back to the day in her mind as she swept her fingertips over the colors of the summers past.

"He was such a scrawny thing when we were kids," Macie laughed as she sat down in the floor next to Aubrey.

"Not so scrawny now though," Aubrey remembered seeing him at the funeral with his tailored suit showing his slender yet muscular build.

"Oh, and this one. Who is that with Samantha?" Macie gave Aubrey a quizzical look and passed the picture to her.

"April Demato," they chimed in unison.

"I haven't seen her in years. She went to Houston after we graduated," Macie said.

"Why Houston?"

"First to college and then I think she married someone from there. How about this one, Aubrey? We were so young."

"Oh, yeah," Aubrey said with disappointment in her voice lowering her head as if she had no interest.

"Are you still holding a grudge against him?" Macie shook her head in disbelief. "He's not the same person he used to be. That was years ago and it is time that you move on and get over all those hurt feelings."

"I got to see that first hand, no thanks to you. Besides, it hasn't been so many years since I was reminded of his antics. It's true that this boy," she pointed a sharp finger at the picture, "is not a boy anymore. You never told me he was a cop. Why didn't you tell me?"

"Well, someone made me pinky swear never to mention his name ever again," she gave Aubrey a less than amused look as she bobbed her head.

"Oh, that's right. I did do that didn't I? Well, I am officially revoking my pinky swear so tell me how he became a cop," she held up a bent pinky finger and then extended it to straighten it and break her hold on Macie's information.

"Fine. You know how much he loved football and his dad had groomed him to become a huge star. He didn't aim to disappoint and in the fall of his senior year he started off great. He loved to hear his name chanted under the Friday night lights. There was even talk about the team becoming state champions under Jason's leadership," Macie began her story with a smirk.

"And then?" Aubrey questioned.

"And then we faced Johnsonville on the third Friday night in October. They had a good team that year too and gave quite a showing for most of the game, but we had edged them out until the final few minutes. They came back to tie things up and we had the ball on the forty-yard line. One badly snapped ball and a broken line left his body vulnerable. He fell to the right to cover the ball and two Johnsonville linemen fell on his left leg. It was broken in three places and his dreams faded with the snap of the local newspapers' cameras. The headline read "High school star fades into the distance," and just like that he was knocked down to the ordinary life," Macie recalled. "Because he had been so focused on athletics, his grades made it seem that he had all the academic potential God gave a goose. He was set to be the star of the show on the Auburn University football field the following fall, but it was over and his father refused to help pay for him to go to college without a scholarship."

"So why go into law enforcement?" Aubrey asked casually as she thumbed through more pictures in the box.

"Simple, that was where Trey was headed. Jason had to come up with an alternative to college now that his football career plans were over. Trey had decided to go into the police academy after graduation, so Jason followed him. As it turned out Jason was good at it and enjoyed the challenge. He liked the daily grind, the projects with the town youth, getting to know the citizens, and they came to trust and respect him," Macie explained.

"So is he a good cop?" Aubrey seemed surprised at the possibility.

"Yeah, he is a great cop. In a short time he advanced to a detective. Trey made detective last year and they are both happy in their jobs."

"Who would have thought a juvenile delinquent would grow up to be the town's most respected police officer," the fact of those words made Aubrey unsure that they could really be true. She could not believe that anyone would respect Jason McNally that much.

"So I'm confused," Macie continued. "Why did you say 'no thanks to you' and when did you see him?"

A mark of embarrassment ran over Aubrey as she quickly returned the photos back to the box and replaced the top. She stood and placed the box on top of the dresser as Macie copied each move behind her. "He showed up yesterday evening at Dragonfly," it was Aubrey's turn to explain her reservations about Jason.

"You are kidding. Why?"

"I might have been floating around the slough in old man Carter's V-bottom and fell asleep," Aubrey turned to face Macie with faux innocence in her eyes and began with very few details. "Apparently, someone called the police because they thought I was dead."

"And Jason answered the call and came to check it out," Macie saw the direction of the story.

"I didn't know it was him at first. I was surprised to see someone on the edge of the water, so surprised that I accidently tipped the boat over and landed in the lake. I was humiliated, but the situation became even worse when I realized who was standing there on the bank," Aubrey felt a shiver run down her spine at the mere thought of the chill of the water and Jason's gaze on her wet body.

"So, what happened?" Macie asked.

"He followed me back up to the house acting like his old self and then I threw him out," Aubrey wasn't ready to divulge all the details of their exchange.

"Well, I can say one thing for you," Macie said raising an eyebrow at Aubrey.

"What is that?"

"You are consistent," she said grimacing as she dropping her head to look at the picture in her hand.

"What do you mean by that?" Aubrey questioned raising her voice slightly.

"You were always good at throwing Jason McNally out of Dragonfly. It has happened quite a few times over the years. Any time he got too close for your comfort you were ready to get rid of him," Macie reminded her.

"It was never without reason," she stated as she felt a confession from deep inside her belly rise up through her throat. "The thing is all morning long I haven't been able to get him out of my head."

"Oh, really?" Macie said with query.

"I have so many other things to deal with right now and I'm not here for very long, but no matter what I'm doing I think of him. He is the last person I want swirling around in my head," Aubrey rubbed her temples as if it would rub him out of her brain.

"So do you think that meeting last night might have sparked something in you?" Macie let loose a mischievous grin.

"No, I most certainly do not," Aubrey said matter-of-factly.

"Years pass, people change," Macie pleaded.

"And deep down people stay the same," Aubrey retorted.

"I give up," Macie rolled her eyes. "You will never see eye to eye with Jason."

"Not very likely," Aubrey said shaking her head.

"Well, let's set these pictures aside because I think we have a scrapbook project to work on," Macie walked to the dresser and took the box. She sat it in a marked box as a "keep" item to go through in more detail later.

"That is a great idea," Aubrey reached back into the closet to continue her search for items that might hopefully relieve her thoughts of the mesmerizing law enforcement officer that circled her head.

"I have another great idea," Macie said.

"What is that?"

"Tomorrow we are going to go to town for lunch and do a little afternoon shopping," Macie smiled proudly at her thought.

"For what?" Aubrey asked.

"I don't know. We could look for scrapbooking supplies, things to help sort through things more efficiently, or a new outfit for the carnival next week," she said hinting to the future hoping Aubrey would be staying long enough to enjoy one of the local festivities.

Aubrey closed her eyes slightly wondering if Macie was setting some type of trap for her future, but decided it would be nice to spend the day in town, "That sounds wonderful. I could use a little time out of the house."

"Then it's settled."

They gave each other huge smiles of endearment and started back to the chore of sorting through the room.

Chapter Six

She stood at the door saying her goodbyes as she watched Macie stroll through the dark and get into her car. Aubrey had been more than grateful for Macie's company, but as the night rolled in and the work came down to the final room, she insisted that it be done on her own time, at her own pace, alone with her mind free and clear to receive the emotions that would surely tread upon her. Although Macie questioned her strength to do so, she finally agreed to be on her way after they had finished dinner.

Over the meal, they had made their plans for the next day and vowed to shop until they literally dropped. Now, Aubrey would spend the rest of the night alone in this large house that she had just spent hours turning upside down. She was no closer to her decision of what to do with it, but there was a better understanding of the power and beauty it possessed. Aubrey was beginning to see it through her aunt's eyes, the wonder it held and the peace it gave. The amazement that she would behold each summer she visited as a child was not only given to her by her aunt, but by this place. She had absorbed it fully today as she wondered from room to room and sorted through its contents.

Giving a final wave goodbye, Aubrey closed the front door twisting the center of the knob to lock it and made her way back into the kitchen to fix a glass of tea. She was exhausted, but content and determined that she at least needed a peek into the very last room, her Aunt Jane's room. She wanted to go through it with a fine tooth comb, but for tonight she needed a short walk down the path of memory lane. Maybe she could limit herself to look through one piece of furniture. Then she promised she would call it a night and get some rest.

She tucked a brownie into her palm and wrapped her other hand around the drink she had poured herself. Her sweet tooth had inflicted itself on her as her appetite had returned, and the double fudge brownies that she had made from the recipe shared numerous times with her aunt in this very house were the perfect treat to satisfy the cravings. With her treat finished, she slowly moved herself with dragging feet down the hall to her aunt's room. Stopping in the doorway she let her head lead her eyes from picture to picture hanging on the wall. Walking into the room she glided a finger across the picture on the dresser as if she were brushing her aunt's cheek. She turned toward the bed and smiled over the comforter containing a paisley print with the neutral colors of tan and beige with a pop of blue that was brought out by the walls. Her furniture was a matching bedroom suite in deep cherry that stood out against the bright white trim. The room had a tray ceiling which gave it openness and depth centered with a drop rounded light fixture that allowed a glow to spill into the room casting shadows on the elegant designer rug beneath her feet. Aubrey inhaled deeply and took in a scent of lily of the valley, jasmine, and musk, hints of the perfume that her aunt always wore. She almost felt her wonderful presence in these four walls. It was a beautiful, comfortable, peaceful room.

Aubrey sat on the side of the queen sized bed and opened the drawer in the side table, but almost instantly closed it deciding it was much too personal of a place to start. She rose again and crossed to the dresser and felt more comfortable searching through the clothing drawers as she took one of the ornate pulls into her palm and drew it open glancing first to see the initial contents then reaching in to it to gain a better sense of what it entailed.

The first drawer she opened on the bottom row was simply lined with carefully folded sheet sets, all arranged together by color and including extra pillow cases. The next drawer to the left, also folded neatly, contained shorts of many different styles and color choices. Above those were equally arranged drawers of t-shirts, socks, underclothing, and pantyhose. The top drawer to the left held a sachet of Victorian rose and more elegant evening wear which Aubrey imagined fit the slender frame of her aunt beautifully, although she couldn't imagine her aunt had found much use for them in her busy life. To the far right of the dresser was a drawer of more practical night shirts and lounge wear which she recalled her aunt wearing as she made breakfast, sat to read a book, or enjoyed her coffee on the back deck as she overlooked the lake waters on a crisp summer morning.

The middle drawer on the top row proved to be the most interesting in the exquisite piece of furniture. It was half the size of the others, but contained the largest treasure. She pulled it open to discover memories of Jane's childhood. Inside it contained photos of her aunt in fashionable outfits as a young girl, smiling with friends or family. Aubrey flipped through them one by one letting a similar grin escape her lips as she found joy in the fun and flair captured in each pose. She looked closely at the details in their posture and the backgrounds as it told so much about the frame of mind of the subjects in the photos. Placing them on the top of the dresser, Aubrey continued through the drawer, searching for more interesting finds. There were souvenirs of the trips taken with friends and companions when she was in her twenties, each undoubtedly with a secret story to tell. Toward the back of the drawer were old appointment books, a couple of watches in their original cases and an elegantly designed book that sparked Aubrey's interest tremendously. She pulled the book from the back left corner and pushed against the front of the drawer with her hip to close it.

Aubrey crawled into the middle of the king sized bed among the mounds of matching pillows and drew her knees up to her chest. She took in a deep breath and let it expel slowly as she opened the journal that sported a dragonfly pressed onto the reddish-brown leather cover. She read the first page written in a stranger's handwriting.

To my dearest friend, Jane.
A place to collect your thoughts.
With love, Kathryn

"Kathryn?" Aubrey spoke the name aloud hoping it would trigger her memory, but came up empty. She was sure that her aunt had friends, but when it came time for her visit each summer, Aubrey knew she put her normal everyday life on hold, took time off from work, and focused on her niece leaving many aspects of her social life in the dark. She continued by turning to the next page and discovering the first journal words written in a familiar script and her heart suddenly skipped a beat as she caught her breath. It was the first journal entry of Jane Todd.

Dearest Journal,

I can assure you that I have not chosen to write to you because my life holds any true excitement. On the contrary, it is quite boring and lacks the sparkle that many humans have, who decide to record their thoughts. I only wish to look back at this book one day to see that I was an accomplished person in my career and hopefully in my life. It was the suggestion of a treasured friend that I make entries into this book to look back on later in life and see how far I have come. I truly hope that one day when I find that I need cheering up, it will fulfill the requirement. I pray that you will become an outlet for my long days, my largest fears, my greatest victories, and my future dreams. It is with these words that I will reveal those involved in my best of times and worst of times, Dickens excluded. I start by thanking Kathryn for her friendship, her ambition, and her lack of sanity (and I say that with love) for she has taught me so much in such a small amount of time about how to be a friend, how to share, how to care, and how to live my life freely. She has been an incredible sense of joy and wonder in the day to day of this career driven person. If one day someone finds this book, that person will discover that once in my life I found a kindred spirit like no other. For that I am always grateful!

Sincerely,

Jane Elizabeth

Her penmanship was breathtaking and the words spoke like poetry to Aubrey. She had never dreamed she would find something as cherished as a journal and the excitement of it was almost overwhelming. She could barely hold her eyes open, but found the words she read so comforting that she had to read just one more entry. She turned on to her side and lay down among the pillows on the bed. As she allowed the words to drift into her soul, she felt her eyes getting heavy and her mind wondering. Aubrey gave in to the pressure of sleep and gently closed her eyes with the journal still gripped in her hands. As she fell into a deep trance, her mind could visualize the words from the journal. She saw her aunt's pen moving across the paper recording her day, her week, her month. There would be so much to learn about this phenomenal person who had blessed her life as a child, and here in her hands was a testament written by Jane herself.

Chapter Seven

Aubrey and Macie had discussed in detail the plan for their shopping adventure and decided it would be best to ride together. So, the next morning after a hearty breakfast and a call to her office in Memphis to check in on her clients, Aubrey gathered her things making sure she had her cell phone, keys to the house, and wallet with her platinum Visa. She wanted a girl's day out to remember and intended to live this day to the fullest. Once she had everything she felt she needed, she headed out the door to go pick up Macie. In the crisp air of the season with the sun beading down like drops of bright shimmering rain, there was a certain immediate happiness to laughing while reminiscing of days gone by and enjoying the top down on her BMW as they drove to the next town over with the wind blowing through their hair, so she had offered to chauffer for the day.

She arrived at the two story pale yellow Victorian style house with potted ferns and blooming mums hanging in baskets from the trim work of the front porch. She stepped up to the front door framed with cement urns filled with numerous flowers, vines and plants. Seeing the decorative doorbell to the left of the door, Aubrey pressed the lit button and listened as the chimes rang a familiar tune.

Macie opened the door of her mother's house and smiled, "Good morning! Come on in I'm getting my things together. I'll be ready in just a few minutes. Hey, thanks for picking me up here. I had to help mom with some things this morning. I thought it would be easier than riding out to my place."

"No problem," Aubrey replied walking into the large living area and laying her purse on the corner of the couch.

"Did you get any more work done last night?" Macie asked in a raised voice as she walked back to the bathroom she had used to freshen up.

"Not much really. I just kind of glanced through the dresser drawers in Aunt Jane's bedroom," she roamed through the room looking at pictures of Macie and her sisters as children. It made a short smile slip across her face. Macie was one of three Sanders daughters, the oldest in fact, and each one had the beauty of their mother's Barcelona heritage with dark tights curls that laid perfectly across broad shoulders and down their elegant backs. The personalities of each had become a combination of fiery Spanish flare and their father's athletic ability, Macie's being much more of a blunt, charismatic, and outgoing nature than her sisters. Clearly Melissa and Maggie had taken in more of the athletic and calm nature of their father, finding a balance in the culture of their heritage.

"Aubrey, don't lose momentum now after you got so much done yesterday," Macie said coming back out of the hallway sweeping through and heading into the kitchen.

Following her Aubrey responded, "I won't, I was just so exhausted that I fell asleep reading."

"Oh, what are you reading now?" Macie asked absentmindedly as she tossed her cell phone and lip gloss into her purse.

Aubrey shrugged, "It's just something that I found. I'll have to show you next time you are over."

"It sounds intriguing," Macie said with a hint of sarcasm.

"Speaking of intriguing, I came through town earlier and noticed a boat at the Marina that had crane like arms on each side. Do you have any idea what it might be?" Aubrey asked as she leaned against the island in the middle of the kitchen.

"Was it rather small like a tug boat?" Macie questioned

sweeping from one side of the kitchen to the other gathering a glass then opening the refrigerator to search for something to pour.

"I guess," Aubrey responded. "It looked strange and there were a lot of people standing around watching it being unloaded into the water. I saw Trey and Jason there too with some of the other officers and some guys in green uniforms."

"That must be the sonar boat," Macie said leaning on the other side of the island and taking a cool sip from the glass. "Trey told me they would be coming into town this week to do research on Majestic Lake. There is some type of technology that has been developed that will scan deep into the water. He said they have used it in the swamps of Florida for a few years to help locate missing vehicles and on the inland waters to find drowning victims in lakes and rivers. Thirsty?"

"No, thank you. Are they looking for a something in Majestic?" worried that something terrible had happened.

"No. Trey says that since we live in a county that contains a lake and other waterways, law enforcement with search and rescue are often asked to search for drowning victims and missing objects. The Wildlife Resources office suggested that they look into purchasing a side sonar boat to help with searches," Macie informed her as she carefully placed the glass into the sink, slung her purse over her shoulder, and began walking back to the great room.

"It seems like it would really benefit the department, but it sounds expensive," Aubrey stood upright and started toward the doorway to the living room.

"They are requesting a grant for it from the state. To get the grant, the state requires a test run be done with an environmental consultant to determine the usefulness of it in the area. They have to look at water depth and check police reports and records for frequency of requests for search and rescue. It is a matter of safety. Since the lake is governed by the Tennessee Wildlife Resources Agency, they are helping with the trial run. That is probably who you saw in the green uniforms," Macie reached for the doorknob to the front door and then yelled over her shoulder. "Mom, Aubrey is here and we are leaving. Love you."

"Wait a minute Macie," her mother's voice rang softly down the stairs and they heard footsteps overhead.

"So what does safety have to do with the boat?" Aubrey continued the conversation.

"It will give them a better idea of what is down there without having to send down divers which can take more time and be dangerous." Macie stopped at the door and waited for her mother. "This system lets them take a look underwater before they even have to jump in which is good if they don't really know where they are supposed to be looking. In other words it can narrow down the search area." Aubrey shook her head in understanding.

Macie's mother found her way down the stairs and making her way over gave Aubrey a huge smile, then opened her arms wide to embrace her.

"Oh, Aubrey, sweetheart, I just wanted to give my girl a big hug and tell you again how very sorry I am about Jane," Mary Sanders was the epitome of the suburban housewife with her classic look of casual pants and a colorful button up top with the sleeves rolled up her arms a quarter of the way. Her familiar dark locks swept back from her light caramel skin in a decorative hairpin. "Now, you know you are welcome here anytime, if you get lonely in that big lake house. In fact, you should stop by for dinner one night this week. Mark, Melissa and Maggie would love to see you as well. Oh, tell me you will," she pleaded.

"Yes, ma'am, of course I will. Just let me know the date and time," Aubrey smiled back with love. Besides her aunt, "Miss" Mary had been her second mother as she was growing up. She always made wonderful dinners and believed that a happy home should be full of children. It didn't matter if the children were not blood related to her. The home had an open door policy and everyone was welcome.

"Good then. I'll get it planned and Macie will let you know when to be here. It is so good to see you," she gave Aubrey a final squeeze and Macie a peck on the cheek before turning her attention back to the stairs to return to her chores.

"Your mom is the best," Aubrey said to Macie with a warm feeling in her heart.

"Well, she did raise three awesome girls, one more awesome than the others," Macie gave her best diva impression.

"You know you are right, how is Melissa doing these days?" Aubrey asked in a smart tone grinning with a proud Cheshire smile.

"Very funny," Macie walked out the front door.

"So, back to this sonar boat," Aubrey followed her out the door and the two made their way to the car in the driveway. "How do they know what is there?"

"The camera sends the images back up to a computer in the boat and it looks a lot like an aerial view of the county when it shows up on the monitor," Macie said as she pulled the passenger door open and sat in the seat. "I think it all sounds pretty interesting. It's guided by a GPS system like you have in your car so they can pin point exactly where something is found, save it on the computer, and come back to the same spot later to recover it."

Aubrey slid into the driver's seat, started the car, and adjusted her radio while putting her sunglasses on and buckling her seat belt, "Will it mean there will be fewer divers needed?"

"It's not going to replace the dive team or the remote control camera that they have, but it should help them find what they are looking for faster," Macie assessed her sunglasses in the visor mirror and after buckling her belt got comfortable for the ride. It was as if they were going back in time to when they were teenagers. The mall was waiting.

"So, is that why I saw Trey and Jason out there?" Aubrey asked as she shifted gears and pulled out onto the main boulevard.

"Probably. They were the ones who got the ball rolling on the project to get one of these boats. Naturally they felt it would benefit the department to have one, but Jason had seen one first hand. He was able to work with one at a training session he did in Nashville. He is training to be a diver," Macie said and Aubrey looked startled.

"Really?" she asked.

"I've told you things are different with him. He is involved with the community and helps out in any way he can. He has taken classes and courses to earn whatever certifications he can to advance his job and make himself a more indispensable officer," Macie bragged.

"So, it seems," Aubrey said not giving in to the fact he could be a better person. She had not been personally convinced. "You are just a wealth of knowledge. You know that."

"It's a small town. I'm not good for much else," Macie said with a giggle.

"Well, good for him for putting in such hard work. I hope they gain the grant for the boat if it is something that will help," Aubrey gained speed as she cruised down the highway.

"You know, they do accept donations," Macie said with a devious tone as if she were asking her to do something illegal.

"Are you hinting at something?" Aubrey asked.

"Well, you did get all that money from Jane's will," Macie suggested.

"That money is to set up my future," Aubrey replied.

"Oh, who are you kidding?" Macie rolled her eyes at the thought. "Your future has been set for years now. All you ever do is work, and yes you are good at it, but you don't spend very much, you don't take vacations or buy expensive gifts for yourself. What are you going to do with that inheritance?"

"I plan to invest it," Aubrey said like it was ridiculous for her friend to even ask, "or at least a large chunk of it."

"That's fine, but you won't invest it all. What about the rest?" she asked. "It was just an idea, but Jane loved this town, loved the people in it. She had a sense of community here. It might be a nice gesture to see that the community gets something they could use. I know they would be grateful."

Aubrey thought about it and how it would be a gift for Jason's cause. She had to put her feelings for him aside and think about the benefits it could have for the community as a whole, "I'll consider it. She did leave me plenty and the people here were always very kind to her."

"They could even call the boat the 'Lady Jane'," Macie laughed.

"Let's not get carried away about this," Aubrey said as she pulled into the parking lot of the mall. "Are you ready to shop?"

"Till we drop!" Macie leaned her head back to bask in the sun one last time before Aubrey found her parking spot.

Four hours and three trips to the car later, the two were finally giving up on any more shopping for the day. They had both spent way over their initial agreed limit and it was almost time to find dinner before going back to Macie's parents to present the fashion show of items they had purchased. Her mother always enjoyed viewing the purchases made by the girls and watching them total the amount of savings as she had taught them when they were children. The savings had been a coaxing tactic used often by Mary Sanders to smooth over her obsessive shopping trips with her daughters to her husband. Proving to him that she had saved him money was a loving game Mark and Mary played for many years. As they walked back to the car, Macie's cell phone began to ring.

"Hello," she said firmly into the phone.

"Hey, Mac, where are you? I've been trying to get you at the house, but nothing for hours now," Trey's deep voice sang through the phone to her.

"Aubrey and I took a shopping trip this afternoon. How are things going?" Macie replied.

"The test run went well," he said.

"That's good," Macie said. "We just got finished and we are going to go back to mom's to try everything on."

"Did you buy so much that you have already forgotten what you bought," Trey gave a chuckle.

"No, but now we get to model them for each other and decide who got the best deal. It's a girl thing," Macie told him smugly.

"Are you going to be around later because I've got something to tell you if you can keep it to yourself," she could hear Trey starting his truck and shifting it into drive.

"Sure, but you already have my curiosity up now. You have to tell me. I'm not going to say anything," Macie piled the last of her bags into the back of Aubrey's car and opened her passenger's side door to get in as Aubrey closed the trunk.

Trey paused for a moment. He intended to tell her the whole story when he arrived at her house, not over the phone, but it was hard to contain the information that he wanted to share with the one person other than Jason that he trusted with his own life. He would give her just enough to wet her appetite. "We found a car in the lake with the sonar today."

"Really?" Macie sounded shocked. "Who's do you think it is?"

"We don't know yet," Trey replied, "but we are going to go back out and get some better reads on it tomorrow. This sonar thing is amazing. I can see why Jason has been talking about it. It could be a huge help in finding people and things lost in the lake."

"So what about…you know?" Macie asked mindful that Aubrey was also getting into the car and could easily hear her side of the conversation.

"We'll have the search and rescue dive team go down and take a closer look, then we will try to pull it out in a couple of days after we evaluate how deep it is and get a game plan together. I'm sure a lot of this will come out in the paper, but I was just so excited at the find and how well the boat did that I had to share it with someone," Trey knew he had already told her too much and that Aubrey was right there in the car with her, but it would be all over town soon and as long as they didn't shout it from the roof tops of downtown he felt comfortable.

"I think it is great," Macie was truly happy for him. "You are already proving that this thing will help the community. They have to give you the grant now."

"Well, they don't have to. They can still say that we would have found it anyway when the lake generated and got low enough or when a fishing boat scanner found it or something," Trey said with doubt in his voice. "They can give all kinds of excuses when they really want to deny something. We aren't out of the woods on this project yet, but it is going to help our case."

"You sound like a lawyer," Macie scolded him. "Quit that!"

"Is it still all right to stop by," he asked.

"Sure, give me a couple of hours," she said with a crooked grin brushing across her face. Aubrey tilted her head quickly to catch a glimpse of Macie's smile.

"I'll pick us up a bite to eat," he offered.

"That would be great, but no pizza. I've had it twice this week and I need a break from it," Macie informed him.

"Yes, ma'am," he told her taking in her words and heading to a mom and pop barbeque place, "how about some, Mama Bell's bar-b-que?"

"Sounds great! See you soon!"

"Bye!"

Macie pushed the red coded button on her phone to end the call and let another smile grace her face as she stared at the pink cased phone in her hand.

"Are you going to tell me what that was all about?" Aubrey settled into the driver's seat and adjusted her seatbelt across her chest as she locked it into place. Once the car engine growled she raised the convertible top to break some of the chill of the evening on the ride home.

"Nothing really. It was Trey. He was just letting me know that they had a good day out on the lake and should know about the grant pretty soon," Macie was careful not to give away too much information.

Aubrey put the car in reverse and slowly backed out from the parking space. "Did he say what they saw, or was it just a bunch of fish and drowned trees?"

"He really couldn't talk about it much, but I think they saw enough to know that it could benefit the department to have it in their arsenal of equipment," Macie couldn't lie to her best friend, so she searched for little ways around the questions.

"Well, let's get back to your mom's and we will try on all of our new outfits. Maybe Melissa will be around and we can get her opinion too," Aubrey added, excited to be having a girl's evening with Macie's family.

"You know, I think maybe we should just head on back to my place and you can drop me off," Macie said suspiciously.

"But I thought we were going to try things on and give each other opinions?" Aubrey was surprised at the sudden change in Macie. Did she say or do something wrong? Macie never refused the chance to spend time together.

"Maybe we can pick it up tomorrow. I'm just tired tonight," she gave a less than convincing yawn.

At first a bit confused, it hit Aubrey like a ton of bricks that her friend's sudden change in attitude may have something to do with the phone call she had just received. Macie had always claimed since high school that Trey was nothing more than a close friend, but perhaps things had begun to shift for them to a more intimate relationship. She could probe Macie for details later, but for tonight she didn't want to stand in the way.

"I'll just drop you and your things off and then you can stop by Dragonfly tomorrow," Aubrey sounded disappointed in the outcome, but was convinced that there was much more to this story than Macie would be willing to share tonight.

Aubrey continued the drive past Macie's family's house and into town then turned sharply past the town square to find a hidden passage to a dead end road. At the end of the road were two small houses, one that inhabited a family of six and an even smaller two bedroom place with the porch light on and a wreath of fall colors on the door. It was a warm and cozy looking cottage and a perfect rental for Macie.

"Here we are. Thank you for the day. It has been wonderful. Maybe we can do it again before you have to go back to Memphis," Macie said hoping that Aubrey would chime in to tell her she wasn't going back to the big city.

"Maybe," was all Aubrey could muster knowing where her friend's comment was leading, "Come by in the morning and we can have coffee on the porch and try on our great deals?"

"It's a date," Macie opened her passenger door and stepped out of the vehicle. She danced around the edge to the trunk of the car to get her bags. With almost more than she could tow, she walked around the driver's side of the car and nodded the only part of her body she could logically control hoping the expression to roll the window down was clear to Aubrey. As if reading her mind, Aubrey stroked the button to send the driver side window down, "Have a good rest of the night, and try to get some sleep. I'm still worried about you."

"I'll be fine. Are you sure you can make it in the door?"

"Sure, I'm a pro at this. Good night!"

"Nite!"

Aubrey carefully turned her car around in the shared driveway so she would not disturb Macie's neighbors. She left the window down as she took her car onto the main street of town. She would take the long way back to the lake so she could hear the faint chirping of the crickets in the trees and smell the fresh cut grass as the lawns received their last clipping of the season. Soon everything would slow down and the winter pace would begin. Soon the flowers would stop blooming and the birds would be flying south overhead. Soon she would have to return to Memphis and she would no longer enjoy these little things that had made her so happy in the past week. Would she continue to dream of the lake and its beauty when she was gone? Would she be haunted by this quant town and its people? Sometimes, she hoped.

Dearest Journal,

Today was a record breaking day for my career. I have sold at least two houses per month for the last six months. Being still fairly new to Walker, I am ecstatic about this accomplishment. I know I am well on my way to becoming a multi-million dollar seller. I have reset my goals to reflect my push forward and I believe that I can accomplish them in record time. Even in a small town, it doesn't hurt to dream big. I have a wonderful feeling that luck is coming my way. What will I do with the lovely commission checks that I will receive from these sales? I have my eye on a cute little lake house in Cedar Grove with a red door and dark gray shaker siding. I think I will have to paint the door, but the rest of it is perfect. With a little facelift it will be just what I need. It has old wood plank steps down to the dock and once I refresh the wood deck and add a handrail it will be the perfect place for me to enjoy my lazy days (if I have any lazy days). I already have the name: Dragonfly, always seeking an adventure, but always returning home, and that is what it will be, HOME.

Yours truly,

Jane Elizabeth

Chapter Eight

Trey paced in the boat skimming his eyes over his watch every few minutes, waiting for a tug, a diving mask, something, anything to emerge from the water. The divers had been under for quite some time and there was no word to the surface yet to reveal their findings. They had gone down on a mission to investigate the submerged car and to devise a plan of recovery, but Trey had a feeling that there was going to be a lot more to this story. He hated that feeling, but it was strong this time and it flooded his chest like the downtown streets of Walker during a rain storm. It had been two days since the sonar boat had found the car deep in the waters of Majestic Lake and the curiosity of what might be in the vehicle had become overwhelming. Jason was on his first recovery dive and that also made Trey nervous. He searched his wrist again for the minutes that were passing so slowly. Why hadn't they come up? What was down there?

"I see bubbles and a tug on the line. We got one coming up," he heard one of the Search and Rescue members call out.

"Well, let's see what we got," said another as he went over to help the diver by guiding the line into the boat.

Trey tried to stay out of the way, but was anxious to see which diver was resurfacing. Reaching the water's edge, the diver first removed his mouthpiece to sweep in fresh lake air, then raised the facemask to his forehead. It was Jason. "That was crazy," he said brushing water from his nose and mouth. "Help me on out fellas." He climbed onto the ladder hanging on the side of the boat.

"So what does it look like down there?" Trey asked as the two men clad in Wildlife Resource t-shirts and shorts each took an arm and helped Jason into the boat.

"It's not what you would think," he replied, slipping his arms from the straps attaching the pony tank to his back as the men held the weight of it. He removed his gloves, headlamp, and mask, and tossed them into a seat on the side of the boat. Then he slid the hood of his wetsuit down from his head. He unlatched the bright yellow harness removing his arms and letting it fall with a clank to the bottom of the boat. He stepped out of it, detached the knife strapped to his inner thigh, and handed it to Trey before he began to unzip the front of the wetsuit.

With a slight tilt of his head and confused look pressing through his eyes and forehead Trey asked quizzically, "Jason, what did you find?"

Jason brushed his hand across his face to remove the remaining drops of water and pressed his thumb and forefinger into the corners of his closed eyes.

"There is a body in the car. It's been there for a while, badly decomposed, and the tags on the car expired fifteen years ago," he said, continuing to unzip the wetsuit and sliding his arms from the sleeves. Jason pulled the suit to his waist exposing his bare chest. "The rest of the guys are taking a closer look. They wanted to try to evaluate the conditions so we lose as little evidence as possible when we bring it up out of the water. It's murky down there, almost too deep to see any details even with headlamps, but the bones are clear. I came on up so we could call it in and get a team in place to raise it," he took a look around and caught sight of the cell phone lying on the dash in the driver's area of the boat.

Taking the phone from the dash, he pressed seven numbers with his moist fingers and raised it to his ear where his hair hung dripping with the musty smell of the lake. "Colleen, it's Jason. Can you put me through to Drake? Thanks." Facing Trey he paused as she transferred his call, "It might be a case of suicide, but I don't think it was an accident. The body is just sitting there in the driver's seat. I don't think it would be in that position if he had been fighting for his life or if he were driving himself into the water. Even someone killing themselves has a slight moment of panic just before they die." He then raised the phone back to his mouth and continued, "Drake, I need you run a plate that expired fifteen years ago. The number is GBS 582. See who it was last registered to. It is on an old dark green Cadillac. Also, see if anyone was reported missing from this area during that same time period. I'll explain it all when I come in later today. I appreciate it." He hung up the phone and returned it to the dash.

"Have you got an idea in your head over this one," Trey queried, helping him get his equipment out of the way of the other divers when they surfaced.

"Nothing comes to mind. I don't know that I've seen the car before and if it sank fifteen years ago, then that was before my time as an officer. I hope we can trace the plate. It might give us a place to start." Jason sat down on the edge of the boat to remove his flippers and then propped his elbows on his knees. He brushed his hands over his dark locks of hair and lifted his head to Trey, "I'm afraid we have a mystery on our hands." He smiled.

Trey returned the childish grin, "Time to put on the Sherlock Holmes hat and find us an old blood hound?" The friends laughed together. "So, what now?"

"The guys from the rescue dive team are trained in preservation of evidence, so I'll leave the rest of the underwater stuff to them. I think this is a little beyond the realm of a newbie like me. Once the car is up they will gather any forensic evidence and we will help with that. It's unlikely but fingerprints might still be there, we just have to be careful how we go about getting them. We'll have to really be careful gathering DNA as well. I guess depending on what we find we'll need to decide whether we take the car to the TBI or not, just because they have the more expensive toys. It's rare that we would have to do that, but if it looks like a homicide, it would be necessary. It's good that our office is pretty much self-sustaining in what we can handle. We can work the case quicker by keeping it local," Jason took a t-shirt from his bag in the floor of the boat. He stretched the knit cotton over his head and pulled his arms through the sleeves, then pulled it down over his well-developed six pack as small drops of water on his abdomen soaked through the white fabric. He then lifted the lid and reached his hand into a cooler sitting to the right side of the boat pulling out a Coke can and popping the top. He placed it in a cup holder and rose from the seat to stand and remove the rest of the wetsuit clinging to his body. Modesty was not something to be concerned about on the job, but he glanced around to be sure there were no other boats in the immediate area. Peeling the suit down, he had nothing to be ashamed of in his physique. His broad shoulders and chest gave way to muscular thighs and a firm backside that would attract even the most prudish woman. He slipped on a pair of jeans quickly, choosing to go commando until he reached the shore and was able to take a shower. Trey simply rolled his eyes, knowing he would never dare to do the same. Jason sat back down on the seat to release the tension in his shoulders that had mounted from the dive and sip his cold drink.

"How did things go last night with Gina?" Trey asked sitting across from him in the boat.

"Yeah, I don't think that one is going to work out." The other men shuffled around the boat keeping watch over the submerged divers still working in the murky waters below.

Trey drew his brows downward, "Really? She is beautiful, successful, and the right age. What makes you think she is not worth your time?"

"There just isn't that spark," Jason explained. "I have been taking her out for a few weeks now and I just don't feel that chemistry."

"Is there someone else you think might have that spark?"

"I'm starting to wonder." Jason drew in a deep breath and sighed, "It seems like I've been through all the girls around here and I haven't felt that heart stopping thing for any of them."

"You know there is one girl in town that hasn't had her shot at you yet," a deceptive grin swept across Trey's broad tan face. His golden eyes shifted to see if anyone else had directed their attention to them as they talked.

"And who might that be," Jason asked with sudden curiosity.

Leaning down closer and lowering his voice Trey said, "She may only be in town for a couple more weeks, so you better make your move quick."

"Sweeney? Are you kidding? I'm not trying that one, she can't stand me. You know that." Jason stiffened and leaned back against the boat seat stretching his arms out across the back.

"That was a long time ago," Trey argued.

Jason shook his head, "Besides she's not in town to see me. She left because of me ten years ago. That's not even in the cards, man."

"Time changes people, maybe she has gotten over all that."

"You didn't see her the other night when I showed up at Dragonfly," the vision of her anger as she asked him to leave a few nights earlier flashed through his mind. She had wanted him gone. "She hasn't changed how she feels about me."

"I wouldn't be so quick to toss that one to the side, man." Trey relaxed against the opposite seat looking out over the water watching the tops of the trees sway in the breeze knocking a few brightly colored leaves to the ground.

"When are you ever going to ask Macie out?" Jason questioned turning the tables.

"You know it's not like that between Mac and me. Besides you, she is my closest friend. We've been that way for years and I don't want to mess that up," Trey escaped into a dream world when he talked about Macie, despite his words his true feelings were written all over his face.

Jason tilted his head and studied his friend's expression, then nodded, "I know how you really feel about her."

"I'd rather have her in my life as a friend, than not have her at all because we tried something and it didn't work out. I don't know if I could handle being without her. She makes me laugh, she challenges me, she just makes things a little more fun, you know?"

"Until she finds Mr. Right and then you will regret that you never made your move," Jason pushed.

Trey looked back at Jason and asked, "When did we start talking about my love life? I thought we were trying to hook you up."

"I'll stay out of yours if you stay out of mine. Yeah?" Jason reached out his hand to seal the deal with a shake.

Trey looked at his hand, then back at his expression, "That's fair."

They shook almost violently as if they were trying to shaking the two exasperatingly wonderful women from their minds.

Chapter Nine

"Well, hello Sweeney," he appeared from nowhere and leaned against the chair across from Aubrey at the two person table she was enjoying inhabiting alone. She had spent her day going through things in her aunt's detached storage building and sorting the older furniture pieces she had found pushed to the back, then she had spent the last couple of hours relaxing on the dock by the lake drinking in the view and her sweet tea while she continued reading her Andrew's book. Because she wasn't in the mood to make dinner for herself, she had decided to take a drive into town to try the food at a friendly meat and three restaurant. Macie had assured her that for local cuisine, it was the best in the area. Her hope had been for a nice dinner alone, but her visitor had stopped that venture with three words.

She peered up at him. "Jason," she replied with static in her voice that displayed her annoyance.

"What brings you here, getting a bite of dinner?" he asked.

She rolled her eyes and exuded a forceful sigh. "Something like that. I enjoy the peace and quiet," she said praying that he would catch the hint.

"I hate for you to have to sit here and eat alone," he took the back of the chair and pulled it out for himself.

"I don't mind being alone. What do you think you are doing?" she asked furrowing her brows in a puzzled expression.

"I'm having a seat. What do you think I'm doing?" he acted surprised at her question.

She was appalled at his egotistical gesture, "I don't recall inviting you to sit down."

"That's all right," he replied, "I don't recall asking." He knew he had her in a fury, and loved every minute of the interaction. Getting under her skin had always been one of his favorite past times.

"Let's get down to it, Jason," she told him, tired from her day and exhausted with playing his game. "What do you want?"

"I was wondering if I could ask you a few questions," he was through with his fun and thought it best to ask her what he came here to ask before she found the need to rise from the table and leave. As entertaining as it was to watch her fume with irritation, he needed to see if she could help him with his latest case.

"About?" her head tilted as she lifted a fork full of chicken to her mouth and savored the flavors of lemon and thyme.

"Can I get you something, Jason?" a boppy little brunette in her early twenties asked him as she swept by Aubrey's table.

"A glass of tea would be good," his gaze followed her slender shape as she briskly walked away to fulfill his request.

"Uhhmmm!" Aubrey cleared her throat to regain Jason's attention and repeated, "About?"

He returned his eyes to her and smiled, "Someone your aunt used to know years ago..."

"I don't know if I will have the answers. I didn't really know any of her friends. She pretty much focused on me when I came to visit," she continued to eat her dinner dipping into her roasted potatoes.

"I'd like to ask you just the same."

Aubrey glared at him with narrowing eyelids wondering just what he had up his sleeve, "Fine, go ahead and ask."

"Have you found anything interesting in Jane's house since you've been there? Thank you, Ashley," he nodded his head in appreciation as the waitress sat a glass of tea in front of him. "Anything out of the ordinary while you've been going through her things."

"Mostly paperwork, things she collected, there are some pictures from years ago when we were all at the lake. You were even in a couple of them. I can make you copies if you like," she told him.

"Well," he said a little surprised at her offer, "maybe I'll come by and take a look at them soon. Anything else?"

"No, just the normal stuff. It's been a real challenge getting through it all and keeping my sanity," she finished her food and pushed the plate away from her a few inches. She took her cup of coffee in both hands to use it for warmth. The food had been surprisingly pleasant, but the chill in the room began to seep into her bones. She leaned forward and placed her elbows on the table propping the coffee cup directly in front of her lips. She wanted to give him her undivided attention. He was beginning to spark her interest. "Macie has been such a help."

He went on, "Does the name Jake Warren mean anything to you?"

"Jake Warren. It sounds familiar, but I can't place him. Why?" She took a sip from the cup and placed it on the table before crossing her arms in front of her, similar to her defensive move only a few days earlier when in the presence of Jason. He noticed and drew back slightly.

"I was just curious," he shrugged off her interest. "Someone had mentioned the name to me and said that Jane was a girlfriend of his years ago."

"Wait," she turned to look away from him as she thought deeply, "I believe I do remember a guy named Jake coming around maybe twelve or fifteen years ago. I was probably in my pre-teens. I didn't see him very much though because she would go out with him on the nights I spent the night at Macie's. He didn't come by the house," then she turned to face Jason with a spark of realization in her eyes, "except for this one time and he was really mad about something. He didn't know I was there in my room and could hear him, but he was yelling at Aunt Jane and cursing her over something. I had almost forgotten about that."

"Have you come across anything with his name on it?" his words were excited as he hoped she might be able to share something of importance.

"No, where are you going with all of this?"

Jason let out a disappointing sigh, "His name has come up in a case we are working on, but he left town years ago so I am really having to dig to find any information on him. Half of the people who knew him back then are gone too, either moved away or..." He stopped silent.

"...or passed. You can say it Jason."

"I'm not here to stir up fresh wounds," she saw the sympathy in his eyes before he could look away from her.

"I am a realist. I know that it happens to everyone," she assured him.

"But the pain is still there," he sounded so sincere. "Anyway, he didn't live here in town very long so I just thought you might have found something in the house that could help."

She lowered her head to stare into her coffee cup, "Well, if I do find something, I'll be sure to let you know."

"Thank you."

As he gripped the edge of the table and started to push his chair back to rise, she raised her hand to stop him, "Now it's my turn to ask you a question." He settled back down into the chair and cupped his hands together on the table in front of him. "I was thinking about making a donation from my inheritance to help buy the sonar boat. Who would I talk to about that?"

He raised his eyebrows in surprise, "I guess you would talk to me, but it looks like we will be getting a grant for the boat and equipment to use with it."

"So, the research turned out well," she inquired.

Not wanting to reveal too much, he vaguely answered, "You could say that. It was pretty convincing."

"Great," she smiled, "I'm glad you will be getting the boat."

He tilted his head in wonder at her monetary gesture, "If you want to help out, I can think of another project that could use the money."

"And what project would that be?"

"It's a community education project called *Officer for a Day*," he explained. "It is designed to help kids understand an officer's job. We want to inspire them at a young age and teach them that we do morc than write tickets and make arrests. There is a lot of community involvement and service in what we do. Kids need to know that we are not the bad guys, that we can be trusted and can help in a difficult situation. We like to have fun, too. There are great events that we can plan for all the folks in town, but all of these ideas need funding to be successful."

She could see his enthusiasm as he unfolded the program's mission, "That is where I come in."

"If you want to be a part of it."

"I'd like to hear more about the specifics," she smiled shaking her head in agreement. "Is this your program?"

"Will it change your mind about donating the money if I say yes?" he had found the catch.

"Not if it is a good program," she told him with certainty.

He studied her face to be sure she was telling him the truth, "Then, yes, it is something I've been working on. I have great ideas and I've even starting putting them down on paper, but it takes time and funds."

"Maybe I can take a look at your ideas sometime, and help you put it into a plan," she offered.

"What do you know about it?" his lips curled in one corner as he questioned her ability.

"I have to put together buyer presentations, research, charts, and many types of paperwork for my job. I might be able to help you fit your ideas into an understandable presentation that will help you get funds from the community or even the state. My money will get you started, but if it is a well thought-out venture you will want to make sure you have the money to continue it," she knew she had him on that note.

"What's your angle?" he probed.

"I don't have one," she sounded taken back that he even suggested she had other motives. He shot her a demanding look and she backed down on her offensive tone, "Macie reminded me of how important this community was to my aunt and how much she cared for the people in it." She lowered her voice and shrugged, "I thought for her memory's sake I might invest a little of my time and money while I am here."

He was impressed, "In that case, I'll let you know when I have something for you to look at. If you are ready to head out, I can walk you to your car."

She shook her head, "You don't have to do that."

"I don't mind. Besides, we have actually spent more than ten minutes together without insulting each other or trying to do any bodily harm. It's kind of nice," he gave her a slight grin.

She smiled back, "Let me go pay my bill and I'll be right out."

"I've got to take care of my drink, too."

"I'll take care of it. It's the least I can do for a hard-working officer of the law." That statement made him laugh.

They both got up from their seats and insisting on taking care of the tip, Jason laid a five on the table and walked toward the door as Aubrey circled back around with her ticket in hand to pay for her meat and three plate, coffee, and Jason's tea. After a polite but awkward parting with the cashier, Aubrey walked out the door into the brisk fall evening air and wrapped her scarf around her neck. She glanced first to her right and then to the left to find Jason leaning against the wall of the restaurant looking like James Dean waiting for his prey.

"Ready?" he asked, burying his hands deep into his pockets.

"Sure," she slipped her purse over her shoulder and began to casually walk toward the parking lot a couple of blocks down from the restaurant.

"So, what has it been like being back in town," he began his friendly interrogation.

"Not bad, actually. I've gotten a lot done at the house, but in town I just feel like everyone is staring at me," she said to him.

"They are not staring at you," he gave a laugh at what he thought was her paranoid thinking.

"Then why do I feel like a piece of Swiss cheese with the holes they are sending through me," she said continuing to walk in a slow paced stride.

He stopped walking forcing her to turn to look at him, "They are just wondering the same thing we all are, how things are, how you are. It's been months since Jane passed and it's the first time they have seen you in town in years. They are just curious about what is going to happen."

She began walking again, "Well, I'm wondering about that one myself."

"Have you talked with Mr. Shipley?" he followed her taking large steps to catch up to her.

"I have talked to him and I have scheduled some appointments with local realtors."

"You aren't even going to consider keeping the house?" he tried not to let the disappointment drip into his words as he kicked a rock along the sidewalk.

"I've been thinking about this for three months. What am I going to do with a house so far away?"

"It would be the ideal vacation place, for some fun, a getaway. Don't you want to keep it in the family?" he couldn't imagine someone other than a *Todd* owning Dragonfly. Her family belonged in that house.

"I don't know. With everything that has happened, I don't know if I even want to keep the house as a memory of her," she blew out a breath of exhausted air from her lungs. She had been through this a couple of times already with Macie and the repetition of the conversation was depleting her energy. "I'm just going to talk to the agents. It doesn't mean that I've made a decision yet. I want to have someone lined up in case I do decide to put it on the market. I have to make sure that they understand that I am a licensed agent myself and would require a percentage for letting them handle the sale. It doesn't make sense for me to try to list it."

"Is that what you are thinking about," he said in disbelief, "the money?"

She jolted her head toward him standing still and straight backed before him insulted, "No, of course not. I could care less about that money. I would trade it all to have her back."

"Whoa, easy, Sweeney," he held up his open palms in admitted defeat. "I'm sorry I even suggested it. I know you better than to think that would be the case. Maybe you could rent it out then it would be available if you ever do need it."

She eased her fury and laughed, "Do you want to rent it from me? I'll make you a good deal."

He smiled at her, "No, I already have my place. I bought mom's and dad's old house down the lake a while ago, so they could move into town. Besides, I'm sure it is worth a lot with all the improvements Jane made."

She looked up at the beautiful night and savored the moonlight and the gleam of the stars. She didn't have a chance to enjoy them in the city the way she did in Walker, "I'm just waiting for that ah-ha moment when it all becomes clear to me."

"Well, my mom says that ah-ha moments don't come to you. You have to go looking for them," he followed her gaze to the stars and took in a deep breath of the cool night air.

"So, what do you do in the meantime?"

"Enjoy the chase," it was simple, but the most encouraging advice she had heard since her aunt had left the Earth.

She lowered her head at the same moment he did and their eyes locked on one another. He was surprisingly close to her all of the sudden and her heart jumped into her throat. She felt a very strange attraction to him like the pull of a bungee cord tightening and releasing with the pressure of the jump. She snapped back to the present and shook her head slightly to free whatever thought had captured her mind for that instant putting distance between them as she began to walk again, "Well, I will be chasing it elsewhere. I'm leaving in a couple of weeks to head back to Memphis, unless I get everything settled before then."

"I'm sorry to hear that you'll be leaving so soon," he began to move with her baffled at the tiny prickles that had raced along his skin in the instant before she spoke.

"Here we are," she pressed the button on her keychain to unlock her car directly across the street from where they stood.

"BMW, I should have guessed," he said sarcastically.

Then she recalled what she had always despised in him and her eyes instantly turned cold, "It's been a pleasure as always, Jason. I'll be heading home now. Thank you!"

"No, Sweeney. The pleasure was all mine," and there it was again, the smug grin that made her cringe.

She quickly stepped off of the curb, not paying any attention to the truck pulling out of the alley across from them. With one swift motion Jason reached out and pulled her back from the road, wrapping his arms around her for protection. She had nearly been hit by overzealous teenagers who had most likely hid in the alley to drink a beer before heading to their next destination.

"Are you all right?" Jason asked her as he felt her tremble in his arms.

She finally released the breath she had pinned up inside of her. His arms felt so strong and inviting as they enveloped her, but after a few seconds she realized who those arms belonged to and she suddenly brushed them off as if they were on fire.

"Thank you, but I'm fine," she said looking in both directions this time before stepping off the curb. She could not find it in her soul to even look back at him. She knew if she did she might let his act of chivalry move her to tears, so she lowered her head and rushed to open her driver's door popping herself into the seat and fumbling to meet the key to the keyhole. Turning the ignition violently, she slammed the gear shift and sped out into the night. He stood watching her taillights fade into the distance and knew that for a moment there had been something that they had never shared before, some spark that he believed neither of them could explain. It made him smile.

Chapter Ten

Aubrey's mind was in a haze the next morning. She had burnt her toast and then scorched her scrambled eggs before sitting down to hover over her cup of coffee. She had been taken back by her dinner guest the previous night. The things he had said both interested her and confused her. He was such an impossible man to read. One moment she could imagine his arms wrapped around her and the next moment she was ready to strangle him. Had she imagined it or did she actually feel some type of energy when she was face to face with him? The thought had consumed her since she woke up. Maybe she would find something to shift her thoughts and make her a productive person because she didn't have time to waste on wondering what was going on with him. Suddenly, there was a knock at the front door and before Aubrey could rise and make her way to answer it, the knob turned and the door opened to a gust of morning air and an energetic young lady. When Macie came rushing into Dragonfly, she brought with her the distraction Aubrey had been hoping for.

"Hello," Macie called out as she closed the front door and whipped through the living room.

"Hello," Aubrey came out from the kitchen sporting a ponytail and old clothes, a reflection of her intentions for the day.

Macie helped herself to one of the leftover muffins that were gracing the stove, pinched off a piece, and placed it carefully in her mouth, "Have you heard the big town news?"

"What news?" Aubrey asked as she refilled her glass from the juice pitcher in the refrigerator.

"Remember the boat that you were asking about a couple of days ago."

"The sonar boat for the police department?" Aubrey turned to face Macie who was already seated at the island in the kitchen.

"Yes," Macie continued with her make shift breakfast.

"What about it?" Aubrey said. As if it were second nature, she reached into the cabinet and pulled out another glass to fill with juice for her friend.

"While they were out there gathering basic information about the depth of the lake and how the computer relays it through the software, they found something close to Williams Point," Macie said, finishing the last bite of muffin and sipping on her juice.

Aubrey stood upright improving her posture as suddenly she became much more interested in the story, "What did they find?"

"Something big," Macie gave a sinister smile. "Are you telling me that you haven't read the paper this morning or seen anything about it on the television?"

Aubrey shook her head from side to side, paying close attention to the information she was being given.

"It made the news all the way up in Nashville. I saw a Chattanooga station's van out there this morning, and I think even Alabama stations are reporting on it," Macie continued.

"I haven't even turned the TV on this morning. I just took my breakfast and a book out on the back deck to spend most of the morning."

Macie rolled her eyes, "Why am I not surprised? I brought my copy of the *Chronicle*." She slid from the stool and walked into the living room where she had laid her purse on the couch. Reaching inside her purse, she pulled out a newspaper copy and began to shuffle through the pages as she returned to her seat at the island. "Here, listen to this," she read it aloud.

"The Walker Search and Rescue dive team was called to Majestic Lake south of Williams Point Thursday morning to pull a submerged car out of the

water, after it was discovered by the Tennessee Wildlife Resource Agency, the Walker Police Department, and the Nashville Environment Consultants Agency."

"What?" Aubrey looked around the room as she listened to the report from the paper.

"There's more," Macie straightened the newspaper in her hands making a loud rustling sound.

"On a training scan of the lake with a side sonar boat, the computer reading displayed that a car was submerged at the bottom of the lake close to the Moonbeam bridge area.

We sent for the dive team to come and take a look because we knew visibility would be a problem. Then after evaluating the situation we had a recovery group come in to bring the car out of the water.' stated Officer Stanley Hall of the Walker Police Department.

What they brought up was a surprise.

Along with the car, they recovered the remains of a man believed to be missing for fifteen years. The man's identification card was found in his wallet inside the car.

The medical examiner will process the evidence and positively identify the remains. The coroners plan to perform an autopsy on the body and work with local authorities to investigate and determine the cause for the individual's death. More information will be released pending the notification of the next of kin."

"So, who do they think it is?" Aubrey had a strange feeling that she didn't really want the answer to the question she had just presented.

"Jake Warren," Aubrey's eyes became dark and Macie laid the paper down, "Aubrey, are you all right?"

"That conniving weasel," Aubrey said through clenched teeth as she looked blankly at the floor and began to pace.

"Well, that wasn't the response that I had expected," Macie relaxed her expression in amusement.

"He knew. He was there," Aubrey was furious.

Confused Macie asked, "What are you talking about? Who was where?"

"Jason!" Aubrey snapped. "He was there when they pulled out the car. He knew whose body it was and then he came looking for me. I knew it wasn't just by chance."

"I don't understand. Why would he be looking for you? Start from the beginning because we are not on the same page." Macie took her by the hand and led her to the couch and motioned for her to sit down. Aubrey obeyed and sat.

"Last night it was late and I was hungry, but I didn't want to have to cook something so I decided to go get a bite at Caroline's restaurant in town. While I was there Jason showed up, sat down at my table and proceeded to ask me questions about Jake Warren."

"What kind of questions?" Macie mused.

"Things like 'Did I remember him?', 'Did I recall Aunt Jane talking about him?', and 'Had I found anything in the house with his name on it?'. The whole time he knew about the car in the lake. He knew about the body. He never would tell me why he was asking the questions. He only said the name Jake Warren had come up in a case he was working on and the rumor was that he and Jane had dated years ago." Aubrey lowered her face into her hands and violently rubbed her eyes with her palms.

"Well, technically it did have something to do with a case, but more than just his name has come up. Maybe he couldn't tell you what was going on. It still hasn't been confirmed yet." Macie took Aubrey's wrists, forced her to lower her hands, and dipped her head to see into her eyes.

"He had enough information to ask and it was certainly enough to go to the newspaper with this morning. He could have said something."

"And the TV stations, don't forget the TV stations," Macie added realizing that it probably wasn't the time to remind her of that.

Aubrey let the conversation lap over and over in her mind studying the questions that were asked and the facts he seemed to already know. She should have known not to let her guard down with Jason. She had been played by him so many times before, but last night she thought he had opened up to her, let her see a part of him that had matured from the childish boy he had once been. Was that all just an act too? Maybe he hadn't changed after all. She had been his piano just like she always had except this time she had let him play a melodious tune on her heart.

Her frustration was finding its way deep into her chest and it burned like a Colorado wild fire, "What if they start prowling around the house looking for something from his past."

"I don't think they will do that. I mean she never knew what happened to him either and besides she's…gone. Jason is going to be investigating this case and he is going to have questions, so we all might as well get used to being asked some things," Macie raised and walked to the back door. The sunlight beamed through the trees creating a subtle glow of red, yellow, and green over the leaves.

"I don't like being blindsided. He should have given me a clue. He could have trusted me."

Macie turned around quickly and jabbed a finger into the air aiming its sharp point toward Aubrey's chest, "There it is."

"There what is?"

She shifted the accusing finger in a stabbing motion as she walked closer as if to attack her, "The same old Aubrey, being defensive when it comes to Jason. Did he know he could trust you? I doubt it. You have never trusted him."

"Would you knock it off, Macie. I don't need this right now," Aubrey stood to release herself of the overwhelming pressure. She saw the beauty that had caught Macie's eye only moments earlier as she stared out the window.

"My suggestion would be to get ahead of this," Macie advised.

"What do you mean?"

"Work with him on this. Cooperate however you can and then you will have a better idea of what's going on. Jane was a part of this whether you like it or not, but if you help him with anything you know, then Jason has the truth when it comes to the relationship." Aubrey opened the back door to let in the fresh sun kissed fall air. Then she stepped out to drink in the beams as they hung from the glowing limbs. Macie followed her and took a seat in one of the chairs.

"That's the thing, I haven't found anything yet and I don't really remember him," she said thinking of the journal, but not ready to reveal it to anyone before she had the chance to read its contents. "Maybe I should call Mom and Dad and see what they know about him. They may be able to shed a little light on whatever happened between them. She would have been more likely to talk to them and shared the relationship, especially with my mom. They were very close back then."

"That's a good idea. Are you going to talk to Jason after you discuss it with them?" Macie already knew the answer, but it was something Aubrey really needed to consider.

"I'll think about it," she found her way to the additional chair and sat down feeling much more relaxed now.

"Don't let your personal feelings for him cloud your judgment on this," Macie pleaded with her.

Aubrey made no promises. Her history with Jason had been so torn and brutal, she continued to find it difficult to get past it. She did not know if she could ever trust him when he continued to disappoint her, but she had a strange feeling that as this mystery began to unravel she would be forced to either confide in him or suffer a broken spirit. What was he keeping from her? She intended to discover his secrets and learn more about the man who the town claimed had been in a relationship with her aunt.

Chapter Eleven

Dearest Journal,

I met the most interesting man today. He came into my office saying that he was new in town and wished to see some of the available houses for rent in the area. Giving me a price range and idea of what he was looking for we researched the rental listings and found a few options for him to view. He had just found his way to Walker due to a job transfer and only wants to rent a place until he is certain that they will not transfer him again. Once he is settled and sure of the path of his employment, he can begin searching for a more permanent place. He is quite handsome and I noticed there was no wedding band on his hand. He has a strong build and when I asked for his number to contact him in case something else became available, he told me to "call anytime" and gave me an almost devilish wink. I believe he was flirting. Being so subtle, it was almost hard for me to recognize. What is a girl to do? I look forward to showing him around town and maybe with a little of my hidden charm, I can coax him into a more personal arrangement. Yes indeed, I hope to be on the arm of Mr. Jake Warren by the end of the month.

Truly,

Jane Elizabeth

She turned around in the kitchen to continue the path back through the living room, repeating the lines of the news story in her head before she dialed the Jackson number to speak with her dad. What was she going to ask him when he answered the phone? What did she really need to know? The truth, that was first and foremost in her thoughts. She finally stopped her pacing, carefully punched the square buttons, lifted the phone to her ear, and prayed that he would be forthcoming with what she felt she needed to know.

"Hello," his voice was steady and low.

"Hey, Dad," she returned.

"Aubrey! How is my baby girl?" his voice brightened when he realized who was on the other end of the line. It had been a few days since he had spoken to his daughter and although concern was always in the back of his mind when she called he was happy to hear her voice.

"I'm not a baby, Dad," she protested as she stepped out her back door and planted herself into one of the chairs in the bright late afternoon sun, "but I'm doing fine. How are things back in the real world?"

"You'll always be my baby. Your mom has had a sinus infection and they have started playing Andy Griffith reruns everyday at dinner time," she could almost hear the smile he was certainly projecting. "Retirement is bliss. How are things really? Are you working your way through the house?"

"She was truly amazing, Dad. It feels strange being here without her."

"I know sweetheart, I know," and with those careful words he felt his heart ache for his sister.

"Macie is the one thing that has kept me sane," she continued. "She has helped when she could and taken me away from it when I have needed it."

"I'm glad you have her with you." It was time to get down to the real reason for the call. "I'm sensing that you didn't call to talk about the house or anything in it. What's on your mind?"

"I need to ask you about someone, Dad."

Concern drew its blanket over him, "Go ahead. Shoot."

"What do you know about Jake Warren?" she heard him take a deep breath and release it slowly.

"Wow, I haven't heard that name in a long time," he replied, as the rush of memories flooded his thoughts. He wasn't a person her father actually cared to remember, but not a name he could soon forget.

"So, you do remember him?" she asked.

"Yeah, I remember him. I didn't know him very well. Janie was very smitten with him, why I have no idea," he began.

"Why do you say that?" she settled in a chair to get comfortable. She could already tell that her father would have a story to go along with his comment and she wanted to soak in every word. It was sure to help not only her curiosity, but the mystery of the relationship.

"Well, there were a lot of rumors around town about him being a traveler. Seems he never stayed in any town for too long, but when Janie started dating him she saw something in him, something different," he recalled.

"They had a good relationship?" she queried.

"Yeah, for a while, but then…" his voice trailed off.

"What happened, Dad?"

"It was hard to get her to fess up to anything when it came to Jake, but we always thought he was running around on her," he steadied his voice. "She said more than once that she had to go get him out of some bar. It seems that was part of his lifestyle. Once he got restless he would start drinking and womanizing then eventually he left. We thought that she could wait it out and he would leave her like he had other women."

"So, you didn't pry," she realized her dad didn't have all the answers she had hoped to discover, but what he was telling her would leave her with an amazing starting point.

"I think she didn't really want us to know everything that was going on, we thought we were respecting her privacy, but we should have pressed her. You see, Janie became very quiet about his activity. Your mom was afraid that he was becoming abusive and Janie was leery of telling anyone. I would have come to Walker myself and took care of him if I had thought your mom was right, but we didn't have anything to go on, so we left her alone. Next thing we knew, he was gone. Jane never said whether she put him out or if he left on his own. We never asked."

"He didn't leave Walker, Dad," Aubrey revealed. It wasn't very likely that they had seen anything about the discovery on the news so far away.

"Sure he left sweetheart, about fifteen years ago," her dad assured her.

"They found his body still in his car at the bottom of Majestic Lake. He never left," she said quietly.

"How? What happened?" he was in shock at her words.

"They haven't said much yet. Locals have gathered what evidence they can and they have sent the body to the TBI. Dad, I need to ask one more thing," she felt her chest tighten. She didn't want to even ask the question, but her father would have a clearer answer than she would, so she had to ask to be able to find the truth.

"Ask me anything."

"Do you think Aunt Jane could have had anything to do with his death?" she questioned.

"Your aunt? No, no! She was a strong lady, but she wouldn't do anything like that," he answered quickly and very sure of himself.

"She wouldn't have, I don't know, maybe hired someone or influenced someone to do such a thing would she?" Aubrey asked to be sure.

"Listen Aubrey, I'm not sure what it was about him, but your aunt was head over heels about him for some reason. She heard the rumors and lived with his lies, but she had strong feelings for him. I don't think she could ever do anything to hurt him, no matter how terrible he treated her," his words were stern and she felt relief sweep over her.

"That is just what I needed to hear," the police would have to look elsewhere for someone to blame. She was without a doubt confident that Jane had nothing to do with the murder of Jake Warren.

"Baby, you can rest on that," he said. "Now, I need to get back to my chores or your mother is going to have a fit. The leaves won't pick themselves up."

"All right, Daddy. Thank you for the information and I'll be in touch with anything I hear."

Suddenly, she heard the rustling of leaves, but assumed it must be a squirrel. There had been no shortage of them scurrying around since she had come here. Then there was a knock at her front door.

"Dad, someone is at the door," she said turning to go back inside.

"You better go see who it is. Be safe, sweet pea. I love you," he said softly in an easy tone to calm her uneasy spirit.

"I love you too, Daddy," she smiled as the words sang from her mouth. She knew if anyone could make her feel more at ease it would be her dad and he had not disappointed her.

Chapter Twelve

The newly fallen brittle leaves rustled under his feet as he made his way through the trees and bushes in the woods only a few feet from the lake. There were still enough on the trees to give him cover if someone should see him, but he did not expect anyone to pay enough attention to see him. He carried his equipment carefully tucked away in a dark green camera bag fitted with a large middle section to house the main body, and numerous sections and pockets that comfortably cradled a standard and a telephoto lens. The telephoto lens had been a special buy for him. He needed to see her, take in the view of her sun kissed skin. He grew closer to the house slowly as not to disrupt the natural surroundings until he found the perfect place to make his afternoon camp. She would never notice him from this area buried among the brush. He was excited to know that his pleasure would be easy as she was outside of the house pacing the back deck in clear view.

He watched her with haunting eyes, seeing her slow movement across the wood as she spoke in a low graceful tone into the receiver of the phone. He wondered who had captivated her attention. He glared through the lens to extend his vision. Her auburn locks brushed across her face as the words poured from her lips. She lifted a hand to sweep the stray locks behind her ear. The movement was stunning to him. He wanted to see her in the daylight, to drink in her beauty. As she took in a deep clean breath, he could see the rise and fall of her breasts. Her figure was perfectly proportioned, just as her aunt's had been so many years ago. He stared at her through the lens of the camera thinking about how her skin must feel, soft and cool to the touch. Her scent would be elegant and tasteful not strong from musk like many women, and her heat powerful. But he was here for a reason, and as attracted as he was to the passion of just visualizing her, he knew he needed to stay focused. He couldn't let his thoughts of what he could do to her interfere with the job he had to accomplish.

Until it was time he would be content to watch her, think of her, dream of her. The pictures would help and he would be sure to have plenty to satisfy his appetite. He would take those back with him and study them. He needed to know her, her schedule, her actions. It would be necessary to gain what he wanted from her. Patience would be more difficult. Having to lay in wait for what he wanted only made him want it more. He could feel himself grind his teeth as he watched. As fascinating as she was, she stood for everything that made him angry. He began to feel the fire of hatred flicker but it wasn't time. He worked to control his heavy breathing. He would have his moment. He would show her, one way or another, the pain he felt. She would know what had been done and only one thing could keep it from happening again.

***

As she finished her phone conversation with her father, Aubrey heard another knock on the front door. She made it to the door and opened it, just as her company was lifting his balled fist to try the knock again.

"Hello, Trey, what brings you here?" she asked surprised at her guest.

"I need to talk to you about something," he said with a sober look on his face.

"Well, I'm on my way out the door. Can it wait for a bit?" she wanted to go to the local library and research the archives for any information about Jake Warren, his presence in town, and his disappearance. She was convinced that she would not find much, but was hopeful that something would be available to give her some type of background on this man. He had not made much of an impression among the town folk according to the few people she had asked about him, but anything she could find might give her a line on the type of person he was in connection with Jane.

"It's best to talk now, Aubrey," Trey said sternly.

She ushered him into the house with a movement of her hand, "Come on in." Then she closed the door behind him. "Would you care for something to drink, a glass of tea, a Coke maybe?"

"No, I'm fine thanks. I'll just get to the point and say what I came here to say," he said after removing his hat. He wasn't in uniform, wearing jeans, a button up plaid shirt, and a ball cap. This was the look she had been familiar with in their younger days. Trey was just the good ole country boy next door, shy and handsome.

"And what is that?" she said because his visit was intriguing her now.

"We found a car in the lake as I'm sure you have heard by now," he began.

"Macie might have mentioned it," she had no doubt that he knew she had the most up to the minute details from Macie.

"And you know a body was found in it," he continued.

"Yes."

"And you know whose body was found," he had never been good at getting to his point when he was nervous and as he rubbed his hat between his fingers she knew his nerves were very much on edge.

"I've heard the rumors. It's a sad situation, but I don't know where you are leading with all of this Trey," she pushed a little to resolve his twitching.

"We have received confirmation from the TBI, Aubrey, and it's him. It's Jake Warren," he finally blurted out.

"You didn't have to come all the way out here to tell me that. You could have just picked up the phone," she glazed at him curiously. What was he up to, she thought?

"Look, I really shouldn't even be here talking to you about this, but I just thought you might need to be aware. There are going to be a lot of questions and speculation about Warren's relationship with Jane. I see some tough roads ahead. You can trust me on that one," he dropped his hands to his sides. "I think I might take that Coke after all," he felt his words becoming pasty in his mouth and needed the drink to rehydrate his throat and as something to hold to keep his hands calm.

Aubrey quickly went into the kitchen to fetch the cold drink from the refrigerator. She was still confused at what he was really trying to tell her, "I'm not sure I understand what you are getting at. Tough how?"

"More than likely Jane was the last one to see him alive. They had a rocky relationship at best toward the end and there were rumors of fights and abuse. There are a lot of things that could come out in the wash about her that you aren't aware of and Mac doesn't want to see you get hurt. I don't want to see you get hurt, Aubrey," he said throwing his hat on the table behind the couch and taking the can from her as she offered it. He took in a long cold gulp.

"You don't know that for a fact, Trey. You've said yourself that they are rumors," her father's words were starting to make more sense to her as well, but she couldn't tell Trey what her father had just confided in her. She wouldn't give them any ammunition to use until all the facts were clear.

"I know that the folks around here thought just as highly of Jane as you do, but behind closed doors a lot of truth can be hidden. We are going to have to look into every angle," he said.

"I understand that. What kind of law enforcement would you be if you didn't search for all the facts, but you'll find that there was nothing more between Jane and Jake Warren than two people and their feelings for one another. She was in love with him," she assured him.

"I'm coming to you as a friend, Aubrey, because I want you to be prepared. Jason is the lead investigator on this and he gets very determined when he is trying to solve a case. You two already have a past, so I don't want it to ruin your future," she stepped back and walked to the window to distance herself from him.

"Now you are starting to sound as if Jason and I actually have a future. You know better than that Trey," she said with a half-hearted laugh.

Trey crossed over to the window until he was standing directly behind her calmly and quietly saying the words to her, "I know that you two go hard at each other for no good reason. You have too much pinned up frustration for one another to see what really matters, and all of that could come out when he starts in on this case,"

She cringed as if a blast of cold air had rushed up her spine, "Is there anything else Trey? I really would like to get on to running my errands."

"Don't let your stubborn streak get the best of you," he said brushing his hand over her shoulder lightly and letting it fall down her arm and then quickly returning both of them back to his pockets.

She turned around to stare at him quizzically, "Where is this coming from?"

"Just do this for me and for Macie, cooperate with us when we need you to, OK," he pleaded.

"I'll do my best, Trey."

"Cooperate with Jason," and there was the real truth of the matter.

"You know I can't make any promises when it comes to him, but I'll do what I can," she told him furrowing her brows. It was as if Trey knew something about Jason that he wanted so terribly to share, but wasn't allowed to tell.

"I just wish the two of you could let it go," he shrugged his shoulders knowing those words were a moot point. Then he turned to make his way back toward her front door. He stopped at the couch to regain his cap. He would finish the Coke on the way back to town.

"You sound like Macie," she told him as she grinned regaining a less serious and more playful conversation.

"Shouldn't that tell you something?" he shot her a crooked smile. "Well, I best be getting out of your way. I've got work to do."

"Thanks for coming by, Trey. I know you didn't have to do it, but I do appreciate the heads up. I really do," she wrapped her arms around him for a friendly squeeze goodbye and to make sure he understood that she had no hard feelings for the things he had said.

"I worry about you and so does Mac. We don't want you leaving on a bad note again. That girl sure is different since you came back into town. She has missed you. I can't stand to see her upset," he said shyly. Aubrey sensed there were more than just friendly feelings between him and Macie, but she was the last person who intended to play matchmaker.

"It will be fine," she assured him.

"Well, I better go." He opened the door and began to step out onto the quaint little porch and down the steps.

"Goodbye, Trey," she yelled to him, "and give my best to Jason." He turned to her with a smirk on his face. "I really mean that."

He laughed, "No you don't, but I will relay the message."

She watched him walk to his truck, get in and start the engine. She was now more confused than ever. What had her aunt been involved in so many years ago?

Chapter Thirteen

Dearest Journal,

Kathryn and I had the most amazing day shopping. I bought a whole new wardrobe for the upcoming season. I have to dress to impress if I want to make my sales goals. We chose lunch at The Meadow and ice cream from The Milk Maid Creamery to round out our day. Johnny will surely give his warning when he sees all the things Kathryn bought. I'm surprised I haven't heard police sirens as of yet, but it is all with good reason. You see, Kathryn shared some wonderful, wonderful news with me today. She is pregnant, which explains her sudden need for all the new clothes. She and Johnny will have their first little arrival in April and I can hardly wait. I want to spoil and love and cherish the gift that will be my god child. This child will not mean as much to me as my precious Aubrey Elizabeth, but I most certainly will love it to the fullest. Maybe having this little wonder in our lives will spark some feelings in Jake to make him think about marriage and kids. He can be a tough one, but then again others just do not know him like I know him. He has a soft side. I just need to work harder at bringing it out in him when we are around other people.

Sincerely,

Jane Elizabeth

Beginning her day with a cup of doctored up caffeine, Aubrey sat in the rocking chair on the back porch of Dragonfly listening to the rustling of the leaves dance their way through the ever changing branches of the trees as the water lapped along the side of the bank. She tossed around the idea of another day of playing hooky from her responsibilities, but thought better of it. Her late afternoon venture the day before to the library archives had turned up nothing on Jake Warren aside from a mention of his name while attending some party sponsored by Jane's real estate firm. He had been as much a mystery to the town as he had been to her family. He had made no contributions that were noted in stories and there had been no interest in his disappearance. Maybe the locals had the same idea as her father, that he had overstayed his welcome and moved on. Gaining nothing from the search, she decided to leave the investigating to Jason and the police for now. If she was going to be ready to return to Memphis in a week and a half, she would need to get back on track with her plans and make her final decisions.

She had packed many of the clothes from the closets to take to Jane's church, who would then distribute them to women struggling or escaping abusive relationships. Often the church would outfit them and help them gain job interviews to advance their new independent lives. In light of her conversation with her father and the proof of Trey's visit, Aubrey knew it would be a worthy cause for the donation.

Her next goal she felt would be to meet with local realtors, ones who could be aggressive if she chose to sell Dragonfly. Although she hated the thought of her aunt's home being taken over by less than worthy owners, she was unsure if she could see herself even vacationing here. Her other option included keeping the house for herself, but hiring a reputable realtor to manage the rental of the property and asking Macie to supervise the overall dealing of the rental as local support. Then she would be able to make trips to see her friend, but not feel obligated or guilty if work did not allow for much time to visit. That too would be something to discuss with the realtors.

She had made appointments with three area realtors that had come highly recommended to her. She had decided to talk with each of them and decide on which would best represent her needs. Aubrey clearly could not list the property herself, being so far away, so she opted to find someone who she felt had her same qualities for the job. Just as many sellers do, she would discuss sale records, marketing strategy, and service in the business before making a final judgment call.

The first meeting had gone well, but Aubrey was not sure of the gentleman's ability to be aggressive. As she had heard her aunt mention many times, he was indeed kind and charming, but not the nose to the grindstone type person she was accustomed to working with in her Memphis office. The next agent followed a similar fate and Aubrey found her concerns rising as she continued to search for an agent more like herself. Nothing had stood out to her about either candidate so far in their presentations. They were certainly qualified and seemed eager enough to put Dragonfly on the market, but Aubrey didn't feel that connection with them or any chemistry with their companies. Maybe her third appointment would be the fast paced energetic go getter she tried to be herself when marketing a property.

She hoped the last meeting of the day would be the very person she was looking for, a young agent named Gina Cantrell, who was suggested to her by Mr. Kyle at the drug store a few days prior. She never recalled her aunt mentioning the name and she had received a concerned response when she had asked Mr. Shipley about Ms. Cantrell, but he confided that she was known for getting the job done. That sounded like just the person Aubrey needed, so after Ms. Cantrell had called the day before to inquire about the future of Dragonfly, she had agreed to meet with her to discuss possible plans for the house.

She walked through the squeaking door of the firm and approached the desk to the left. Sitting behind the desk was a slightly overweight lady in her mid-forties with a phone receiver pressed between her left shoulder and ear. As she rustled through the papers on her desk she caught a glimpse of Aubrey and sported a quick smile. She drew up her right pointer finger and swished it in the direction of the other side of the room. It was easy to take the hint and Aubrey turned to find her place on the couch. This firm had been the home of her aunt for almost twenty years prior to her accident. As with many real estate firms, her aunt spoke of cut throat tactics and odd friendships within the firm, but once you were past the hard exterior, she claimed there were some allies that were trustworthy.

"I'm sorry about that. May I help you?" the deep southern drawl of the plump woman behind the desk was almost hypnotizing as Aubrey lifted her head to answer.

"Yes. I'm here to see Gina Cantrell. My name is Aubrey Todd," she stood to walk closer to the desk and present her hand in introduction.

"Ms. Todd, it is so nice to meet you and let me give my condolences for your aunt. She was always such a lovely woman," the lady crumpled her brows in concern for the loss.

"Thank you."

"I'll dial Ms. Cantrell and let her know that you have arrived," she picked up the receiver to the phone and pressed four round buttons, "Gina, Ms. Todd is here to see you. Yes, I'll tell her." She returned the receiver to its holder and gave Aubrey a wink, "She will be right with you."

"Thank you, again." Aubrey made her way back to the couch, but was not seated very long when a very attractive young woman in a tailored blue suit came down the hall and made her way across the room. She wore her hair up in a twist with trails of sandy blond ringlets embracing her face. Her makeup was artistry and the three inch heels made her long slender legs very shapely with each stride. She was a stunning business woman and matched Aubrey in the way she cared for and carried herself.

"Ms. Todd," she said extending her hand, "please follow me to my office. I believe you will be very interested in the presentation I have to show you." Aubrey followed the beauty back down the hall into a small area that housed four offices. It was apparent that the area had been added on to the building after the initial structure was built, but that could only mean that business was doing well. The young lady motioned to Aubrey to have a seat in one of the burgundy padded chairs across from her desk.

"I will say that this is a little unusual, as I'm sure you will understand. I normally conduct presentations in the home that I wish to list," Ms. Cantrell noted hoping that Aubrey would give her a cause for straying from the normal procedure.

"My apologies, Ms. Cantrell, it's just that right now I am still very up in the air about what I intend to do with the house and thought it best to first meet with you to get more of a feel for what you and your company could do should I decide to go ahead with the listing. The details will all be worked out at a later date, if I choose to do so," she explained.

"I understand," Gina replied. "The important thing for you to remember is that it would be my honor to, in your absence, locate that special buyer so that the lake house sells for the best price possible. After all, isn't that the reason I was asked to give you this presentation!"

"I certainly hope so," Aubrey felt a little uneasy with her, but the agent was much more of the antagonistic type she had been searching for.

Gina took out a three ring binder and handed it to Aubrey, opening the front to display the cover page, an outdoor photo of Dragonfly taken simply from the middle of the driveway.

"If you will continue through the presentation materials, you will notice how I precisely pinpoint buyers for the home by using the MLS as a buyer location tool as well as local media and social media," Gina pointed out the bold text of each page.

"I will provide you with a list of who I believe are your targeted buyers and the means by which I intend to seek them out.

I will email you a list of buyers for the home each week that I intend to pursue, giving you a full layout of my marketing plan to get these buyers into your home to see the beauty and amenities of Dragonfly.

I will convince you that I am no ordinary agent. I believe in going beyond the call of duty to ensure your home sells.

My ultimate goal is for you to perceive me as an agent who knows how to succeed at her job, thereby establishing the professional verification required for you to feel confident and secure about listing your home with me and my firm.

Luckily, since you are also a successful agent, you will understand that eighty-five percent of my work is done behind the scenes. The result, of course, being a satisfied seller who is confident that I am on the job, shopping the listing in ways many never think possible.

I hope this presentation has established a sense of security, confidence and trust that is needed in order for you to feel comfortable listing your home with me."

Aubrey gave one last quick glance through the binder then closed it and laid it flat in her lap over her crossed legs, "Ms. Cantrell, you certainly have a well thought out presentation and I will take your ideas into consideration in the next few days as I make my decision."

"Well, thank you. As you know I also manage property for rent, but I thought it best to give you my qualities as a seller's agent, since the word around town is that you probably will not be staying with us," she replied.

"That is something I am weighing into the decision as well," Aubrey noted. "This is such a nice, quiet, and friendly town. I can see my aunt's attraction to it and I may decide to keep the house. There is still so much to think about and many conclusions to be made. It would be a beautiful place to live or call a vacation home."

Gina twisted uneasily in her high back office chair, "Well, I look forward to hearing from you soon and I hope I will be able to help you." Her smile became more unrealistic with each passing moment.

"Thank you, Ms. Cantrell," Aubrey let the corners of her lips upturn slightly as she raised from her seat and offered her hand.

"And Ms. Todd," Gina continued standing and shaking, but not allowing Aubrey to retreat. "I am truly sorry for your loss. Jane was an amazing woman and a great agent. She was a caring person and I don't believe the rumors about her for one moment."

Aubrey was stunned by the last few words and pulling back her hand, she narrowed her eyes with perplexity, "Rumors, what rumors?"

Gina looked startled at her reaction, "Well, the ones about the man they found in the lake."

"I'm afraid I don't know what you are talking about," Aubrey said quizzically tilting her head in amusement.

"Oh," Gina presented a sly demeanor, "maybe, I've said too

much."

"Not at all," Aubrey probed, "please fill me in. I'm interested to know what is being said about my aunt."

Gina was unrelenting, "As I said, I don't for one minute believe that she was in any way involved in the death of Jake Warren, but it has circled around the office that since they were dating she might have had something to do with his demise. Some of the older members of the community have mentioned seeing her with him that night. Many recall the trouble of their relationship, the cheating and booze. It seems she was the last one to see him alive and someone mentioned they had been in an ugly disagreement, but I know she was much too kind to have done any real harm to someone."

"Is anything else being said?" Aubrey questioned.

"Just that they wouldn't blame her. Apparently, Jake Warren was not a respected man in this town."

Aubrey had to know, even though she really did not want to ask, "Just out of curiosity, can I ask you where they might be getting their story, the people around town who are talking?"

"Well, I'm not one to gossip," Gina feed her the bait she wanted her to bite, "but I believe it was overheard between Detective McNally and one of the other officers."

It suddenly became very clear to her. This had been the very thing that Trey was trying to warn her about. He knew where Jason was going with his investigation and wanted to make peace before there was even a war. But there would be a war. Jason was not going to succeed with his allegations.

Aubrey lifted her head and smiled as if none of it truly bothered her, "Well, thank you for the information and for your concern for her memory. I'm sure it is all just stories and speculation. The officers will get to the bottom of it."

"I'm sure you are right," Gina came around from behind her desk and lifted a hand toward the office door. This was Aubrey's hint that the meeting was over and Gina had accomplished all that she had set out to do, whatever that may be.

Aubrey turned to make her way through the door and glanced over her shoulder as she glided down the hallway, "Thank you again for your time and the wonderful proposal. I will certainly keep you in mind when I make my final decision."

Gina walked briskly behind her escorting her to the front of the office building, "Thank you again for the meeting."

"Have a nice day, Ms. Cantrell," she spoke the final words as politely as she could through her clenched teeth.

"As well to you, Ms. Todd," Gina returned the comment.

As she closed the door behind her, Gina stared out the glass and in a haunting tone stated, "That is one woman this town doesn't need. The quicker she leaves Walker, the better."

Chapter Fourteen

"Can I help you," an average height dark haired young officer approached her looking as if he were fresh out of the academy. His uniform was pressed to precision and his hair trimmed to the perfect length above his navy collar.

"Yes, I'm here to speak with Jason McNally," Aubrey said trying her best to be calm with her demeanor although her blood boiled with fury. It was imperative that she talk to him to get an explanation and she knew if she came across angry it was less likely that they would allow her see him.

"I believe he is on the phone right now," the young officer stated. "You can have a seat and wait."

She did not intend to wait as if she were in line at the DMV, "No, I need to talk to him right now," her jaw felt locked. "Please tell him it is Aubrey Todd."

"I'll see what I can do. Wait here," the officer turned to walk to the back of the station, around the corner to the left, no doubt to Jason's office, to warn him of the persistent woman demanding to see him.

Aubrey backed up slightly to see seats in the corner of the small waiting area, but chose not to use one of them. She needed to make a presence when he entered the room. She needed to let him know that she was upset, even as she struggled to control her temper through her words.

Jason came around the corner of the back offices with the under-experienced officer in tow behind him. His half-hearted smile struck a match of frustration in her because she felt he was careless toward her feelings. He had to know she was concerned about something. She didn't make social calls to the police station. The officer would have undoubtedly made sure he was aware that she was anxious to see him. His long stride through the building toward her just made her more furious that she had to deal with him at all.

"So, I hear there is a beautiful woman out here demanding my presence," he said smugly as his white teeth gleamed through the half-hearted smolder.

Straight faced burning with a fierce glare she replied, "Don't flatter yourself, and you can wipe that fake smirk from your face."

He toned it down to a grin knowing that she was not amused with his playfulness, "Sweeney, to what do I owe this pleasure?"

"How dare you," she pressed her lowered voice through clenched teeth.

"What are you talking about?" he asked.

"You know exactly what I'm talking about," she began to lose her cool and raise her voice. "You are trying to run down my aunt's good name, trying to pin a murder on her."

He licked his lips to moisten them and removed all traces of the excitement of seeing her here. Jason lowered his voice and bent his head to whisper in her ear as he took her bicep in his grip, "Look, can we talk about this in the back."

"No, we can talk right here," she said while looking down at the hand that held her arm.

"Aubrey, you are causing a scene," there was a sharp sternness to his voice. "Come back here with me and I'll explain."

"Fine," she snapped at him, jerking away from his grasp. "Get your hand off me." Shaking his head he turned around and began walking to the back of the station to a non-mirrored conference room where they could talk in private without being observed. Aubrey followed him with her head held high determined to make her point to him no matter his defense. He strolled through the door and stopped to turn around and motion Aubrey in to the room with an inviting outstretched hand. She walked in and all but threw her keys on the table. Jason closed the door with just enough force to hear it latch into place and then strode across the floor to the table.

"Now, do you want to tell me what this is about?" Jason began as he pulled out a chair for Aubrey.

"I've heard you are the lead investigator on the Warren case and are blaming Jake's murder on my aunt," she sat down in the chair next to the one he had pulled out for her solely to make a point that she was not accepting anything from him including a kind gesture.

"Sweeney, I have to look into any leads," he sat into the chair across the table from her so he could be face-to-face with her.

"I don't see you looking into Harry at the hardware store or Katie at the pharmacy," she accused him.

Jason brushed his hand down his face and released a sigh, "Harry at the hardware store," he said narrowing his eyes with sudden irritation, "and Katie at the pharmacy do not have a direct connection to the victim."

"Oh, and because my aunt did you think naturally she did it," Aubrey spat out in haste.

"I didn't say that, but I do have to check into the story," he reminded her.

"She wasn't a violent person and you know it," she arose leaning over the table and lowering her face within inches of his.

"Well, her reputation in town says that she wasn't but I have to go with what I know," he said motioning to the chair as if to let her know she needed to take her seat. "A detective has to look at things a little more blindly where every suspect is on an even road. Not only did she know him, but she had a personal relationship with him."

"So, that's what you are basing all of this on, the fact that they were dating?" refusing his offer to sit back down. She turned away from him and began to walk across the room with her arms folded over her chest. "They had a relationship so she must have done it."

"I wish you would stop putting words in my mouth. You have no idea how hard this is," he said standing and walking over to her.

"No, I get it. She is the prime suspect," she turned to face him once again.

"She is the *first* suspect. Naturally we always look at the closest relationships first. She had a motive. There were people in town that had seen him leaving the Pub with women other than Jane, and suspected that he had cheated on her," he revealed not knowing if she had been aware of Jake Warren's infidelity.

"And I believe she knew it," Aubrey made known, "but loved him anyway or she wouldn't have stayed with him. They must have been trying to work things out. It would have been just as easy to break up with him."

"Normally we would bring her in, ask her questions, and get it out of the way," he said. "The sticky situation we have here is she's not alive to tell her side of the story. We have to research and dig a little deeper to find something."

"To find what?" Aubrey asked.

"The truth, Sweeney," he answered. "I'm just trying to do my job and you have to let me. The quicker I find the truth, the quicker I can determine if Jane is a legitimate suspect and whether I need to continue investigating or not."

"A legitimate suspect?" she began to pace again.

"Yes," he answered and sat down on the top of the table letting one leg dangle from the edge. He crossed his arms over his chest tired of being forced to defend himself and his occupation.

"So you really think she might have been involved," pleading with him now for his honest opinion.

"I wonder if she knew anything, yes. I must look at the evidence and determine whether the person remains a person of interest," he knew that was not what she wanted to hear, but he refused to sugar coat it for her for the sake of her feelings. His job was important to him.

"Is that what she is to you, a person of interest?" she asked.

"Right now, yes, but I hope we can find enough evidence to release her from that list. You wouldn't want us to leave it hanging out there, not knowing the truth, would you," he took a more settled approach for her to think about hoping she would determine that what he was doing was just part of the process and would benefit her in the end.

That wasn't the case, "I can't believe this. I will not have you ruining her reputation."

"I'm not trying to ruin anything. With the circumstances it just might take a little more time. I'm going to go with the evidence no matter what it is and you have to get used to that," he told her. "This isn't about you or me, not about our past, our present, or our...you have to set your feelings about me aside. She is not a suspect because she is your aunt. Believe me, I wish it were the opposite."

She had finally had enough and stomped over to him within inches of his rugged face. "Then by all means, continue your investigation, detective," she blurted out.

She walked past him and turning the doorknob with force as she stormed out of the room, down the hall, and into the main office area. He immediately jumped up from the table and followed her.

"Hey, wait," he shouted after her.

She stopped and snapped around to face him, "No, Jason, forget I even came here. I can't believe...fine, you do your job," she turned around looking at all the staring officers. "Just stay away from me in the process. You'll find out the truth. You'll find out she had nothing to do with it," she stepped back to be face-to-face with Jason and raised a finger to his chest. "You'll know I was the one telling the truth all along." Quickly she turned and started for the door.

Under his breath he muttered quietly, "I hope you're right, Sweeney. I really do."

She stormed out of the station feeling the tears swell in her eyes, but unable to stop her fast pace until she knew she was well out of the reach of Jason and his interrogation methods. She knew she had just fallen right into his trap. He probably planted the rumors himself just to get that type of rise out of her, and she had just fallen for it. Now he knew the effects this case had on her feelings and how he could turn and bend that emotion to his will, breaking her spirit if he needed. He would certainly use her love for her aunt and her vulnerable state against her. He had not been forthcoming with his intentions in the case. Nothing about the situation had come to light for her, but it might have for him. She wondered if she had just made a terrible mistake by coming into the station to see him.

Chapter Fifteen

There was a knock on the front door of Dragonfly, although Aubrey was not expecting anyone. She swept through the living room picking up the shoes and jacket that she had so carelessly thrown on the couch earlier, tossing them into the closest bedroom, and closing the door behind her. One thing she had learned by being out on her own was how to project a clean house even when it was in a mess.

She came back into the living room and walked over to the entryway to open the door, not looking through the peephole to get a glance at her evening caller, but simply opening the door to face whoever was going to drain the last of her day's energy. When she turned the knob and opened it, she was face to handsome face with Jason. Why was he here? Hadn't he done enough damage to her family's name, to her Aunt Jane's memory, for one day? She only stared at him. Then she rolled her eyes imitating an annoyed pre-teen, turned her back to him leaving the door open, and walked back into the living room. She crossed over to the back window to take in the beautiful ripple of the evening waters on the lake.

"Well, hello to you too," he said as he closed the door behind himself and followed her.

Aubrey turned back around swiftly and asked, "Are you here to make some more accusations toward my family?"

"Sweeney, I'm not taking sides. I thought I made that clear at the station," he answered.

"Jason, you can't keep doing this," she said with a begging tone.

"I'm just conducting a thorough investigation like any good detective would. You have to understand that," he replied to her plea. "Look I don't want to start this again. I came over here because I didn't like the way we left things at the station, so I wanted to see if I could smooth it over a bit."

"Oh, so you didn't like what I had to say about the situation," she immediately became defensive with him as if to continue the fight that had been pursued only hours before.

"I didn't like that you stormed out and I don't like that we are fighting," his words remained calm. "The truth is I could really use your help."

She cackled with a fake laugh, "Now, you want my help. To do what, get a clear conviction of my aunt? She's not here to defend herself so if I help get you what you want it should be an easy case. You can be at dinner with some trashy blonde by 7 p.m. with the case solved. Is that what you think? Well, I'm not going to help you do that." She attempted to walk around him, but he stepped in front of her.

He took her shoulders in his strong hands and with a sharp shake he looked deep into her eyes to help convince her that his request was honest. "I want your help so that maybe we can clear your aunt."

"I'm supposed to believe that?"

"Believe whatever you want," he retorted, "but I know you were at the library looking for information on Warren. You want to find out his story just as much as I do."

Was he following her now? How did he know about the research? "Well, I hate to disappoint you, but I didn't find anything."

"Do you want her name cleared or not?"

Aubrey tried unsuccessfully to calm herself and with a blaring gaze fired back at him. "You know she didn't have anything to do with Jake's death. You know Jane wouldn't be involved in that," she clarified.

He released her, "Are you asking if I personally believe it?

Between you and me, not really, but I can't prove it. Then, I have my superiors breathing down my neck about it. I can't convince them unless I eliminate her as a suspect. Come on, Sweeney, you have seen all the detective shows, you know how this goes," he shifted away from her and began to raise his own voice to her, growing tired of the back and forth banter getting him nowhere.

"She just couldn't have been involved," she gave him the words as if it were a fact in his case.

"We have to start with what we know. She was dating him at the time." He returned to rehashing the same story hoping for some new information from this almost intolerable beauty in front of him.

"That still doesn't mean she had anything to do with his death, Jason." She decided to return the tit for tat game.

"But it could mean that she knew who did," he revealed. "If she didn't actually do it, she could have been an accessory, or she might not have had a thing to do with any of it. It's already starting to eat at me and I have to find out for sure," he looked at her trying his best to find some spark in her that she understood the awful position he was in between his work and her.

Aubrey couldn't believe that he was going after her again, arguing as if they were still kids. Who did he think he was and who did he think he was dealing with? She thought he knew her aunt better than that. She felt a rage building in the pit of her stomach. She thought he believed in the person her aunt was, the loving caring community member everyone would miss in Walker.

"Let me determine what really happened and if she had no part in it I'll be the first one to file the paperwork proving it." He said in a calm, quiet tone that eased her anger slightly. "You have to know that I don't want this to turn out badly. I don't want you to be hurt."

"As if you really care about my feelings in all this," she said, now exhausted by the anger she had for him. Aubrey turned her back to him and glared out the window to the back porch. "And why should you care anyway? It's just another case to you."

"I do care," he said wanting to show her how much he cared, but knowing she would reject him the way she felt toward him right now. "You have no idea how much I care."

He stepped close enough to take her by the shoulders and turn her back to face him. He was looking down at her as she stretched her head upward to see into his amazing blue green eyes.

"Sweeney," he paused taking in a deep breath, hesitating, and thinking carefully before he shared too much with her, "you mean more to me than you think. If you believe this is easy for me, to investigate a case where your family is involved, then you don't know me like I thought you did. I don't want to see the evidence I find, and I don't want to draw the conclusions I do. I don't want to hurt you. I know how much you loved your aunt. The sight of your face as you were leaving the funeral has haunted me for months."

"You weren't at her funeral," she snapped.

"I was part of the motorcade that delivered her to her final resting place. I wasn't sure how you would feel about me coming to the funeral, so I attended the visitation the night before when I knew you weren't there and volunteered as an escort the next day."

She was taken aback by his confession. He had insisted on being there, being a part of the worst day of her life, but she couldn't focus on that right now, "and you would go through all of that for someone you now think murdered Jake Warren?"

"Right now, I'm following this case where the evidence leads."

"And what you have discovered is leading straight to my aunt, is that what you are trying to tell me," she interrupted his explanation.

"I have to do my job. That is what I'm trying to get through to you. What else do you want me to do?" he asked.

"I want you to find my aunt is innocent. Everyone in town believes she is and so do I. She just wasn't the type of person to harm someone else." Her father's words echoed in her mind as she spoke.

"I have to go where the trail leads and I just have to hope that she is not at the end of that path," he said.

"I told you before," she pulled away from his grip. "You'll learn the truth. Now, I think you have overstayed your welcome," she said staring into his eyes deeply so he could feel what he had caused in her.

Suddenly, she could no longer stand to look him in the face. She turned and walked to the front door and opened it. He had been in this position before and as she hung her head, her heart in pain, he walked past her and through the door. As he crossed the threshold, he stopped one last time, turning his head only slightly so his gaze would still be focused downward. It was a long shot at this point, but he decided it might be worth taking the chance.

"You broke my heart," he raised his voice just enough to release the ache he had held inside for ten years. "When you left Walker, you broke my heart."

"Broke your heart?" she questioned. "You've had a terrible way of showing it," she took a step toward him in defense.

"You never would let me show it. You were too busy doing the same thing you are doing now, being defensive and shutting down your emotions around me," he said lifting his eyes to meet hers.

"You picked at me, teased me, called me nicknames and taunted me."

"When we were children, yes, but I cared for you so much. I begged for the day each summer that you would change your mind. Since you were sixteen years old, I prayed that you would come back." He looked as if he were in agony just saying the words.

"Jason," she said slowly and curtly.

"Listen, I don't know why I feel the need to confess all of this now, but I have always cared for you even when we were kids. Don't you remember your mother telling you that a boy will pull your pigtails because he likes you and doesn't know any other way to show it?" he asked.

"You hear those things, Jason, but it isn't always true. Sometimes you…you could just be cruel." She felt her voice shake with her reaction.

"I know, I know, and I'm sorry for those childish things, Aubrey, I really am," He had called her by her name. He never did that. She saw a glimpse of regret in his eyes as he took a step closer. "That was then and I can't change the past, but this is now and you have to know. I think about you, and what might have been."

He had a broken heart? She felt as if hers had just been ripped to shreds with pieces lying in her past, pieces on the door step of Dragonfly, pieces buried with her aunt and pieces now lying at his feet. It was one thing for a man to admit his feelings for you. It was another to realize that you shared those same feelings. Maybe her mind had tricked her when it came to the past, and he had not been as cruel as she thought she remembered. Maybe it wasn't anything more than childish games they had been playing for all these years, or maybe with age Macie was right and he had truly transformed. Could it be possible that she had let her grudge carry on too long? It was just so hard to let those barriers down that were now her only protection since her aunt was gone. Maybe she just refused to see what had always been there?

She was so confused. He was her childhood bully each summer, he criticized her, he had grown up with her, he had longed for her, and he had feelings for her. She never even knew.

Aubrey could feel her heart fluttering, and her pulse racing, and she was sure that it all showed clearly in the expressions on her face. Suddenly, in this moment she had an incredible urge to be kissed and not just any kiss, but a kiss that was mysterious to her that she never could have dreamed existed, a kiss from the sweet passionate lips of Jason McNally.

He turned around and began to walk down the steps of the front porch, but she couldn't let him leave.

"Jason, wait," she called out to him.

He slowly moved back around, his head tilted to the side and his eyes staring down at the wooden porch, with a sad look on his face and his hands in his blue jean pockets. He looked like a scolded little boy, hoping to bypass a punishment for something he should not have been doing.

As he lifted his head and cut to her heart with a sparkle in his stare, he answered, "Why? Why, Aubrey?"

She stood there in complete silence with tears welling up in her eyes, her mouth slightly open, not knowing what to say. Thank goodness he seized the quiet opportunity, taking her into his arms, and closing his eyes gently as he pressed his lips softly to hers. The masculine smell of his skin heighted her desperate need for him. She was frozen in time, and she wanted more. Jason pulled his head back and looked into her hazel eyes deep with mysterious hues to gauge his next move. Then he took a tighter grip, one muscular arm around her waist and lifting his other arm across her back to hold her head in his hand. She wouldn't get away from him this time, and he pressed harder against her lips crushing them beneath his. His body leaned into hers and she knew she was pinned against the open navy front door of Dragonfly. She felt hot from the passion of his mouth covering hers and the steam of their bodies embracing one another.

Not realizing it, she had wrapped her arms around his neck running her fingers through his hair, completely accepting his advances and eager for more. She rolled against the door until they were inside the house and his back was flat against the wall. His tongue slipped between her teeth and caressed her tongue as his breathing became a passionate pant. He released his hand from her only long enough to push the door closed then returned it to its rightful place on her body. This was not a view for the passers-by. His hands began to smooth over her back, down her sides, over her hips, and cupped her backside before finding their way again up her back squeezing her closer. She pulled back and looked at him with shock in her eyes.

"Are you all right?" he asked with a racing speed in his breathing.

"I don't know. I can't think," she replied.

"Don't think, Aubrey, just feel," he told her.

She rolled her eyes in pleasure and leaned her head back to face the ceiling. He took full advantage and pressed his warm wet lips to the nape of her neck biting her slightly to demand her attention. She took in a deep quick breath as her mouth opened in surprise and sheer delight. She rolled her head to the side and let him take her in as she released a quiet moan and closed her eyes. She was wrapped in the arms of a man she had never wanted and yet she couldn't resist.

Chapter Sixteen

The knock on the door startled Aubrey from her daydream and she immediately went to open it. Her fingers shook as she searched for the knob. She freed the door of its lock and coaxed it to open, Macie shuffled her way into the lake house as if she had a broom behind her sweeping her forward and she briskly sat her things down on the table behind the couch.

"What was so important that I had to come over as soon as possible?" she asked as she shifted her weight and headed to the refrigerator to help herself to a drink.

"Not even a 'Good Morning' or 'Hello'?" Aubrey stood dumbfounded at the lack of a friendly gesture.

"Hello," she said sarcastically with her head still deeply in the refrigerator searching for the liquid that could set her thirst at ease, "Now, what is so important?"

"I need to talk to you about…Jason," Aubrey replied shyly as she rang her hands nervously in front of herself.

"Ahh, yes. How did it go at the station?" her nonchalance shocked Aubrey.

"How did you hear about that?" Aubrey stood at the island terrified at the words. She knew she might be the talk of the town, but could not imagine it had circled around that fast. What other information had already made its way through the gossip chain? The birds chirped brightly outside the window, but inside Aubrey's shoulders began to ache with tension.

Macie closed the refrigerator and popped open the top of the Coke can. She drew a long cold swallow then continued, "It's a small town. Word gets around, babe!"

She sat down at the island and patted the seat next to her sending Aubrey a message to sit.

Aubrey shook her head and let herself fall onto the stool, placing her elbows on the tabletop and setting her forehead in the center of her hands, "Just great."

"So, what happened?" Macie inquired.

"I had interviewed with the last real estate agent, a girl named Gina who apparently knew my aunt and had made a few deals with her in the past. So far she has my vote for a listing agent, although there is something odd about her that I can't put my finger on, but anyway, we concluded our meeting and as I was standing to leave she gave me her condolences," Aubrey revealed.

"That doesn't seem so bad," Macie replied.

"It was what she said next that stirred my anger. She told me that she had enjoyed her business dealings with Jane and she couldn't possibly believe the things that were being said about her. When I inquired about what she meant by that, she said that she knew the police were looking at Jane for the Warren man's death, but she just didn't believe that Jane really had anything to do with it. What she said made me so furious that I went to see the one person that I knew was responsible," Aubrey's anxiety begin to bleed through her once again as she relived the conversation. She stood to move around and release some of the pent up energy.

"So you hashed it out at the station. You've been in arguments with Jason before," Macie arose to follow her friend into the living room. "It will blow over and soon things will be back to normal for you two."

"Well, he must have gotten over it pretty quickly. He showed up here about an hour after I got home."

"That's strange for him to follow you home. What did he say?" Macie became intrigued at the story.

"More than I was ready to hear," Aubrey shifted as if she were suddenly uncomfortable talking about the situation, but she followed the unspoken rules of friendship and finished the tale that she had begun to weave.

Without releasing too many intimate details, Aubrey relived her encounter with Jason biting her lower lip as she recalled his arms around her and taste of his kiss.

"The excitement was almost too hard to control, so I finally made him leave, but he swore that it wasn't over. He said it is only the beginning for us," she dug the palms of her hands deep into her eyes rubbing them with such force she saw specks of color when she opened them again. "I am so embarrassed. How did I not realize that he actually felt anything for me?" she looked at Macie puzzled at the thought.

"Because you were too busy hating him and everything he stood for growing up. Trey and I always believed he had something for you, but he never would admit it to us, not to himself and certainly not to you," Macie beamed.

"Wait, why did you and Trey think he had something for me? We were at each other's throats most of the time. He teased me, played pranks on me, called me his little pet name," Aubrey's voice rose as she remembered her childhood with him. She ran her fingers through her hair down a similar path that Jason had pressed his fingertips through yesterday as he nipped at her neck and…

"That's the thing. He never did any of those things with other girls. He never showed them that much attention, not like he did with you."

Aubrey sighed shaking the heated thoughts from her mind, maybe she hadn't noticed because she saw it as something else, as negative attention.

"So, what are you going to do now?"

"I don't know. It complicates things a little," Aubrey sighed as she sat down Indian style on the couch pulling her legs into a half yoga position. Macie handed her the cup of coffee she had left on the island.

"What is complicated? He likes you, you like him." Macie sat down on the couch facing Aubrey drawing her legs under her and shifting back onto her heels.

"Macie, I'm only going to be here another week and a half.

Besides, I don't know how I feel about him. I only know how I felt in the moment, but that doesn't make a relationship and I don't know if I could handle something long distance if it did," Aubrey laid out the facts like pages of a book.

"Are you still going to sell the house and just go back to Memphis?" Macie had concern written on her face.

Aubrey finally had a reason to keep the house and she was still going to let it slip through her fingers, "I can't stay here. I have a life in Memphis. I have my job, my apartment, and I have friends there too."

"Yeah, like the suited up stuffed shirts at the office, or the corporate do-gooders downtown. That city is full of fun, music, and excitement and you haven't taken advantage of any of it. I think you are looking for something more, something that feels like home," Macie told her.

"I'm looking for success and a career, and..." she stopped.

"And love, maybe." Macie finished her phrase whether it was a fact in the situation or not.

"Don't call it that," Aubrey snapped.

"Then what should I call it...like, lust, a fling? What's it going to be?"

"I don't know, but it can't be with Jason, it just can't," Aubrey shook her head. She didn't want to accept that the tension she and Jason had felt for so long was released into a flow of passion and it felt right. He couldn't be the one. "Besides, it's not like he has even asked me out or anything. It is not a relationship," she groaned. "This is why I don't do this."

"Don't do what?"

"Don't date. Don't fall for guys. It's just ridiculous." Aubrey rubbed her temples as if she could rub away the thought of his touch, of his lips.

"So maybe you just play it by ear and see where it goes."

"Maybe."

"It sounds like you have a lot to think about, but not tomorrow night. Tomorrow night you are going to let it be." Macie returned the subject to the present and smiled as a plan formed in her mind to bring some more of the hometown charm to Aubrey's less than willing soul.

"What do you have in mind?" Aubrey asked knowing her friend was up to something.

"The Indian Summer Festival," Aubrey began shaking her head from side to side before Macie could finish her proposal. "Wait, let me finish. It is a good chance for you to get out of this house and away from your worries for a bit. There are rides and games, and of course cotton candy and funnel cake. Who doesn't like a good funnel cake, huh?" Macie tilted her head and waited for a response hoping for the best.

"And what is the catch?" Aubrey asked.

"No catch, just a little fun. Everyone in town will be there so you can see what the town is like when something special brings it together. It is only one night. Come on, say you'll go with me," Macie clasped her hands together as if she were in prayer and with a silent "Please" running around her lips she closed her eyes and playfully pretended to beg.

Aubrey took in a deep breath and let it out in a loud sign, "Oh, fine. I'll go, but only for you. It does sound like it might be fun."

"It will be, I promise," Macie stood to take her can back to the kitchen and get her things from the table. "I have to run, but I'll call you later. So, we are on for tomorrow?"

"Yes."

"I'll pick you up around six," Macie tucked her cell phone into her pants pocket.

"No, that's all right. I'll just meet you there. I have some things to get in town anyway, so I'll run a few errands then head on out. It's at the city park, right?" Aubrey stood and followed her to the front door.

"Yeah, I'll see you there. Don't stand me up," Macie laughed half-heartedly because she was afraid that it might be a possibility.

"I won't. I'll see you then," Aubrey waved as Macie briskly floated out the door similar to the way she had breezed in. She couldn't help but stand in awe of her friend, always happy and full of life. Why couldn't she feel the same?

Aubrey closed the door and returned to her vision of Jason and the day before. What would she do about the situation? They had such different lives. Jason was a respected person here and he wouldn't think of coming to Memphis with her. She in turn could not leave the life she had built there. She was important in her real estate firm, a top seller for years now and she had worked hard to get her position and gain the respect of her peers. Macie was right about that though, they were only her peers, not true friends. She didn't let herself have friends in Memphis afraid that they might interfere with her career. It began to bog down her mind and she decided she needed some fresh air and a more peaceful place to think. She took the cup of left over coffee and made her way out the porch door to sit in the Adirondack chair.

***

He gleamed at her as the shutter clicked once again. This time she had smiled as she peered out onto the water. He hadn't seen her with that smile before. She was beautiful when she smiled, just like her aunt had been. And didn't the baby blue cotton dress flatter her long frame when it caught just right in the breeze. He could see it cling slightly to her breasts. Now what had made those perfect peaks swell so? She must have something or someone on her mind. This would be a treasured photo. For the second time in three days his lens had found its mark on the back porch of Dragonfly, but tomorrow would be special. It would mean the most to him. He would have the one thing he had come to Walker to find, but his patience was important and he couldn't lose sight of that, so he would continue to wait and watch. The time would soon arrive.

Chapter Seventeen

Aubrey walked into the lights of the carnival rides and looked around at the children running to the games, the elder citizens hand in hand, and the moms and dads snacking on their fair favorites. It brought a smile to her face that Macie had talked her into being a part of it. She felt for the first time since she had come back to Dragonfly that she was a part of a community. The kindness of the town and its people were starting to make her feel as if maybe she could find a place here.

"Is your world as happy as I am to see you here," Jason's voice behind her made her heart skip a beat. She felt his arms wrap around her in a gentle squeeze as his body pressed against her back. She was happy to be here. She was happy to be with him.

"I was just taking it all in. I guess I've never really experienced it before. I always left before the Indian Summer Festival to get back in time for school. It really is the event of the year, isn't it?" she said to him.

"Well, it isn't much, but there is always a good turn out and the town becomes very proud and united when the festival comes around," he told her and she could feel his hometown pride as he kissed her temple then rested his head on her shoulder brushing against her cheek.

"I can't believe I missed this," she added and turned to face him breaking his precious embrace. "I have to go find Macie, after all she did invite me."

"I've got to catch up with Trey anyway. I just wanted to let you know that I'm glad you came," he smiled down at her as she stood on her toes to lay a soft kiss on his cheek.

"I'm glad too," she said as she grinned and shyly walked away.

***

"Macie!" Aubrey shouted across the swing ride where she saw her friend standing with a cardboard cone of cotton candy.

Waving, Macie looked relieved and started walking toward Aubrey, "You made it! Oh, I'm so glad you are here. There is already drama in this place. The Baptist Women's Board is pitching a fit because they think the Methodists have a bigger tent for their cake sale than they do for their pies and cookies. Mr. Harold tried to break up the argument and save Mr. Shipley before they gave him down the road on how the tents are arranged. Everyone knows the Baptists can't be put next to the Methodists. You can't put the dancers from Ms. Bell's school next to the Girl Scouts either. It's just a mess and before the night is up there is normally a yelling match over some junior high boy. That's why the Girl Scouts have to stay in the clubhouse. Since Mr. Shipley is in charge of the tent assignments they all want to blame him, even if he does buy an even amount from each tent," she finally came up for air. "That is why I stay clear of all of them and stick with cotton candy and funnel cake." She gave Aubrey an enormous smile and raised her eyebrows. "So, have you seen Jason yet?"

"He actually found me first. I was barely in the gates," she gave a sweet grin.

"It sounds like he was anxious to see you," Macie noted as she pulled pink fluff from the cone, tilted her head back, and opened her mouth wide for the treat.

"I think he might have been, but I told him I was here to spend time with you and maybe we would run into each other later in the night," she gave a shy shrug with her shoulder as she beamed.

"Are you kidding me? I would have left you on the side of the road if Jason McNally were after me," she laughed peering around at the swishing sound of the rides. "I love you Aubrey, but Jason is a hottie. You need to go find him and spent that time with him. I'll be fine."

"No, way! Not in a million. I'm still not sure how I feel about him. I mean he dropped a lot of information on me in a very short amount of time. I still don't know what to think about it all. I need some time to get a clear mind," she said looking up at the *Ring of Fire* ride in front of them and shooting Macie a devious grin, "and I know just what to do."

Aubrey grabbed Macie by the wrist and insisted that they ride the largest, scariest ride at the event. They had been in line waiting for about fifteen minutes, catching up on the town gossip, when Aubrey heard footstep behind her. Macie's face bared a cunning smile and brightened as she stared behind Aubrey.

"You know the carnies are out here drinking beer while they are putting these rides together, don't you?" she heard that beautiful familiar voice behind her.

"I'm sorry, I haven't heard anything about that. Is it true or are you just too afraid to ride the big kid rides?" Aubrey returned ready to play Jason's game. It felt oddly similar to their school days, but not as harsh. This time it was playful. She turned to see his stunning blue green eyes as they sparkled now like they had never before.

"I'm not afraid to get on it, but Trey here gets sick on these things. I hate to ride it without him," Jason stated.

"Oh, I see, so because Trey can't ride it and you don't want to ride without a friend," she said smugly as she noticed Trey rolling his eyes at her out of Jason's view. "That's all right. The ladies will ride it and you can just watch from over there," she pointed to the *Exit* gate on the other side of the ride.

"I believe I hear a little bit of a challenge in your tone, Ms. Todd. Do you think I won't ride it?" Jason said as he tickled her playfully.

"I don't believe you will Mr. McNally. Do you care to prove me wrong?" she smiled brightly at him daring him to accept.

"We can do this Trey. We are big boys, just suck it up and get ready for the ride of your life," he demanded to his friend. Trey didn't seem very impressed with the game.

"Next up," said the tall fire-haired carnie as he opened the *Enter* gate.

"It's time," Aubrey said smacking a high five with Macie and giving a quick kiss in Jason's direction before walking swiftly to find her seat.

"It's about time," Jason muttered under his breath staring at her in complete admiration before following her footsteps and taking his place on the ride with her.

After trying their luck, Jason's words seemed to ring true finding only Trey's stomach was a questionable mark for the speed of the *Ring of Fire*. Macie and Trey left to find a drink to settle the queasy feeling Trey had and a seat on solid ground for his nerves. Jason was approached by a fellow officer working security for the event, so Aubrey found it to be a perfect time to do some festival exploring. She worked her way through the carnival rides, around the skee-ball slides, passed the numerous fall-themed crafts for sale and found a semi-local bluegrass band belting out "Rock me momma like a wagon wheel," one of her Old Crow favorites, on the ancient bandstand close to the clubhouse. She stood enthralled in the music as the band changed strides and began to play an Earl Scruggs classic. She giggled as couples took the floor to clog and do-si-do. Her laughter wilted to a simple smile as she listened to the timing of the music and the clank of the taps on their shoes hitting the wooden floor. She thought to herself *I truly hope I am this happy, healthy, and excited by life when I am that age.*

When the song was over, the lead singer of the band announced a short break, but encouraged the dancing to continue to the more modern sounds of country music selected by the college-aged disc jockey they had hired to "spin tunes" while they took a rest. The DJ, a youthful boy with bright crystal eyes and dark hair, chose to start off with an uplifting tune by Keith Urban which let both young and old strut their stuff as if there were no age barriers. With the last line of the sultry Australian sound, the youngster began to slow the fun down and adapt to more folks while playing Patsy Cline's *Crazy*. As the song began to play gentlemen turned to their wives for a romantic stride, teen boys took hands of young ladies to guide them to the floor, and even small children whose parents had taught them well focused their efforts to the dance. Aubrey stared in wonder at the beauty of it all. As the song drew to a close she thought of Jane and how she wished she were here.

"Would you care to dance?" she heard a smooth voice say from behind her.

Aubrey bent her head slightly to the left to see Jason close to her ear with a hand subtly placed in the small of her back. She blinked her eyes to flash him a twinkle and let a slight grin curl up from the corner of her mouth.

"Sure, why not." It was just a dance after all.

As they moved onto the dance floor the DJ began to play Lady Antebellum's *If I Knew Then*. The lyrics of the song echoed through Aubrey's mind as she moved with his strong yet gentle body. She wondered if things would have been different if she had known Jason's feelings when they were younger. He drew her tighter to him, taking her right hand and pressing it too his brawny chest. She could feel the steady beat of his heart under her fingertips. He kept his hand over hers as he slowly moved her around the dance floor. She could no longer hear the screams of children on the carnival rides or the bells ringing on the games. She only heard the music deep in her core. She only felt the beat of his heart in rhythm with her own.

Her knees began to weaken and she wondered if she would be able to continue to move. As long as his arms were there to catch her she would stay lost in them. He bent his head and pressed his cheek to hers.

"I have waited so long to have you in my arms like this," he whispered in her ear.

She closed her eyes and let him consume her. Her body shivered with his words and a breath escaped her lips. As they swayed together in the early fall breeze, their bodies began to move as one and their minds focused only on one another. The scars that Jason had left on her heart so many years ago began to heal and she felt that maybe she would let him into her life after all. Maybe with all their history and all they had been through, she could finally, truly forgive him and move forward.

"Aubrey, the music stopped," he said quietly in her ear.

"What music?" she opened her eyes and glared up at him taking a step back to soak in the beauty of this man. Aubrey could only hear mumbles in the background as they stood still staring at each other. He bent down to kiss her and she suddenly found the voices familiar and broke the connection of the pull between them, not allowing him to succeed with his intent.

"Aubrey," Macie's voice became clear and she stepped further from Jason. He had totally captivated her soul once again. It was already becoming hard for her to resist.

"I'm right here Macie," she said not taking her eyes off of Jason.

"Yeah, I can see that. Did you hear what I said?" Macie asked.

Aubrey blinked her eyes and shook her head slightly as if to clear her mind. She looked at Macie a little confused and bothered by the interruption, "I didn't quite get that. What were you talking about?"

"We ran into Chera at the drink stand. Remember her from when we were kids? She lives in Chicago now working at a news station with the production crew. Anyway, she is in this week for the festival and to see her parents. They had told her about Jane and that you were staying at Dragonfly for a while and she wants to see you. I told her when I found you we would head toward the House of Mirrors," Aubrey tilted her head and twisted her face in disapproval. She had hated the House of Mirrors since she was a little girl and had run face first into one of the mirrors causing her to have a knot on her forehead for a week. "Not to go in. The pink flamingo game is next to the mirrors and I want to win one."

"Well, then I guess we will head to the House of Mirrors to visit with Chera and the flamingos," Aubrey started to walk away with Macie and remembering Jason twisted around to give him a wink, "We will catch back up with you later?"

"Count on it," he hadn't moved. He only gawked at her in amazement. What was he thinking all these years letting her spend so much time away from Walker? Why had he not searched for her when she hadn't come back? He now felt that he might regret not making that move, but he knew she was here now and he intended to enjoy every moment.

Chapter Eighteen

After catching up with Chera and her wonderful Chicago life with the handsome fiancée and newsroom job, Aubrey decided she needed a bathroom break.

"I'll go try to find Trey and Jason," Macie said turning to head toward the game tents.

"All right, I'm going up to the clubhouse to the bathroom. I think I will grab us a funnel cake afterward so meet me over by the food trailers," Aubrey told her licking her lips at the thought of the sugar covered chaos of fried dough.

"That sounds delicious. I'll see you in a few minutes," Macie walked away with a slight skip in her step.

Aubrey began to make her way toward the clubhouse. While there were portable bathrooms set in many different areas of the carnival, the walk to the clubhouse to go indoors and use regularly cleaned ones were worth the trek up the hill.

Aubrey walked inside the clubhouse and was greeted by Girl Scout Troop 241 selling home baked cookies, pies and other delicious treats to raise money for a camping trip. Undoubtedly they were on track to gain a few merit badges. Aubrey smiled brightly promising to look at their goods on the way out. She turned to the left and headed in to freshen up. Once in a stall she heard giggling voices as two older ladies entered the bathroom.

"I can't believe she said that," one of the ladies said as she entered the stall next to Aubrey.

"And she wonders why people talk," the other lady stayed close to the sinks.

"Wasn't that strange about finding Jake Warren's car in the lake? I always thought it was fishy, no pun intended, that all of a sudden he left town and no one ever heard from him again," an oddly husky voice said.

"Well, I always thought that something happened to him and he didn't just up and leave," the other lady joined in the conversation.

Aubrey heard a flush in the stall next to her and the door swung open almost violently.

"Everyone knew he drank all the time, so a lot of folks wondered if he just fell off a bridge somewhere or wandered into the lake after a drinking binge," the husky voice stated as she turned the water on.

"I heard momma talk about him years ago, hanging out at Gus's Pub and going home with all kinds of women," another faucet turned on making it harder to hear. Aubrey focused to eavesdrop.

"Josie said her cousin got caught with him once by his girlfriend at the time," the husky voice lady turned the water off and pumped the paper towel dispenser three times.

"Was that when he was with Jane Todd or before?" the older voice asked.

"I don't know when it was, but I know he cheated on Jane. Josie said there were a lot of times he was seen flirting with other girls." the husky lady clarified.

"I wonder if Jane had something to do with that car being in the lake. She was the last girlfriend he had before he took off and she had a lot of friends in town that would have protected her," the older lady considered as she in turn shut the water off and pumped the paper towel dispenser.

"You know her niece is at her lake house. I heard Jane left it to her in the will," the husky voice whispered as if it were a secret.

"The one that used to visit in the summer time when she was younger?" the older voice questioned.

"Yes, I've seen her around town too. She grew into a rather

pretty girl that looks a lot like Jane," there was no longer any sound of movement between the two ladies. "Anyway, the story is Jason McNally was assigned to the Warren man's murder case and since she has been back in town, he has become very friendly with her."

"That must be the girl I saw him with earlier. Isn't that a conflict of interest since her aunt was dating the man they just found dead?"

"I wouldn't be too concerned. I hear he is using it to his advantage. He is just seeing her to try to get information so he can make a case against Jane for the murder, then he'll be done with her. The captain seems to think Jane was involved, but since she is no longer alive it is going to be harder to prove," said the husky voice.

"So that's why Jason is with her? Well, that makes a little more sense. They were never close when they were kids, and she doesn't live here. Besides, he needs to be with a local girl."

"In any case, I don't think she is planning on staying around long. Becky in Mr. Shipley's law office said she heard that the Todd girl is going to sell off Jane's things in an auction, take the money, and head back to Memphis. She said the niece is career-minded just like Jane, except she loves the big city. She just wants the money for the place and wouldn't think of moving down here anyway," the husky voice said in an upscale phony tone as if she perceived Aubrey to be a snob.

"Well, I'm glad Jason is not really interested in her. He is such a studly thing," said the older lady.

"Are you kidding? You don't have a chance," the husky voice said with a laugh.

"Not me! But you know my daughter is still single..." the conversation trailed off as both ladies walked out of the bathroom and went on their way.

When she was sure of their departure, Aubrey slowly slipped out of the middle bathroom stall. Before she even glanced at herself in the mirror she knew her face was pale and lifeless. She washed her hands, dried them with a paper towel, then dabbed the damp paper towel over her face and neck. She had heard every word, studied every syllable that had spewed from the mouths of the two unknown voices. He was only after information to conclude her aunt killed Jake Warren. How could she have been so blind? Had he been so charming, and his kiss so mesmerizing that she was unable to see what he was actually after? She lifted her fingertips to brush across her lips remembering the pressure of his kiss only days ago at Dragonfly. Aubrey was in pain with the enlightenment. Her head began to spin and she felt dizzy so she anchored herself by gripping the sink with her hands. She looked again in the mirror at her vacant face. How dare he!

Macie had found Jason as promised and while laughing at an older man's frustration at the OK Corral gunslinger's shoot off game they approached the clubhouse finding a disheveled looking Aubrey.

"Are you full of funnel cake yet? Hey, what's wrong?" Jason asked seeing the blank expression on Aubrey's face. "You look a little pale. Are you sick?"

"Is it true?" she asked staring at him.

"Is what true?" he replied bewildered at her question.

"All those things you said. Is it true that you just said them to get closer to me?" she asked pleading for an answer.

"Aubrey, I don't know what you are talking about. What things?" he reached out to take her arms and pull her closer to him, but she pulled away putting up her hands to signal him to stop trying to comfort her.

"That you care for me, how it broke your heart when I didn't come back, that you haven't found another girl that you could see yourself with, was it all just to get information from me about my aunt?" her voice became persistent for the answer.

"Look, I don't know where you heard that, but you got some bad information. I wouldn't do that to you," he insisted.

"Really? How long after I left the station did your captain send you after me? What did he tell you, to earn my trust, seduce me if you had to, and then pump me for information? If you got me in bed, then that was a little "just dessert" for a job well done," Aubrey's eyes sparked with amber fire as they widened in anger.

"You told me you made him leave. Did you sleep with him?" Macie quickly questioned.

"Mind your own business, Macie," Jason snapped at her.

"I fell for it hook, line, and sinker, didn't I?" she began shaking her head slowly while never taking her eyes off of him. "I don't believe it. I fell for it, and I fell for you."

"Who told you that?" he asked.

"It doesn't matter who said it. It's just like when we were kids. You are still trying to play me like a fool. You needed me to trust you, so you could solve a case. It was all for the job. Well, not this time. I'm not a child anymore," she inched closer and closer to him to look him in the eyes, trying to read any signs there that he might be telling the truth that it was all a mistake.

"I am well aware of that and I'm not playing a boyish game. I may have tricked you or teased you in the past, but the one thing I never did was lie to you, Aubrey, ever," he emphasized to her as he looked deeply into her hazel eyes.

"I have to get out of here," she blinked her eyes to come back to her senses, drawing her arms to her chest and closing into herself before turning to leave. "I can't be around you."

She began walking toward the game tents with her arms crossed and her head bowed as if defeated. Jason was frozen where he stood, blind-sided by the words that she spoke in anger and hurt.

"Well, what are you standing there for?" Trey asked him. "Go get her."

As Jason began to move he heard a harsh voice belt out at him and saw Macie's finger in his face as she stepped between him and the path Aubrey took. "No, you stay away from her. I don't know if you are telling the truth or not, but you are going to stay away from her."

"Macie, I swear to you I don't know where she heard it, but it's not true. I do care for her. I think I'm falling for her," he confessed to his friends.

"You just need to let her settle down for a bit," Macie saw the fear of losing Aubrey in his eyes. "I'll go after her and make sure she is all right." He shook his head in agreement.

Macie found Aubrey sitting on a wood-carved bench just outside the gates of the festival with her face in her hands and tears running down her cheeks. A cool wind was beginning to blow in and she could smell the spice of the sausages from the nearest food trailer, but food was the last thing she could tolerate. Macie softly plopped down beside her, put an arm across her shoulders, and drew in a deep breath. Aubrey looked up at Macie and flipped her head to shake back the streams of her auburn hair blowing across her tear stained face.

"I can't believe I fell for his deceiving tricks. I really thought he cared for me and I was starting to have feelings for him too. I'm so stupid. Just because we are adults doesn't mean the juvenile games are over," Aubrey analyzed as she sat with her arms crossed and stared up at the clear night sky.

"I don't think he was lying," Macie told her wiping the tears from her chin.

"How could you not think so?" she asked.

"I've spent a lot of time with him over the years and all the girls he has dated, he never got too close to any of them. But his eyes have had that funny sparkle ever since you came back into town. When he heard of Jane's death, his first reaction involved you. He wondered if you might come back. He just told me that he thought he was really falling for you. I looked in his eyes when he said it, Aubrey, and it just didn't seem like a lie to me. He hasn't ever lied to you, has he?" she drew from memories of their childhood and forced Aubrey to look back among all of the ups and downs of the summers here with Jason.

"No, I guess he hasn't," she replied. Standing, she turned to face Macie. "I need to be somewhere quiet. I'm going to head on home."

"I'll call you later to check in," Macie stood, gave her a hug and whispered. "Think about giving him another chance."

Aubrey pulled back, "Thanks, Macie, for watching over me."

"Anytime," Macie said as she turned to walk back to the festival.

Dearest Journal,

I am in a very awkward situation. It would appear that something strange is going on with Jake. I haven't heard from him in a couple of days and it seems odd that he hasn't done so much as call. When he is here, he seems bothered by something or his mind is a million miles away. When I ask if something is wrong, he claims he is just fine and brushes me off. Deep down I think he is hiding something from me. I need to do some investigating to find out what is going on. I don't want to be nosy, but I need to know he is safe. I love him and if we are going to progress in our relationship, I need to know he is in this with me. Maybe I'll fix a nice dinner this weekend and we can talk.

Sincerely yours,

Jane Elizabeth

Chapter Nineteen

The drive home was silent, but long as Aubrey turned up the country station on the radio and rolled down the windows to allow the night to leave her breathless as it hit her face. She had taken the long way home in order to let her thoughts circle in freedom in her head hoping for some resolution to the situation. Then with no results and still fuming from her confrontation with Jason, she decided to make her way back to Dragonfly. She was feeling more than betrayal, she felt a tight pain in her chest that she was convinced was the result of the emotions she had let herself feel for him. To find out it was just a game was causing her physical and emotional pain. What if Macie was right and those were not his intentions. Maybe they even had been at first, but he had found something deeper for her. It was all just too much and she was tired of thinking about it. She pulled into the driveway and set it all free to trade it for a good night's sleep.

The door was open about a half an inch as Aubrey approached the front porch of Dragonfly with her keys jingling in her hand. She thought for a moment replaying her departure in her head. Had she left in such a hurry that she didn't close the door tightly? It was possible because it wouldn't be the first time she had left it unlatched just enough that the wind blew it open, and there had been a breeze this evening. She stepped up to the door and slowly drew her fingers over the knob, examining it as she carefully pushed the door open. There were no lights on in the house. Strange she reflected but again it was not impossible. Aubrey would often forget to leave a light on especially if she left the house during the day when lights were not needed.

With only a slightly uneasy feeling she opened the door widely and walked into the house. Closing the door behind her, Aubrey opted not to search for the light switch on the wall but to feel her way into the living room and find the glow of the Tiffany style lamp on the corner of the sofa table.

"Welcome home," she heard the man say and she stopped instantly becoming quiet hoping he couldn't see her in the shadows, but he had been there creeping around in the dark for some time and his eyes were adjusted to the night.

Aubrey was unable to make it to the sofa table before the man wrapped his hand around her throat from behind. She jerked to break free from his grasp with failure. His other arm then wrapped around her chest pinning her arms in a strong hold to subdue her, while at the same time tightening his hold on her throat. She could feel the hardness of his chest vigorously against her back. The sudden movement caused her to struggle for air and sent a cold chill down her spine. Her house had an intruder. The man placed his head next to Aubrey's left ear.

"You must be her niece," he croaked from deep in his throat. "I've heard about you," Aubrey tried to break free from the man's grip like a child wiggling from his mother's grasp to get to the floor and play.

She trembled in his arms frightened at his actions and numb by his words. She took in anything that she thought she might be able to recognize later, if she lived through whatever was to happen next. His strength was aggressive, his voice rasping, and he smelled of cigarette smoke, a decent brand that didn't give off such an offensive stale odor.

"You have something in this house that I need," he said through clenched teeth. "Where is the box?"

Aubrey shook her head as best she could with his hand still on her throat. "I don't know what you are talking about," she strained to get the words out of her mouth.

"The box with the dragonfly on the top, where is it?" he repeated with frustration.

Again, she tried to shake her head.

"Well, I guess we will just have to find it together," he gave her a nudge in the direction of the hallway leading to the back of the house.

The stranger began to make his way to the master bedroom. He seemed very familiar with the direction of the room and the layout of the house even in the dark. She concluded that he had either spent time here before, or he had just spent some time searching for his prize already. He kept Aubrey in front of him continuing to push at her back with his chest. The box had been a treasure of her aunt's and he assumed it would be in the most protected place, her bedroom.

"Open the closet," he let one arm go so she could open the closet door. "Now find it," he pushed her to the floor where she fell to her knees causing slight carpet burns. With a hand on her neck from behind, just to make sure she knew he was still there, he snarled at her to search through the bottom of the closet. He made certain with the pressure on her neck, that she was aware he was able to overpower her at any moment.

Aubrey searched through the piles of things. She sifted through clothes, shoes, cardboard boxes, and mementos, but she didn't see a wooden box.

"It's not here," she told him hoping he would ease the weight on the back of her neck.

She tried to remember from the summers that she had spent in the house if she had ever seen the adored box he was looking for and vaguely recalled a dark wooden vessel that held favored souvenirs from her aunt's childhood. Could that be what this stranger was seeking? She couldn't recall where Jane kept it or what else could be in it.

"Get up." She arose to her feet feeling the tug on the back of her shirt from his strength. She turned around to face him only to see the fury in his eyes as the moonlight came through the cracks of the blinds. As her eyes had now adjusted to the dark she looked around the room and noticed that he had already gone through the drawers of the dresser and nightstands, leaving them disheveled.

"You know where it is. You probably found it already," he was becoming very agitated and impatient. He grabbed her by the top of her arms and shoved her hard against the wall knocking wall art from the nails and overturning the picture on the dresser of her Aunt Jane and her dad embracing on Thanksgiving Day five years ago.

She felt her back strike against the wall and send a surge of pain up her spine, the back of her head slamming against the pale blue paint that Jane chose so carefully. In a long legged stride taking only a few steps to arrive in front of her, he raised his arm across her throat choking her and pinning her tightly against the wall with his burly body.

"I'm tired of playing games. I'm sure you have been all through this house," he said in clear anger. "Where are you hiding it?"

He let her go and she stumbled around him to the other side of the room. He turned around to face her as she coughed to regain her breath. Again, she shook her head to let him know he was not going to gain access to the wooden box.

"You worthless piece of trash," he raised his right hand across his body and brought it down on the smooth flesh of her right cheek. The blow caught her off guard and the rush of pain tore through her face like a flame of fire brushing over her. She fell to the bed with her head tilted to her left exposing her now red cheek and throat. He felt his frustration turn to heat as he stared at her unconscious body. She looked so much like Jane he thought. He decided that if she would not make it easy for him to find the treasure that he desired, then he would certainly not make it easy for her to forget him. As he grazed a hand over her now throbbing face, he crawled on the bed straddling her limp, lifeless torso.

He took her in inch by inch carefully glancing over her body pale in the same creeping moonlight. He bent over her to smell her hair and breathed in the sweet aroma of roses, and then he dipped down close to her and licked her neck. "You taste like..."

Aubrey lay on the bed quietly calculating the perfect time to reveal her plan of escape. She just needed a few more seconds to control her breathing and make sure that he was in the right position to do the most damage. Feeling his warm wet tongue breeze across her neck, her heart skipped a beat. He was too close. He mumbled in her ear with a gruff sound that generated frost in her soul. While balancing on his left hand, his right hand moved around the side of her breast letting his thumb travel across her nipple which she was sure would awaken his senses. Fear covered her, stunning her and protecting her until the very moment came to have her revenge. She had to remain calm as he stood from the bed and took her legs to drag her to the edge of the bed. He straddled her bent legs and steadied himself to unbuckle his belt, reaching into his jeans to release his length. She knew she was lined up perfectly.

The blow to his groin doubled him over, causing him to fall on top of her. She quickly pushed him off with all her strength, but he grabbed at her arm to steady himself and to keep her from getting away. She knew she had to make her next move swiftly and clawed at his face with her free hand to release herself from his clutch. She was able to stand and get past him as he writhed in pain on the floor. Aubrey ran into the spare bedroom, stumbling as she moved, able to close and lock the door behind her. With adrenaline flooding her veins, she pulled a chest of drawers in front of the door. She hurried to the far side of the room and dropped down onto the floor drawing her knees to her chest. She could hear his footsteps in the hallway, searching for his prey.

It suddenly occurred to her that she still had her cell phone in her pocket from her trip to the festival. She released her knees for a moment to gain easier access to her pants pocket. Reaching deep in her pocket and praying that it hadn't fallen out during her attack, she felt the hard plastic cover on her phone and pulled it out dialing 911 as fast as her shaking finger would allow. Tears dripping down her face, her voice quivered as she spoke to the calm female on the other end of the line.

"Please help me. I have an intruder in my house. He attacked me. Please help me!" she cried beginning to lose control to fright.

"Try to stay calm ma'am. Stay on the phone with me and we will get to you. Does he have a weapon?" the lady asked.

"I don't believe so. I haven't seen one," she answered.

"That's good. Are you in a safe place?" the lady asked.

"I...um, I'm locked in a bedroom, but," she heard his stern

voice call out as he banged his fist against the door.

"Come on out pretty. I'm not done playing with you," he threatened.

"Ma'am, we have tracked your phone and I have an officer on the way," the sweet voice said. "Does he know where you are?"

Lowering her voice Aubrey spoke slowly and softly to the lady on the phone, "Yes, he knows where I am. He is trying to break the door down."

The intruder began using his shoulder to make his way into the room after her and she decided that since he had realized she was in there, she would let him know exactly what she was doing hoping to detour his determination to obtain her.

"I'm talking to the police. They have officers coming and you will be arrested," now standing, she screamed out toward the door as she placed her phone on speaker so maybe he would hear the lady on the other end of the line.

"Ma'am, are you there? Is he in the room? Ma'am can you hear me? The officer will be there in a few minutes. Try to remain calm and put any barrier you can between you and the man," she said with a sudden hint of fear in her voice.

"See, I have them on the line. I've told them what you look like and what I've done to you. They are coming after you," Aubrey shouted. He continued to bang against the door. "They will be here soon to get you. Do you hear me you maniac?" she had a sudden fit of determination to make sure he knew she hated him.

Then there was silence except for the steps she heard walking away from the door. It had worked! He resolved that if he stayed, he would probably end up in jail. As much as she wanted him to ultimately pay a visit to a cell, for now she just wanted him gone out of her house.

"Ma'am? Ma'am, what happened? Are you still there?" the lady's voice had fear of what might be occurring on the other end of the line, but was relieved when she heard Aubrey's voice return.

"I'm all right. I think he is gone." She breathed a sigh of relief, sank down on the floor and began to cry.

Chapter Twenty

"Let me in, let me in," Jason screamed at the officer as he came barreling through the door of Dragonfly. "Where is she? Where is Aubrey?"

"Jason, wait. Calm down," Trey quickly turned away from the officer that he was talking to in order to intercept the panic of his friend.

"Trey, where is she?" Jason demanded as his face began to heat up with a fearful fire that he was not sure he could control.

"She's outside on the back deck with Mac getting some fresh air," Trey replied placing his hand on Jason's chest to hold him back as he started toward the back door. Trey had sent Aubrey out to let her collect herself, thinking she might be more comfortable opening up to Macie, and he was sure that if Jason interrupted them he would not be able to reign in his fury when he witnessed the results of the attack. He needed to calm Jason down first and prepare him before he saw her.

Jason moved over to the window and felt all his breath seep from his chest as he saw Aubrey with her back to him standing out on the deck, a blanket wrapped around her shoulders and arms. He needed to see for himself, that she was able to stand on her own two feet, but what he found was the fear that he had for her, the fear for her safety, for her life. In that moment, all the years of teasing and denial had turned into emotions that were melting him. All he wanted, all he believed he needed was to take care of her.

He turned only his head back toward Trey, "What happened?"

Trey began to repeat the story that Aubrey had shared, "There was an intruder in the house when she came home."

"Trey, how did he break in?" asking for the facts with his detective instincts.

"She either left her door unlocked or he simply jimmied the door open. The lock wasn't broken," Trey told him. "It's possible that he slipped in from the back deck if she left the sliding door unlocked."

Jason began with his own conclusion, "She lives in a big city. She always locks the door. Jane didn't believe in deadbolts so he could have used something as simple as a credit card to break in."

"I've got officers scouting the area," Trey informed Jason, "but I don't think he hung around. They found a set of footprints on the south side that lead down toward the dock then cut back into the woods. They got hard to track after a while."

Jason crossed back over to the window. With his heart pounding in his chest like a greyhound during a race, he raised one arm to rest it across the pane of the window, his other on his twisted hip. His eyes began to glass over as he saw her talking arm in arm with Macie.

Running his hand through his hair he asked the burning question that made his soul tremble and his knees buckle beneath him, "Trey, did he…" His throat became dry and he forced his voice to remain steady as he struggled to find the words. "Did he rape her?" the fire of the question barely escaped his lips.

"No," Trey replied quietly. "She said he was looking for something and when he couldn't find it he became agitated. Then it turned violent. He attempted…well, that was when she made her move and was able to escape."

With a quick jerk of his head, it only took Jason two steps for him to be face to face with Trey, his eyes glowing with hate.

"What do you mean it turned violent?" Jason demanded. "Is she hurt? Tell me!"

"He must have thought that she was holding out on him, so to try to make her tell him what he wanted to know he slammed her against the wall and then back handed her across the face. She already had a pretty nasty bruise on her cheek and more on her body when we found her."

Jason's hands drew up into fists wishing that there was something or someone that he could hit. He wanted to feel the soft flesh of the person who had hurt Aubrey under his knuckles pulsing with pain. He began to pace slowly between Trey and the window to calm himself and finally stopped again at the window to stare out at the deck.

"She was not even supposed to be here, Trey," he said through clenched teeth in a low growl. "She was supposed to be having a great night at the festival." He turned to glare at Trey with glazed eyes. "I was going to try to convince her to stay, but we got into that fight about…it wasn't even important what it was about. She should have been there with me," his eyes dropped to the floor and his breathing slowed. "If she hadn't heard the things she did and she hadn't gotten so upset," he looked back up at Trey shaking his head trying to get the thought of a stranger's hands around Aubrey and her fright as he abused her out of his head. "I should have been here with her."

"Jason, don't even start thinking that way," Trey reassured him. "This isn't your fault."

"But she wouldn't have come home and she wouldn't have found him here," Jason said. "He wouldn't have gone after her or hurt her. He would have just looked for what he wanted and left."

"You don't know that," Trey stepped closer and laid a hand on Jason's shoulder. He dipped his head to force Jason to look at him. "Hey, it happened the way it did and you can't change it. Now she needs you. You can't deal with this like you would one of your cases. Be strong for her."

Jason looked eye to eye with Trey, "I don't know if I can do that. How do you handle this when you are in so deep? I could deal with it if it were just a domestic dispute case I was working, but what do you do when it's more."

He took a deep breath and regained himself. Trey was right, he would have to try his best to look at things less like an officer to be able to help piece things together and help Aubrey get past the terror of being attacked.

"I'm going to take care of this," he assured Trey. "We will have every officer the force can spare to work on this. I'll be in early tomorrow and start making some calls and interview everyone in the neighborhood to see if they have seen or heard anything strange lately."

Trey lifted his grip from Jason's shoulder and shook his head, "Jason, you are not getting anywhere near this case. You are too close."

"So what am I supposed to do," he asked, "just stand on the side line and watch?"

"Not just watch, but give us some insight. She might feel more comfortable telling you things. She might remember something when she is with you. Your instinct and training could help us find this guy faster if you just focus on her," Trey said with firmness. "You can't go looking for this guy on your own. Promise me you won't try. You are in way too deep."

"Yeah, all right," Jason finally agreed as he stared back outside as the moonlight surrounded her.

Jason opened the door and walked out onto the patio quietly closing the door behind him so not to disturb the conversation between the two women. Macie looked back at the door and seeing Jason appear decided it was time for her exit. She gave Aubrey one last gentle squeeze.

"I'll call you first thing in the morning to check on you. Are you sure you don't want me to stay," she asked.

Aubrey only shook her head, so Macie took the empty coffee cup from her hand and started toward the door meeting Jason's glance as she passed by. He tipped his head toward her as if to assure her that he was ready to take over and comfort Aubrey. With no words spoken Macie understood his intent and left them alone, opening the door and letting herself back into the living room to get her things and head home for the night.

Jason took Macie's place standing to the left of Aubrey looking out over the lake with his hands tucked in his pockets. In the late night breeze there was no trace of a crime, no trace of a crushed spirit, no trace of a wounded woman. On the patio of the Dragonfly the story was very different. Aubrey only stared out at the water, not ready to face him just yet, not knowing how he might react when he saw the damage. She would only focus on the water and its calm rippling sound against the bank. They stood there in silence for what seemed to him like an eternity, his heart pounding in his chest waiting to break free and search for the answers he wished to find. Finally, when he could not take it anymore, he spoke.

"Aubrey, I am so sorry," Jason pleaded. "Can you ever forgive me?"

"I couldn't breathe," she replied quietly still staring out over the dark night.

"I shouldn't have let you go. I was just so…I shouldn't have let you come home alone," he said with such regret in his voice.

"His hands were so strong and I couldn't breathe," she could begin to feel the stranger's fingers wrapped around her throat again and blinked her eyes to close out the memory.

"I know. If I could change what happened…" he pleaded once again hoping for forgiveness.

She closed her tearful eyes and the wet drops began slowly trickling down her face as her voice became weak and trembled, "I tried to call your name, but I couldn't breathe." She began to weep softly.

He was taken aback by the confession and felt a blow to his heart as if he were hit in the chest with a sledgehammer. He moved toward her wanting so desperately to hold her, but afraid that she might reject him.

"Aubrey, please look at me," he begged ready to see the damage to her skin, wanting to know the damage to her soul.

"I just don't understand why, Jason?" she turned to look him in the face and saw the fear erupt in his blue green eyes that sharpened when they viewed her bruised cheek. "I couldn't give him what he wanted. Why did he do it?" Fire burned in him and his hands instantly became fists again at his sides as his mouth refused to close from his shock.

"He will pay," Jason said in anger not able to take his eyes from the bruise. "I promise you. We will find him and he will pay for what he has done to you."

She burst into tears again trying to get her emotions under

control. Unable to settle herself she turned her head to the right to once again look out over the water. She took in a deep breath and as she did the blanket fell just enough that Jason caught sight of the four horizontal marks on her neck, the violent shadow of fingers that lingered from her assailant. His blood boiled with anger at what he saw. He closed his eyes and turned his head away from her. He could not stand there and continue to see the aggression that was left behind until he was sure he could control the rage it unwrapped inside him. When he felt collected he turned back to her with hatred on his face for the intruder that had forced a temporary wedge between them.

"Let me take you back inside. You need to rest," he told her.

She turned back toward him knowing what he had seen because it was clearly written on his face, "Give me just another minute or two before I go back inside," she said swiping at the fallen tears on her cheeks. "There are still policemen in there and I really don't want them to see me so scattered."

"I don't want to leave you alone out here," he began to ease back into himself.

She took in another composing breath, "I'll be fine. It's just for a minute. I'll be in soon."

"I'll have my eyes on you," he assured her.

"I hope so," she forced a crooked smile.

Trey continued his conversation with a burly gentleman in a blue uniform, jotting down notes as the man spoke, and shaking his head with each phrase as Jason and Aubrey stood listening to another officer replay the story that Aubrey had so carefully told him. Jason could see that Trey was finished when he folded his notebook, tucking it into his coat pocket, and shook the man's hand. He turned and let his head fall before stepping over to meet Jason who had already begun walking toward him.

"Jason, we have scoured the area and we haven't found anything but the partial footprints. He knows we are out looking and is probably long gone by now," Trey could barely look at Aubrey feeling so sorry for her pain. She was Macie's best friend and he knew this situation would be the focal point of their future conversations.

"You have searched down by the lake and dock?" Jason

inquired.

"Yeah man, nothing. We checked the whole area but he was careful and didn't leave anything behind, not so much as a cigarette butt," Trey added.

"I'm going to stay here with Aubrey tonight. I don't want to take any chances that this guy could come back after her. Trey, could you…"

He interrupted, "I've already called it in. We will have a car coming by every hour."

"Thanks! I appreciate it," Jason reached out his hand and Trey took it firmly in a shake then they finished with a pat on each other's shoulder. This was business, but it was also personal and they both felt the courage, fear, and duty it required.

"I'll, see you in the morning, Jason."

"See you then, Trey!"

Trey looked around Jason to find Aubrey's eyes pale and unresponsive, "Try to get some rest tonight, Aubrey. We will be watching out for you, I promise."

"Thank you, Trey. You are so kind," she struggled to find a smile for him.

Trey called out to the other officers that their work was done for the night. It was time to take the information they had gathered and get started on solving this case. Navy blue uniforms adorned with medals and badges filed out of the front door of Dragonfly as if they were toy soldiers in a Christmas play.

Aubrey watched as they strolled across her porch and stepped closer to the door as Jason gave them a final wave and closed it locking it behind them.

"Did I overhear you say that you were spending the night?" she asked him.

"Listen, Aubrey, before you even try to argue. I don't feel comfortable leaving you here alone tonight," Jason shook his head and raised his hands in protest of what he knew she was about to say. "He came here very determined, looking for something specific and he didn't find it. He is still out there and he might decide to come back and finish what he started."

"You heard Trey. They didn't find a trace of him except the footprints leading out of the woods. I'm sure he is not stupid. He has to believe that the police are watching the house now," she retaliated.

"But you will be safer if you have an officer on the property, in the house," he demanded.

"I don't need a babysitter," she argued, "or someone hanging over me asking if I'm all right every time I move."

"I'm not trying to be a babysitter or watch your every move," realizing he was becoming defensive, he lowered his voice. "Just let me stay the night."

"I don't know if I can be alone with you," she croaked.

"What?"

"I'm not sure I can trust myself, or you with my emotions right now," she felt her head begin to spin. "It's been a scary night for me and I'm afraid if you try to comfort me…"

He took her chin into his hand and lifted her head to face her, "More than anything I would love to take you in my arms and make this pain go away, but I've worked these types of cases before and I know it can be traumatic for a woman. I will wait until you feel that you need me, that you want me. For now, we will put all that has happen between us to the side, and focus on you."

She believed him. He was an officer and if anyone understood how she felt right now it should be him, regardless of their deep feelings for each other. First and foremost he was an officer, "Fine, you can stay the night, but I need you to understand something about me. I'm never going to be the one that falls helplessly into a man's arms or hopelessly into his bed. I've learned how to protect myself. I'm just not that type of girl, Jason."

"I don't have to be that type of man, Aubrey," he assured her. "Tonight is not about anything like that. Tonight you are a victim and I know that a victim needs space, not to be coddled, or touched, or embraced. You need to have your comfort and find control again. I'll gladly sleep out here on the couch, but if you need me I'll be right there beside you."

"Thank you, for everything," she let it slip out so quietly he almost hadn't heard the words, but the emotion behind them were piercing and he felt the prick in his heart. She didn't want to admit it, but she needed him more than anything tonight and was silently glad that he had protested against her being alone. She reached her arms out and wrapped them around him laying her head on his chest, but only for a moment. It was a start and as much as he enjoyed the touch of her embrace he didn't want to push, ever. She let go of him just as quickly and brushed at the tears seeping from her eyes.

"Are you hungry?" he asked.

"I don't think I can eat," she answered. She suddenly shuttered, "I need a shower. It's as if I can still feel his arms around me, touching me, forcing…" she closed her eyes to remove the memory then continued, "I have to wash him off."

Jason understood the dirty feeling her attacker had left behind. It hurt him to have to watch her relive the scenes in her mind. It showed so clearly in her expressions.

"Don't lock the door and call out for me if you need anything. I think you will mostly just need your time alone, but if something should happen I want to be able to get to you. I'll fix you something to eat because you need your strength to get through this," the tenderness in his voice amazed her.

"All right," she agreed to his request and began to make her way to the bathroom.

Chapter Twenty-One

Aubrey walked toward the master bedroom, stopping at the doorway, and suddenly she was unable to move. She hadn't returned to the room while the policemen were asking questions and examining the damage. She could now see the broken glass from the picture frame that fell when she had hit the wall. There were wrinkles on the comforter where she had laid anticipating her escape. The closet doors where she had knelt, the mess he had made in her aunt's room, a stranger who had no business being there. The scenes flashed one by one in front of her, his growl, his hands, his force, and she began to pant unable to catch her breath.

"I'll take care of this," she hadn't heard the steps of Jason behind her, and flinched at his voice. "Easy, it's just me." Not thinking he reached out and put a hand on each of her shoulders and an image flashed through her mind of her intruder's hands in the same place only hours before when he had thrown her across the room.

She jerked away from him and he realized he had made the wrong move. She pushed him aside and ran down the hallway to the guest bathroom slamming the door and locking herself in. Jason followed her and reached for the door knob attempting to give it a twist, only to find it would not move. He could not get to her to apologize. He leaned against the door, his forehead making contact with the wood, and softly spoke to her hoping that she was on the other side listening to him.

"Aubrey, I'm sorry. It was too soon. I want you to know that I am here to help. I'll take care of you," he could hear her sobs through the locked door. He had said what he felt he needed to and knew she needed time. He turned to go back to the kitchen when he heard the door unlock. He shifted around and watched the knob slowly turn to the left. A beam of light seeped out from around the edges as she opened it slightly. He began to walk back toward the bathroom and placed a hand carefully on the wood to force it open. She stood looking into the 3'x5' mirror dressed in her shorts and a tank top she had worn under her white twill button up shirt that was now lying in a heap on the floor. She examined the bruises for the first time. As he watched, she lifted her hand to her face and touched her purple swollen cheek. Then she glanced down at the four stripes at her throat. She had previously been unaware of the soreness of her shoulders until Jason's hands had touched them. The pain and bruising ran all the way to her wrists. He stood in the doorway stunned, unable to say anything that would make her feel any relief. No wonder she had jumped and ran from him. How could he have been so careless as to touch her in such a way? He had wanted to comfort her so badly, and for a moment, lost sight of her fears.

"I need my clothes," she finally said in a whisper.

"I'll get them for you," he responded. "Where are they?"

"In the top drawer of the dresser there is a t-shirt and a pair of gray shorts," she inhaled deeply, brought a hand to rub her temple, and closed her eyes as she breathed out.

"I hate to ask, but…um…underwear?" he questioned her shyly.

"I actually have a pair in the linen closet in here," she said. A habit that was passed down from her aunt, always hide a spare pair in the bathrooms. You never know when you might be caught in the bathroom with guests in the house, especially when changing your swimsuit after taking a dip in the lake.

He left quickly to gather the things she needed with the vision of her wounds and damaged body clear in his sight.

Jason walked into the bedroom and tried to look at it the way she had seen it through her eyes. The distress still lingered in the room. Would she even be able to sleep here tonight? He knew she would do her best. She hated for things to get the better of her. He knew that from first-hand experience. She certainly had never allowed him to get the better of her. A slight smile ran across his face at the thought. He bent down in front of the dresser to retrieve the gray shorts that had been disturbed by the intruder. He also picked up a few other items and tucked them in the drawer trading them for the t-shirt she had requested. He would finish the clean-up while she showered. It would give him a chance to look for any clues left behind that the other officers might have missed. He was sure that they had been thorough, but he wanted to take a look for himself and then he would remove this bad memory for her. There should not be a trace of what had happened in that room when he was finished. She should not have to see it like this ever again.

Before returning to Aubrey, Jason wanted to offer her one more comfort. She would surely be in physical pain soon, if she hadn't been already. He swept through the kitchen to get her a glass of water and pain reliever. Then he returned to the bathroom to deliver the order. He knocked softly on the door and she opened it a fraction of an inch.

"I have your things."

"Thank you," she reached out and took her clothes from him.

"I brought you something for the pain," he saw her eyes through the crack in the door. "Go ahead and take it. It will help."

"Is it that obvious?" she asked.

"It is obvious that you have been hurt badly tonight, physically and emotionally," he replied.

"Thanks," she said as she took the pills and water. "I'll be out in a little while."

"Take your time. I'll be here," he told her reassuringly.

This might be a long night for them both, but he would keep his word. He intended to be her strength if she needed him to be.

Aubrey reemerged from the guest bathroom forty-five minutes later. With her comfortable clothes on and her hair still wet, Jason could tell she was much more calm and collected. He had found a few things in the kitchen and was able to throw together enough to call it a meal. He knew that she would need to have something, but was well aware that she would not want to eat much. She made her way to one of the high chairs that rested at the island in the middle of the gourmet kitchen. Jason laid out a plate containing some grilled cheese sandwiches and two small bowls of tomato soup. He had prepared a couple of glasses of tea, wondering if she would ask for something stronger.

"It's not much, but it should help you feel better," he said handing her a plate from the cabinet.

She took it and smiled at him gently, grateful to have his company. She was finding that she needed him more than she thought she would need anyone.

After filling his plate he came around the island to sit on the stool across from her. There was a solid ten minutes of silence until he asked his first question about the break in.

"Aubrey, do you know why he was here?"

She knew he would start to question her at some point. After all it was his job, even if this was not his case. She also knew that he was genuinely concerned, and if they were going to spend time together, she should tell him what he wanted to know.

"He asked about a wooden box with a dragonfly on the top," she replied taking a deep breath in and releasing the built up tension that had emerged in her back and shoulders.

"Have you seen this box before?" he asked.

"I vaguely remember seeing it when I was young. Aunt Jane used it as a keepsake box. I think there were a few jewelry pieces in it, maybe letters from Dad when he was in the military, and other little mementos from friends and her childhood. I can't imagine what would be in the box that he would want so badly."

"I think we need to find that box. We need to know what is so important, what could be worth breaking in to get," he took the empty plates and put them in the sink to handle in the morning. He turned to remove the rest of the food and found Aubrey picking at another sandwich half.

"They're really good," she said with the mischievous grin that Jason had missed all night.

"My specialty. The secret is a lot of butter on the bread," he blushed slightly.

"Jason, I'm sorry about before. I didn't mean to…"

"There is no need," he interrupted. "I wasn't thinking. It was out of line for me to touch you."

"I knew it was you, I had heard your voice, but the hands, they felt like his hands and my body reacted regardless of what my mind knew," she explained as she stood from her seat to face him. "But I can see, and hear, and know that you are here now." She placed her hands on his chest and let them slide up around his neck, and then she lifted her head to kiss him.

He did not want to make the same mistake twice. He gently unwrapped her arms from his neck taking her hands in his and kissed her forehead. Her emotions were still too unstable for him to feel comfortable in this situation.

"My mind is drained and I feel so tired," she said turning from him loosening her hands from his.

"You need to try to rest. I'll camp out on the couch so I'll have access to the doors. You can more easily rest in the bed," he assured her letting her know he intended to stand guard tonight.

She shook her head in agreement, "Then I guess I will head off to bed. Thank you again, Jason, for being here," she dropped her head as if she were ashamed at her attempt to kiss him before. She should have known he was only here to protect her. It was his duty as a police officer to do so, especially since she was an outsider. "There are blankets in the hall closet and a pillow as well. Please feel free to use whatever you need."

"Good night, Aubrey," he stared at her trying to read her, but falling short. She would be hard to find emotionally for a while, but he wanted so desperately to know that side of her. His patience would become the key.

She felt his eyes on her, but refused to look up, "Good night, Jason." Regardless of his intentions she had feelings welling up in her and she didn't know what to do. She had to take one last look at him and as she lifted her head her heart leaped. Even with her spirit broken she was falling for him.

***

The screams came tearing through the night waking Jason from

161

his sleep. Jolting up he looking around to find the source of the noise and then it occurred to him that he was at Dragonfly and the sound was coming from Aubrey's room. He kicked off the chenille blanket he had wrapped around his lower half and ran to her room to find her still asleep, but thrashing in bed fighting the darkness. He rushed to her bedside and instinctively he tried to bring her out of her nightmare.

"Aubrey wake up," he said in a soft voice as he took her by the arms and gave her a gentle shake.

"No, let me go. I don't know where it is," she shrugged to get loose from him.

He shook her a little more, trying to free her from her fright by brushing his hand across her forehead. She sat up in the bed and awoke fighting him, still screaming.

"Let me go, please," she cried out.

"Aubrey stop, it's me. It's Jason, baby. It's me," she opened her eyes and looking deep into his alarmed soul, her eyes widened in horror of what had just happened. She melted into his arms with fear. She felt comfortable against his chiseled bare chest. Her eyes burned with tears as she came to her senses and realized it was a nightmare. She pulled herself tighter against him to feel his pulse racing almost as fast as hers as his arms wrapped around her. He had been afraid for her.

Jason felt a deep pain sear through his chest as he held her and felt her tremble in his arms. His heart sank as he thought of her typically strong demeanor and realized how weak one man had made her. He felt for her weakness, knowing it took away her control which was causing her grief. He let her back away from him taking her chin with one hand and brushing back a loose piece of her auburn hair that was covering her purple-hued cheek. He stared into her glowing hazel eyes and then pulled further away. His actions questioned her emotional instability. He wanted to know if it was real, not just a feeling of fear that was causing her to reach out to him. Her eyes told him that she needed him, that she was afraid and wanted him to embrace her.

This was the moment he had waited for, when she chose him. He took her firmly, but tenderly, holding her, waiting for her next move. She backed away from him slowly gazing up into his face.

Then she did what she felt was right, she leaned into him with a kiss. It was sensual, and gentle, and dangerous.

"Aubrey, wait. This is not how you want this to be," he proceeded with caution giving her a chance to think before she took any further actions toward him, and giving her a way out if she needed it.

"I don't know what I want. I'm not sure what is going to happen between us in the future. I just know what I feel right now," the passion on her face lured him in and made him want her.

"When you come to me, I want it to be right," he tried hard to resist his feelings in order to focus on her.

"I just need to be lost, away from this place," she looked down so he wouldn't see the tears glazing her eyes.

He lifted her head once again and softly admitted, "I think you are already lost. I want to help you find your way back to your life, and into my life."

He took a chance on telling her he wasn't just an officer looking out for a citizen, but he was a man concerned about his love. He just hoped she believed him this time; that he was pouring his heart out and telling her the truth no matter what people in town might say. He kissed her delicately as she closed her eyes and tears fell down from her cheeks and onto the bed.

"Don't leave me here alone. Stay with me," she whispered pressing her forehead to his and softly sweeping her palm over his cheek.

"For as long as you need," he laid her back down in the bed and covered her as she turned over to her side. Jason still believed that he needed boundaries with the situation, but he felt he had made progress with her and her barriers were already starting to fall. He lay down behind her on top of the blankets and wrapped one arm around her waist. She reached her arm over his and entangled her hand with his. She needed to be able to touch him before she could fall into a slumber. He held his face against her rose scented hair and gently kissed the back of her head before moving around to kiss behind her ear. She was already drifting back to sleep, but he would be awake for the rest of the night.

He could feel the strength of her grip on his arm and a soft painful murmur as she dreamed. It had only been a few hours and it was happening for the third time. Although he couldn't sleep, he knew that she must and allowed her to reach for him if she needed to. No matter if she slept with trepidation, as long as she slept because she needed her rest. With her nails digging into his flesh, tighter and tighter became the squeeze on his forearm, and he had no doubt that when he found daylight the following morning, he would have reminders of this night. She would leave red scratch marks behind and although painful, he would gladly bear it if it helped her. It was worth it to him because she had been through too much tonight. He held her tighter to absorb her anguish as her heart raced and her head shook. Still holding her eyes closed and shifting with panic, it passed as quickly as it had come. She would release her tight grasp on him and her body would release its tense pressure. Her breathing would again be slow and steady and he could relax until the next episode. He was more than willing to endure this for her.

Chapter Twenty-Two

She slowly opened her eyes to let the warmth of the light seep into her. Aubrey had managed to finally fall into a deep sleep with the knowledge that Jason was there with her to protect her not only from her attacker, but from her own head and the dangerous thoughts that circled in her mind. She rolled over expecting to find him there and reached out to an empty pillow. He was gone. Had it been a dream? No, his kiss was real, his embrace warm. She could still feel the pressure of his arms wrapped around her in the night. She felt the heaviness of panic tighten within her chest. It was becoming hard to breath. Where was he? He said he wouldn't leave. He had made her that promise.

The door knob of the bedroom turned and with a sharp click the door began to open. She sat up in the bed and drew her knees to her chest. Slowly the door moved with a creaking sound and she could feel fear shooting through her body but no sound would escape her lips. Suddenly she saw a beautifully familiar face peer from around the half opened door and she released her pent up breath in relief.

"Oh, you are awake. I didn't mean to disturb you. I just wanted to check on you," Jason said with kind words to sooth her weary spirit.

She allowed her head to drop onto her knees as she expelled another deep sigh.

"What's wrong? Do you feel all right?" he asked.

She raised her head with a frightened look on her face as she realized she would live with this type of dread each day for a long time. She would question everything around her in her daily life. Noises would jolt her and sudden movements would cause panic, but she didn't want him to think she wasn't handling it. He would know how vulnerable she had truly become. She didn't want him to know that side of her, at least not yet. Her feelings for him and what had happened last night were still unstable. What had she been thinking?

"Nothing is wrong. I just wasn't sure who was on the other side of the door," she replied breaking down some of her barriers toward him.

He widened the opening of the door and stepped in, "I didn't go back to sleep last night, so when the sun came up I decided to get up and make us some coffee." He walked over to the bed, sat a coffee cup on the side table, and sat down on the edge next to her. He raised his hand to brush her hair from her battered and swollen face. "I am sorry if I frightened you, Aubrey," he could see her reservations more clearly than she realized.

"I think we need to talk about last night," she knew it might not be best to start with this conversation, but she wanted to get it out of the way so she could begin healing physically and emotionally.

"What do you want to talk about?" Jason asked with a good idea of the subject she had in mind.

"Jason, last night I wasn't…" she let her eyes roam around the room buying time and searching for the perfect words that would not be a hard blow to his ego, "I wasn't myself."

"In what way?" he asked.

She drew in a gasp as she let her eyes roll around taking in the quiet of the morning. She was trying hard to avoid his gaze, but she came back to him and decided to be direct.

"I work a tremendous amount of time. I'm proud of the things I have accomplished. I don't believe in wasting time, so I don't have hobbies, and I don't have relationships, I hardly even date, and I don't have casual sex. I work."

He leaned forward and brushing his palm over her left temple as he swept his lips softly across hers. He stroked her hair continuing his fingers down to settle in the center of her back and he pulled away just enough to find his connection to her, "Aubrey last night you weren't in a good state of mind and you tried too hard to act like everything was fine. I want you more than you could ever possibly know, but I meant what I said to you last night. I want you to feel the same for me."

"You are amazing, smart, and heroic. Any girl would love to have you in her life."

"But right now I'm looking out for you and I'm satisfied with that," he took her hands in his covering them with his strength. "You have been through something traumatic. You need time to come back from that. In this day and age most men wouldn't understand that, but I do. I honestly respect your choices."

"I just want to be up front with you, so you don't feel like I'm dragging you down a dead end road. I know what guys like you expect from girls," she gave him a sheepish grin as if embarrassed.

He drew back releasing her hands and his expression turned to disappointment as he tilted his head, "Do you? Do you know what I want, what I need?"

She realized that she had said more than she should have, but she couldn't think quickly enough to bail herself out of the direction this was taking. Up front and honest would have to do, "You had a reputation."

"Can you only think of who I was in the past?" he was almost accusing with his words. "Stop being so concerned about something so superficial. Let me decide how to best deal with what I'm feeling. My teenage reputation was spawned from what every tough jock expected me to be and what some cheerleader spread eagle on the hood of a car wanted from me. That wasn't me, it isn't me. You need to see who I really am, who I have become now."

She felt the guilt seep into her stomach making it churn inside, "I am trying. I want to know you, the real you. I just don't know what you expect of me."

"I expect you focus on getting through this one step at a time," he told her. "Can you do that?"

She shook her head.

His face relaxed with relief that their little talk was over. "Are you ready to get up?"

"Yes," she answered. "I'll be out in a few minutes." He arose from the bed taking his cup and turned to leave her alone to dress. "Jason," he turned back to face her, "thank you for the coffee."

"Sure."

She stood at the window overlooking the back porch, draped in a quilt to warm her weary body, watching the rain fall onto the wood planks with a tapping rhythm that made her eyes heavy. She heard the sound of plates clinking from the kitchen where Jason moved around fixing breakfast.

"They will have a hard time finding any additional evidence now, won't they?" she asked.

"The rain will affect the outcome, yes. But hopefully he left something physical behind that the water can't wash away," he wanted to ease her mind, but he knew the likelihood was very slim that they would find anything after the rain. It had begun around midnight with a break around 3 a.m. then reappeared just after daybreak.

She raised her hand to her face and brushed her cheek. He had left something behind that she would not soon be rid of, but she knew that Jason was hoping for something more substantial, something to help find him and build a case against him.

"They won't find footprints and lifting a fingerprint off something that has been saturated by the rain will be hard," he continued, "but maybe there is something out there."

His words weren't very satisfying for her. She knew in her heart that they might never catch her intruder, and she simply prayed that he decided not to make a second appearance.

"So, I guess you will be off to work soon," she assumed. It must be getting close to eight o'clock.

"I have to go in for a little while, but I'll be back soon and after I stop by my house for some things, I'll be here with you for the rest of the day," he said as he piled mounds of scrambled eggs onto a plate he had set on the island.

She turned around quickly to face him, surprised at his response, "Jason, I don't want this to interfere with your job."

"No, the captain refuses to let me work your case. He seems to think I'm a little too close to the victim," he shot her a grin before placing the skillet into the sink. "I am still on the Warren murder case though and I have some leads to look into and research to do."

"Why are you staying here?" deep inside she was grateful, but her heart wanted to know the true reason.

"I'm not leaving you alone. Besides, I've got all I need right here. I can hit off your Wi-Fi for internet service and that will give me access to the police station's mainframe," he told her. "Once I'm in I can search the database for what I need on the case. I have to go to the station to get copies of the file. Once I'm set up to link straight in, I can do what I need to from here and it will also let me check my email. If you have a printer and some paper around here, then it will be the perfect work from home environment." It was as if he had taken days to think through every detail and plan it out carefully. "Besides, I would just be hanging out at my desk to do it so I might as well be here and keep you company. That way I know you are protected."

"What about tomorrow, or the next day, or the day after that?" she wondered. "You can't protect me all the time, Jason."

"I can try my best. As I said I can do a lot from here for now. Macie will be off this weekend and she has offered to come by and keep you company when I can't," he had it all figured out. "In fact she will be by shortly to stay for the time I need to run to the office. You can leave the house if you like, as long as one of us is with you. And of course there is the cop detail coming around every hour for at least the next week maybe two."

"A prisoner in my own home," she walked into the kitchen when he motioned for her to sit down because breakfast was ready to be served, "that's what he has done to me."

"It's only for a little while, until I know you are safe," Jason assured her taking the blanket from her shoulders, folding it in a messy uneven square, and walking to the couch to place it on the arm for safe keeping.

"In two weeks I'll be back in Memphis," she quietly reminded him of her plans.

He sat on the stool next to her and took a piece of bacon from the plate. He took a large bite and refusing to look at her chimed,

"We will discuss that later."

She left that topic alone for the moment as she raised her glass of juice to her lips and sipped. She had already insulted him and thought it best to enjoy her breakfast rather than argue with this handsome, fearless, daring man who was so bent on protecting her.

Chapter Twenty-Three

He had taken a shower to prepare for his trip into town and came into the living room in tailored khaki pants and dress shoes with his button up dress shirt still open down the front to reveal tightly chiseled pectoral muscles that allowed her heart to almost leap from her chest at the sight. She had never envisioned a man with such beauty and depth before. Even his walk was daring and calculated when he was focused. She could see a shadow along his left side, but couldn't make out exactly what it was and he caught her staring.

"See something you like?" his glance was enough to send a chill down her spine.

"I was just noticing your left side. Were you hurt?" she stepped carefully closer and lifted a hand eager to touch him but was unable to force herself to reach out.

He almost fumbled, curious to know what had found her interest and realized his art was visible with his shirt open.

"That is the result of a dare made by a bunch of immature sixteen year old boys," he said moving his shirt out of the way for a clearer view.

"What is it?" she wondered.

"A tiger in orange and navy for Auburn."

"I remember now," she muttered quietly recalling a shadow along his rib cage the last night she spent in Walker as a teenager. She found her bravery and swept the tips of her fingers across the drawing of the strong, courageous animal.

He looked at her confused, "I'm sorry, what?"

She quickly drew back and tried to cover her recognition, "You were an Auburn fan, I remember."

"I was supposed to play ball there, but it didn't work out," he returned his shirt and tried to go about his business of preparing for work.

"Do you regret not being able to go to college and play football?" he should have known that Macie would tell her the story.

"No, I think I am exactly where I was meant to be doing what I was meant to do," he moved closer and his lips found their mark on hers so tenderly that she sighed.

He made his way to the kitchen hopeful for a cup of leftover coffee and the design of a leather bound book caught his eye.

"So what is this?" he picked up the book from the kitchen counter brushing his fingers over the soft creases curved into the shape of a dragonfly.

Startled from her view of his body as he strolled through her home, she realized he had said something and drew her eyes to the object he was holding in his hands, "Oh, yeah, that is something that I wanted to show you. I found it while I was cleaning in the back bedroom a few days ago. It's my Aunt Jane's old journal. I've been reading through it a little. I've found out things about her that I never knew, all her deep dark secrets," she said giggling.

"Oh, really," he smiled and began to flip through the pages admiring the penmanship of the owner. It surprised him that she was willing to trust him with content of the book.

"No, not really. She was pretty predictable for the most part," she admitted. "I have read a few passages from it, but I haven't found anything shocking as of yet."

"So, what type of things have you found in it?" he asked. He brought the book over to Aubrey and handed it to her sitting down next to her on the couch and pulling his shirt together one button at a time.

She felt her pulse jump slightly, he was so very close. "She refers to someone named Kathryn in the book, but there isn't a last name. There is also a handwritten note in the front," she turned to the front page as a reference, "from someone by the same name addressing her as if she were the one who gave her the book as a gift. I've tried to remember someone named Kathryn, but for the life of me I don't recall anyone by that name. The more I have thought about it, I don't rightfully recall many friends at all. Sure she knew most everyone in town, but I can't remember any true best friends. I always thought that she was buried in her work and didn't have time for friends."

"You know she may have had a life that you knew nothing about," he doubted that Aubrey could have known the background of her aunt when she was young. Adults often had a way of living double lives when it came to children. "Maybe she had them and you just didn't know about it."

"I guess maybe she could have. I always wished for her to have that close best friend, the one that would do anything for her," she stared at the book letting her mind get lost in the words that her best friend had shared only a few days ago. "I think everyone should have one."

"Just like you have Macie," he stated.

"And you have Trey, yes," she knew he understood.

"We have been fortunate to find them and have them in our lives."

"It has turned out well for us," she smiled and he returned her expression. "It's funny because we grew up only seeing each other for a few weeks in the summer. We would call and write letters during the school year, but when I came here it was as if I had never left."

His smile drifted away and he stood up from the couch, "Until one summer you didn't come back." He walked away from her because he needed the space. He had feared having this conversation with her, but the curiosity behind her disappearance for so many years had eaten at him for long enough. He had an opening to find out the truth and had decided to take it.

"Macie and I kept in touch," she blurted. "We would meet in Nashville every couple of years and she came to Memphis once.

We called and sent emails." She laid the book on the coffee table carefully as if it were glass and followed his path to the window. She wore a look of wonder on her face.

"But you never intending on coming back here, did you?" he sounded angry and bitter.

She knew she was entering a painful territory with him, but she wasn't sure how treacherous it had become. Her voice lowered to a gentle sigh, "No, I didn't," she stood behind him as he stared out to the lake. She needed to touch him, settle his nerves, so she raised her arms to entangle them around his waist and turning her face to the right she slowly laid her head on his back between his shoulders. "When I left, I put Walker behind me and I had no intention of ever coming back."

He stiffened his posture, "Did you really hate me that much?"

"Hate is a very strong word, Jason."

He took her arms and unlocked them from his waist and brushed them to his sides taking a step forward to separate her from him, "It's the only word I can think of that would keep you away so long." He walked away leaving her standing alone in front of the window.

"It wasn't all about you," she said afraid to turn and face him.

"That doesn't answer my question," he raised his voice. "Did you? Hate me?"

She twisted her head to speak over her shoulder straightening her body in defense, "I didn't hate you. I just couldn't be around you." She turned completely around to gauge his reaction.

He raised his head and looked down at her with a bruised ego and hurt seeping through his face as his jaw line became rigid, "I see. Being around me was that hard for you."

"Do we have to talk about this now?" her heart begged for his questions to end. She didn't want to do this to him. "Can't we just let it go?"

"I need to know," he pressed.

She swallowed hard and dropped her head down to stare at the ground. She couldn't bear the way he was looking at her, "I didn't see you then the way I see you now. You were young and juvenile. I thought the worst of you, yes, but…"

"The day I saw you at the lake in the Carter boat, you looked at me the same way you did when we were fifteen," he queried for the truth.

"I did," she responded.

"And now?"

She looked up and found his gaze, "And now I don't. It took me a little time, but I see the changes in you. Macie had told me, but I wasn't ready to listen. Even after you came here and kissed me, I had to keep you at arm's length until I discovered the real you for myself. I always have my guard up with people. I guess that included you. But last night, when I was attacked, you were all I could think about, the only person I wanted to see come through the door. I was afraid something was going to happen to me and I wouldn't have that chance to rediscover you."

He didn't make a sound, didn't give her a reason, only closed the space between them as he reached for her and drew her close to him. He lowered his head to crush her mouth with his, and breathed life into her weary soul. Her first reaction was to push him away, but her tense body relaxed as she felt his warmth and she permitted her arms to move from his chest to wrap around his neck as she ran her hands through the dark waves of his hair. He lifted her from the ground to allow his passion to envelop her. His lips parted to take her in and release himself to her. Neither had been attentive enough to hear a knock at the door. They were too enraptured by the power of the moment. The knock came again, only louder and more direct. He separated himself from her and sat her carefully back on the ground. Her head was spinning and for a moment she feared that she had become too dizzy to stand on her own. Her eyes never left him. Her heart was soaring at an unthinkable pace, and he was going to leave. He made his way over to open the door after catching the third knock and a voice from the other side asking if anyone was home. Her body still in shock would not move.

"Come on in, Macie," she heard him say. "I won't be gone long." He had tucked the edges of his shirt into his pants as he gave his attention to their visitor, and she hadn't even noticed the movement. He walked back to a chair at the dining table and removed his holstered firearm, wrapping it around his back and slipping his arms through the deep tanned leather. He pulled the gun from its cradle and made his safety checks as he always did anytime he was dealing with weapons and slid it back into position. Then he took his suit coat from the back of the couch and slung it over his shoulder. It had been effortless for him to prepare his body for his job. He stepped back in front of the stone-faced Aubrey and bent to whisper in her ear, "I'll be back soon and we can finish this."

She blinked her eyes quickly as he pressed his lips to her forehead, then turned and walked out the front door closing it behind him.

Macie dropped her purse on the sofa table, then with a raised eyebrow and a crooked smile she asked, "And just what was that all about?"

He was true to his word and made his way back to Dragonfly in less than two hours. She had been tight-lipped with Macie about their morning conversation, but it ran over and over in her mind as she prepared for his return. She couldn't let him get to her in such a way. Her plan was to direct his interest elsewhere and she thought of the very thing that had brought on his line of questions, the journal.

Once he had changed clothes and was settled, she brought the journal back to his attention. He sat on the couch and she sat next to him, raising her feet to the couch and curling her legs beside her. Careful not to rest on his shoulder, she opened the book and handed it to him.

"How far back does the writing start?" he asked letting her direct his thoughts. He had evaluated the actions of the morning and felt that maybe he had pressed too hard. She could still be in a vulnerable state and the last thing he wanted was to push her away. For once things seemed to be going in his favor.

"There are entries dating back about twenty years or so," she answered showing him the date of one of the entries she had read earlier.

"Did she write a few times a week?" he flipped through the pages.

"No, she wrote maybe once or twice a month. Then again, sometimes she would go months without writing anything. It depended on what was going on in her life. I suppose she wrote what she felt was important to remember at the time. There have been entries about things that happened in town, things she enjoyed, new businesses that opened," she sighed and looked down at her hands. She realized she had been wringing them in front of her. "It made me realize something."

"What would that be?" he wondered, hoping it might concern them both, but not receiving his wish.

"She wasn't just the brutal workaholic that I always pictured," she smiled. "There was joy in her life."

He chose to let go of the event from earlier in the morning. It had become clear to him that if it had affected her she was not willing to show it. His kiss had more than likely frightened her instead. "How far have you read?" he continued.

"Just a few entries. There is so much more to discover."

He handed the book back to her, "Keep reading. You may be surprised at what you find."

Taking it she replied, "I hope so."

As she flipped through a few pages, Jason noticed a piece of paper peeping from the pages in the back. "What is this tucked into the back."

Aubrey let her mouth drift open as she thought carefully about what to tell him concerning the note she had placed between the pages, "I had almost forgotten about that," she stood and walked over to the window to take advantage of the natural light of the day. She took the envelope in her right hand to again read the suspiciously typed address on the front. "It came in the mail."

"Is something wrong?" he asked noticing her bewildered look as she stared at the paper.

"It's just…well," she let her index finger slide over the typed letters then handed him the envelope. "Open it."

He took the envelope not letting his eyes leave hers as he carefully raised the flap and searched for the contents. The folded paper was new and crisp. He laid the envelope aside, unfolded the page and began to read.

Time to leave, city girl, before you get hurt. Pack your bags while you still can.

His expression turned cold as he stood, and carefully studied the black typed words. He read it again to examine the tone of the sentences. When he turned to face her once again, his eyes burned with fury.

"Why didn't you tell me about this."

She rolled her eyes at him and said with cynicism, "Because we talk all the time, right. We are such good friends. It couldn't have been the fact that our...whatever we have here, has been a rollercoaster ride the past few days."

"Yeah, there's the sarcasm I love. Can you knock it off for now and be serious for a minute?" he insisted.

She eased back into herself, "Sorry, it's just a natural reaction with you."

"As happy as I am that you have your sense of humor intact..." he took another look at the letter.

"I didn't think it was that big of a deal at the time," she moved to stand in front of him, "It's just a letter."

"When did you get this," he demanded.

"This one I received in the mail yesterday," she answered quietly, "the other one came a couple of days before that."

"There's another one," the pitch of his voice rose with surprise. "You should have mentioned it, if not to me why not to Trey?"

"Things have moved at such a pace around here lately, I've had a hard time keeping up. Besides, I didn't think much of the first letter," She crossed over to the drawer beside the refrigerator and pulled it open. She reached in to remove another similar envelope and read over the address on the outside before closing the drawer. Turning to face him she handed him the envelope and stood silently to gauge his reaction.

"It wasn't really a threat, just someone who didn't want an outsider in their town. Some folks can be that way, and I wasn't going to be here long anyway. But then the second one came and..."

"I'm calling Trey and getting him to take a look at these." She understood and shook her head in agreement. It was time to let him do his job. He made the call to Tray and bagged the letters so if there were prints or any fibers on them, they would not be lost or rubbed out.

After working on his computer for much of the afternoon, Jason treated Aubrey to a dessert he had picked up on his way home that morning. Aubrey had focused on restoring the bedroom from the destruction that had been a reminder of the previous night, replacing the photos and exchanging the bedding with one of the quilts that had been stored in the closet.

She decided to cook dinner for him and had forgotten how much she enjoyed it. There was simply no need for it in Memphis when it was only for her. They chose to end the relaxing night with a movie, but Aubrey drifted to sleep shortly after the movie began.

He lay there quietly on the couch and watched her as she slept. She still grasped his arm tightly from time to time which was wrapped around her. Her breathing would quicken as she would squeeze him. That must be the time when the dreams became hard for her to face and she would tense hoping he was still there. He hoped that tonight the dreams would be calmer than they had been the previous night.

***

As each day passed she became a little bit stronger. Most of the time she had walked around the house in a daze and he would watch her with worry in his eyes about the things she wouldn't say out loud. He still couldn't find it in his heart to leave her in the house alone. During the times he would need to go to work Macie and Trey had agreed to watch over her and keep her occupied, escorting her on her errands and staying with her until he was able to return. Even Macie's mother had offered to come to take her turn as a watchful den mother over the bruised lamb, so she never had to feel lonely. But even though she would be surrounded by people who cared deeply for her well-being, inside he knew she would still feel very alone.

He struggled with his plan to make all of that hurt go away. He wanted more than anything for her to feel whole again. But he knew that time would have to heal that wound. She would ultimately have to find her own path back to who she had been before. He would be there to help her, but could not do it for her. She would have to find her own strength.

Chapter Twenty-Four

The days passed and she became more comfortable with his presence in her home. Jason had followed leads on the Warren case to no conclusion, but had learned a great deal about his personality from interviews with locals and research into his past, much of it he had chosen not to share with Aubrey because he felt she wasn't ready to view that side of her aunt's life. He also made regular contact with Trey to see if there had been any new discoveries on Aubrey's attacker. Macie had been more than willing to fill in when she was needed to keep an eye on Aubrey, but with no activity, Jason had become more relaxed about insisting that someone watch her every move.

Macie had spent time at Dragonfly earlier in the evening while Jason had been at the office, but her sister was going to be home from college for the weekend and had asked that they go out to a movie for the night. Aubrey had never cared much for the theater, sitting in uncomfortable seats in the dark, dealing with the sticky floors and talking people around her, never sure if you received your money's worth for the entertainment until the movie was over. It was not how she had wanted to spend her Friday evening, but she didn't want Macie and her sister to miss the adventure so she begged Macie to go on and leave her so they would arrive at the show on time. Reluctantly, Macie had agreed only because she was certain that Jason would be home in a reasonable amount of time after she had left.

Aubrey had once again been in the mood to make a sensationally delicious dinner. She turned facing the kitchen sink to stare out into the sky that had begun to grow dark with the early evening, a sure sign that winter would be upon them soon.

She washed her hands then taking a step to the side she picked up a rather large knife to use to cut onions for the pasta dish she was sure Jason would enjoy for dinner. There was something about creating a fabulous dish that made her want to listen to Otis Redding and dance in the kitchen. She turned the music up a little and swayed as his crooning voice belted *These Arms of Mine*. She was making precise slices in the produce when she felt a hand touch her shoulder. She gripped the knife and as panic struck her, she gasped and spun around lifting her weapon to a striking position to the right side of her temple. She screamed as she pressed her back against the countertop in terror. Shaking with hysteria, she saw his blue green eyes glazed with shock and blood beginning to seep from the slash on his chest. He recognized her horror and felt her unwillingness to breath. Lowering her arm, she let the knife fall to the floor as her hand shook uncontrollably. He took her wrists and she began to sink to the kitchen floor tears streaming from her hazel eyes. Closing them she moaned a painful noise and cried for what she had done to him, for the feelings he had released in her. She was ready to kill him in fear. He hadn't realized how much terror she still harbored inside her. She continued to shake as the reality of it sank into her heart. How would she live each day? How could she continue to take each step? She opened her eyes to find Jason staring at her wanting to help, to protect her but unsure what avenue to travel. Something as simple as an unknowing touch had triggered that memory for her and caused such a violent reaction from her. He reached out and took her with one arm, resting her head on his opposite shoulder and letting her grip his back so tightly that her nails began to dig into his flesh through the gray t-shirt he sported. He was numb to the physical pain of the cut on his chest because her emotional state was too severe.

"Shhh, It's all right," he winced slightly, but became more focused on her. "I thought you knew I was behind you, or I wouldn't have touched you. I said your name."

"I'm sorry. The music was up and I didn't hear you." She pulled away from him to see the red wetness soaking through his shirt.

He shook his head in disagreement, "I should have known better than to come up behind you like that."

She looked at him with tears burning down her face leaving red streaks, "Is this how it is going to be from now on? Is this how I'm going to react every time someone touches me or reaches out for me? I thought I was starting to get better, but it's just never going to go away, is it?" He helped her back to her feet and walked her to one of the stools at the island. As she sat down, she stared at his chest and he realized why she was so focused on him. He began to feel the sting burning his flesh and reached for a towel that hung over the edge of the sink. He soaked it under the stream of water from the faucet, rang out the excess, and pressed it to the cut. Satisfied that the damage was under control, he turned back to address her.

"You felt it all over again, didn't you?" his eyebrows furrowed in concern for her, "That easily it came back into your mind, what he did, and how you felt."

"Yes."

"It didn't matter that it was my touch, you felt him didn't you," wondering if it had happened before and she had chosen to keep that hidden from him.

"Yes. I can't live like this Jason," she wiped at the dark circles under her eyes that had grown over time since her attack. "I can't do it."

He wrapped a hand around the back of her neck bringing them face to face, "We are going to get him, Aubrey. You won't have to live like this much longer. We are going to catch him. I promise."

"Stop making promises when you know you might not be able to keep them," she whispered as he pressed his lips to her forehead for a soft kiss.

He loosened his hold, "That's why I'm here. I need you to come down to the station with me."

"Why? Has something happened in my case?" her nerves were

finally beginning to settle and the quivering was subsiding.

"Trey has arrested someone in connection with the letters that were sent to you. He is also questioning her about the break in. He needs you to come down to the station and listen to what she has to say."

"She?" Aubrey was surprised by his use of the female pronoun to describe the person.

"Yeah. Trey wants you to observe the interrogation. He believes she could be connected to what happened to you."

"I don't know," she said unsure that she wanted to face the person that could be responsible for her sudden reaction and uneasy nature.

"It might help the case and put all of this to an end," he said thinking that he might have to convince her of the benefits of being there watching Trey do his job. She wouldn't actually have to come face-to-face, only be present to answer any questions that the officers might have in connection with the arrested person.

His persistent tone must have worked because after a few moments of thought she replied, "All right, I'll do my best," she reached up to him to remove the towel and see the damage she had caused. He held tightly to the towel, not wanting her to see the wound. She gave him a stern look and he gave in, removing the towel resembling a tie-dyed fabric with swirls of red, pink, and white. She gasped a short breath taking in what she had done. She flipped the towel over and blotted away the remaining blood around the still trickling separated skin. It wasn't deep, but in just the right place to keep the blood flowing. She knew there were bandages in the linen closet in the bathroom, so she immediately stood up and started walking down the hallway.

"Where are you going?" he didn't think it had been that bad, not enough to need such attention. He had been hurt in the line of duty before and after some time it would clot on its own, so he thought, but it appeared she had read it differently.

"We need to doctor up that wound," she told him. "Go ahead and take off your shirt." He saw no need to argue with that request.

She returned after only a few minutes and she brought with her bandages, medicine to disinfect the wound, and medical tape. As she walked into the room, she stopped in her tracks seeing him carefully removing the heather gray fabric to reveal ripples of strength and sturdy arms fading from their previous summer glow. She had not seen him so beautifully undressed since the night of her attack when he had consoled her while the nightmares crept into her sleep. He reapplied the towel and forced pressure to try to stop the bleeding. Coming back to herself, she walked over to him and removed the towel once again wiping to eliminate the seeping blood. The bleeding finally stopped and she took advantage of it by applying the medicine and the bandage. Her touch was cool to his bare skin, and the pressure of her fingers made him jerk. He took in a deep breath and pulled his hands back down to his sides so she could finish her work. Once she had secured the gauze and medical tape, she swept her fingers lightly over his chest, up to his shoulders and down his arms slowly. He was so striking and he wanted to understand her and protect her. Moving her hands back up his arms, he suddenly gripped her elbows and she stopped, realizing what she had been doing. He demanded her attention and she looked up at him. He lowered his head to brush his lips lightly across hers taking her into his arms. She could feel her pulse begin to race and she knew she could not control it; she didn't want to control it.

Dearest Journal,

Something is most definitely wrong in my relationship with Jake Warren. He has started spending less and less time with me and more time with his friends at Gus's. I have also begun to notice stares and whispers as I walk through town, stop in stores, and attend community functions. I am starting to suspect that there may be someone else in his life. I have heard tell about the signs and know all the stories by heart, but I do not want to make assumptions. I need to know the truth of his actions. I'm not sure how forgiving I could be if it turns out to be the worst. I love him, but is that enough? I've talked to Kathryn and it frightened me that she may know something that she is not telling me. I'm sure she feels she is protecting me, but I need to know. She is such a dear friend, but I feel she may have made a promise to her husband and possibly to Jake that she does not wish to break. I believe she is committed to that decision. She does not talk to me about Jake anymore. I'm not ignorant of these situations. I can see it very clearly for myself even if the details have not been revealed to me yet. I do not like being in the dark and it is about time that someone admitted their faults to me. I need to know if this relationship is worth the heartache I have begun to suffer.

Excruciatingly yours,

Jane Elizabeth

Chapter Twenty-Five

Trey walked into the cold room with its grayish blue-toned walls and metal table and chairs. He was holding a file that contained any information he had been able to find on Gina. For most of her life she had been a model citizen of Walker, but over a five-year span she had tried her hand at college and at life in a bigger city, neither of which had been a success. She had been arrested in Atlanta for drunk driving that ended in a fine, but her record while she spent a year in Dallas was what interested Trey.

She had been a secretary for an investment banker who had embezzled around a half million from the bank and stored it in an offshore account. She had eventually had the charges dropped by convincing a judge that she had only been a worker for him through the bank and she was in no way involved in his illegal activity. Trey wanted to keep this type of information handy in case her character came into question during the interrogation. He strolled over to the table and slammed the file down letting the page corners be seen as they fanned out from the edges of the manila folder.

"What is all of this about?" Gina asked very calmly. "I have a showing this evening and I need to be out of here in time to meet my buyers."

"You might need to postpone that for a bit," Trey advised.

"Why?" she said with innocence as if there must certainly be a mistake for her to be in this room. "Is someone going to tell me why I'm here?"

Trey wasn't about to fall for her games and chose to go ahead and get to the point, "Gina, where were you last Friday night?"

"I was in the firm's booth at the festival."

Ahh, the alibi Tray thought. He had assumed she might have one. She wasn't a foolish woman by any means.

"We were handing out samples of apple cider and drumming up business," she continued.

"All night?" he probed.

"Yes, from six to about ten," she wiggled in her seat bringing her hands down to her sides. She seemed very uncomfortable.

"And there are witnesses?" Trey continued making a mental note of her body language.

"Yes, what is this all about?" she had a more serious tone to her voice now.

Still unwilling to answer her question, Trey pressed on "What is your relationship with Aubrey Todd?"

Gina settled back in her seat, suddenly stiff and straight-backed in the metal chair. Almost as if she had found a surge of confidence, she crossed her arms over her chest, "I had a meeting with her last week about listing her aunt's house. Other than that, I barely know her."

"So, you are familiar with the inside of the house."

"No, she insisted on meeting me at the firm."

Trey had a quizzical look across his face, "You've never been in the house?"

"No," Gina became concerned and raised her volume in protest, "and I'm not answering another question until someone tells me what this is all about."

He had watched her be both defensive and aggressive in her responses, with no head way in either case. He thought that she told more through her actions, so he watched her carefully as he finally gave her the explanation she had demanded.

"Her house was broken into a few days ago and she was attacked. You don't know anything about that?"

"It's a small town, Detective," she said rolling her eyes at him as if to say *Of course I've heard about it*. "I don't know what it has to do with me." Then it occurred to her why she had been asked to come to the police station. It was as if she had been hit with a ton of bricks, "Wait a minute. Do you think I had something to do with that?"

Trey blinked and leaned in to read her closely, "I think there are a lot of unanswered questions."

"I can't believe this," she shouted, throwing her hands up in a reaction of surrender. "Why would I want to break into her house?"

"I think you had something against Aubrey," Trey remained calm through her outrage.

"Yeah, well, I think you have been working too hard or you have gone off the deep end," she turned in her seat to face the two way mirror. Jason, Aubrey, another officer and the district attorney were on the other side witnessing the entire conversation. Jason occasionally glanced over to Aubrey to gauge her response as Gina spoke, but nothing about the situation made her change her expression. She watched closely as Trey uttered his questions and Gina responded to each one.

"Why did you leave the notes that were found in Aubrey Todd's mailbox?" Had there been proof that the notes were from her? Aubrey gasped.

"What notes?" Gina readjusted the way she was sitting and he noticed that she was becoming nervous and jittery.

"Threatening letters were put into the mailbox at Aubrey's lake house."

"I didn't send any letters. This is insane. You can't prove those letters were from me."

There it was, the opening to use the information he had on her, "The lab tested the saliva on the envelopes used to seal them. We simply had to compare the DNA on the licked flaps with the DNA on file from your arrest in Dallas three years ago. It came back a match." The evidence they had found that linked Gina to the letters was solid. How would she explain her way out of this? "

Her eyes widen and she could not find the words for a response. Trey knew he had her for the letters and all he needed now was to press her enough for her to confess to sending the attacker too. "Unless you give me an answer that makes sense, I am going to link the letters to the break in and then you are in some big trouble, Gina. I suggest you just come clean."

She didn't even flinch at the mention of the break in, "I didn't have anything to do with a break in."

He had hoped she would fold, but she was standing her ground, so he had to back up and try to get her to admit to the letters so he could continue to hold her for more questioning, "But you did send the letters. The evidence is clear on that one, Gina."

"All right, yes, I sent the letters," she confessed. "That's not a crime."

Wasn't it? Aubrey thought. There was no real harm done, only threats. If the threats were acted on then it became a true crime. Gina might be right. If they didn't have hard evidence to link her to the attack, then they couldn't charge her with anything.

"Why did you send them?" Trey needed the full explanation to build his case.

"I had heard that she was going to sell the house and I would stand to make a good amount in commission if I got the contract on it. I even had a possible buyer lined up, but then I met with her and she seemed skeptical about selling it. It was as if she had seller's remorse before she even put it on the market. I just wanted to give her a little encouragement to list it so I sent the first letter," Aubrey felt the room grow cold as she told the story. She folded her arms and Jason could see her caving, becoming lost in herself. That was the last thing he had wanted for all of this. He felt her slipping away from him as they watched and he knew that she would fall farther away from him before it was over. She almost looked like a hurt child as she listened.

"And the second one?" Trey continued.

"She should have left after the first one, but it didn't seem to convince her. Instead, I found out not only was she staying in town, but she was making moves on Jason McNally. I was seeing Jason and I didn't need her to come between us," she lowered her voice and leaned over the cold metal table with piercing eyes. "At that point it was a matter of killing two birds with one stone, so I sent the second letter and made it a little more interesting so it would send her packing for good," Jason couldn't tear his gaze from Aubrey.

"But she still didn't leave or list the house with you?"

"No."

"So you thought you would try one more time and get a little assurance that your plan was going to work," Trey went for his mark.

Gina sat back in the chair as if she had been insulted, "No, after the second letter I waited to see what was going to happen. There was still a chance she would list the house with me and as for Jason, I decided he wasn't worth it."

"Oh I think he was worth a great deal to you. I think you paid off the masked man to go in and scare her, take something important of hers so she wouldn't feel safe, only he took it a little too far. Not that you cared as long as it made her leave."

"No," she snapped back.

"I think you got jealous of the new girl in town moving in on your man."

"I want my lawyer." She was beginning to see red, and before she said something she regretted she needed legal help.

"That was it wasn't it?" Trey put on an act as if he had just realized her true reason behind the scheme. He egged her on in hopes that she would break, "She was going to take away your deal, your money."

Gina slammed her open palms on the table and the witnesses in the other room jumped, "She shouldn't be here. She doesn't belong here."

"And then she swept in and grabbed your man. So, you needed an easy way to get rid of her," Trey's pressure was finding its way into her head and he knew he had to continue. Jason watched Aubrey close her eyes as if she were in pain watching the display.

"I worked hard to get to his level after what happened in Dallas, and she messed up my shot with him," Gina screamed. "She doesn't deserve him. She's a worthless piece of crap like her aunt. She's an outsider, always has been and always will be. She should have gone back to the city. He is too good for her." Aubrey's heart sank.

"So, you sent someone to scare her didn't you, someone to

make her go back."

"I said I want my lawyer," she demanded.

Aubrey ran out of the room, and down the hall searching desperately for a way out of the station. She had heard all that she was able to listen to and suddenly found it hard to breath in that small room. Gina hated her and had threatened her. She saw the red glow of a sign that said 'Exit' and threw all of her might into pushing the bar to open the door. She ran out into a downpour of rain. Within seconds she could feel the chilly bite of the water as it covered her from head to foot. It would cover the sight of the tears that had decided to fall from her eyes. She was cold and didn't know where she was going to run, but knew she couldn't stay here. She picked up her pace as she started around the edge of the parking lot.

"Stop!" she heard a strong, low voice call out from behind her. She stopped, but was terrified to turn around. Slowly she curved around to face him, her arms now crossed over her chest.

Jason was jogging to catch up with her and just as wet as she, "Why? You heard what she said in there." Aubrey shouted out at him.

"You can't listen to her. She's only looking out for herself," he tried to assure her, but her mind was made.

"What if she's right?" she asked him. "Come on, Jason, I am a city girl. What am I going to do in a po-dunk town like this? I shouldn't have stayed this long."

"You are doing what your aunt wanted," he told her. "You have as much right to be here as Gina. Hers is just one opinion in a town of people."

"I'm living in someone else's house, terrified that some strange man is going to come in and rape me or worse," the rain continued to beat down on them. "This isn't where I'm supposed to be. This isn't my life. I don't belong here."

He was close enough to touch her now so he took her by the shoulders, "Are you trying to convince me or yourself?"

"I'm trying to face reality," she wiggled free from him and took a step back. "I need to go back home so everything in Walker can go back to normal. You and Gina can continue with your lives."

He became furious at the thought, "Oh get real, Aubrey. I don't want Gina. She and I went out before you ever came into the picture and it was over before it ever got started. You saw her in there. I was never attracted to that, to her."

"Well, clearly she wants you."

"What about what I want?" he began to raise his voice. "What if I want you?"

She had to get through to him, "Did you think this would turn into some big love affair, Jason, and I would pick up and move here for you? Did you think I would really stay in Walker, that I would just drop everything, give up my life, to be here? We have been playing house with each other and I don't like games."

"Then stop playing games," he demanded. "Do you want more from me?"

She gave him an angry motion with her hands, "I don't want anything," then she lowered her gaze.

He shook his head, "Something is eating at you because I don't think this is just about us."

She raised her head with renewed courage and said the words that she knew would break his heart, but worse, it might also break hers, "You're right, because there is no us. Just let it go. This is over. We, or whatever we could have been, is over. Gina is right, I don't deserve you."

He felt as if she had driven a knife into his gut, "I think you should let me decide that."

"I am going to decide it for both of us. I'm going back to Dragonfly and pack my things. I'll be gone in a couple of days," she was firm and stood very still in front of him, scared to the core of what she was saying and how it would affect the rest of her life.

"What has you so spooked, Aubrey?" he demanded as she turned her face from him. "Gina? You're going to let her get in the way of being happy," he reached out and took her face in his hands and forced her to look at him. "Don't let her do that."

"It's not Gina. It's me. I don't know who I am anymore," she took his wrists in her hands as he held tightly to her. "Tonight I was so horrified at a touch that I turned a knife on you and drew blood. I cut you and didn't think twice. I could have killed you. Do you understand that?"

He let a slight grin sweep across his face, "I did something that

I shouldn't have done. That was not your fault. It was an accident. You wouldn't have stabbed…"

"Yes, I would have," she interrupted, "because I have been afraid and I have reached so deep inside myself to try to find the strength that I once knew. I would have killed you if you hadn't stopped me. I can't live like that anymore."

"I don't believe that," he said lightly as he brushed his thumb across her wet cheek.

She needed space between them and pulled at his arms to release herself from his hold, "I am so sick and tired of being afraid. So, I'm going to deal with it my way. No more hiding, no more waiting for something else to happen. I'm going back to Memphis, back to the way it was before all of this chaos started and I'm going to live my life my way. I can't be in Walker, I can't live in Dragonfly, and I can't be with you." She turned and began to walk away from him.

He called out to her, "You can't leave and act like it all didn't happen. You can't act like we didn't happen."

She stopped and turned back to face him, "Don't be so sure. And you need to call off your goons. Gina knows that you have evidence on her, so she isn't going to be sending anyone for me. It's about time they find someone else to watch. You can come get your things after I'm gone. I'll leave a key with Macie. I don't need you in my house anymore, and I don't need you in my life."

She turned to walk away from him, but his sense of being reasonable left him lurching for her. Taking her by the wrist he spun her around and wasted no time sweeping her into a strong embrace and pressing his lips painfully to hers. His heat oozed into her as if she were invaded by an elixir that dripped through her veins killing her anger and feeding her soul.

He released himself from her angling his head back to stare into the deep dark pools of her eyes, but he couldn't release his grip on her, "Please, tell me you don't mean that. Don't do this. Don't leave like this, not again."

She put as much force as she could muster into the palms of her hands, and forgetting his injury pressed his chest until he broke the hold he had on her. She began taking small steps backward to put distance between them, keeping her hands raised and shaking her head in disagreement even before the words slipped past her lips. "I should have kept my word and never come back to Walker," and with that she circled around him and walked away, leaving him standing alone in the rain.

Chapter Twenty-Six

Jason walked back into the station to find Trey coming out from the interrogation room. Trey knew not to ask about the outcome with Aubrey. If he wanted to talk about it, he would. Jason got straight to business, his love life put on the back burner. Duty called for him to get his head back in the game.

"Find out anything else?" he asked.

"She will admit to the notes," Trey answered, but began to bite the inside corner of his lip. "She wanted Aubrey to sell the house so she could get the commission and try to win you over. I can't get her to admit to the attack, but Chase and Johnson still feel that she could be responsible."

He recalled the other officer and DA who witnessed the line of questioning Trey had dealt her, "So, what do we do now?"

"If she won't admit to sending the guy into the house there's not much we can do. She was right about the charges. A couple of letters aren't enough to hold her," Trey hated that he didn't have more evidence to hold her on.

"You are going to let her go?" Jason said in disbelief. He had hoped there would be something else that he had missed from his general conversations with Trey prior to Gina's arrest.

Trey lowered his head almost ashamed to face his friend, "We have to, but I'm going to have a team keep an eye on her for the next couple of days. If she goes anywhere close to Aubrey we will know." He looked up at Jason, "We can monitor phone calls too. Whoever she hired to scare Aubrey took it too far and now Gina knows it. Maybe she will try to get in touch with him again, then we will know who he is. I really don't believe that she will come after Aubrey now that she believes we are on to her and the guy probably has his money and is long gone to the next job anyway." His words didn't make Jason feel any better, but he knew Trey would do whatever he could for Aubrey.

Jason drew in a deep lungful of air and released his frustrations as he blew out, "You are probably right. Gina is not above using scare tactics, but I don't think she really wants to hurt anyone. She probably didn't even know much about the guy. I just wish she would give us a name, so we can make sure he won't hurt anyone else." He rolled his eyes and shot Trey a disgusted look, "You can use Aubrey's detail to keep an eye on Gina. Aubrey made it very clear that she is tired of being watched."

That gave Trey an opening to express his concern for his friend without interfering in his private life, "Something wrong?"

"I don't understand her, man," he revealed. "She refuses to let herself feel anything for anyone."

"She'll realize one day that her mind has nothing to do with it." It was the best advice he could come up with for two people that were so determined to not be together. Trey had watched how things were playing out and knew that both of them were so stubborn that they were going to have to break each other completely down before they would ever be able to build a future. He wondered if Jason could keep a watchful distance, "Are you really going to leave her alone?"

Jason quickly reaffirmed Trey's suspicion, "You know better than to even ask that. I've waited too long for this chance with her."

"I'll make the call to change the detail."

"Thank you," Jason said with a nudge of his elbow to Trey's arm. "Can you take me home? I rode with her and she took off so I'm without a car."

Trey laughed. Aubrey was something else, "Let me wrap a

couple of things up here and I'll be right out."

***

His eyes were becoming heavy as he stared out the window at the bright light that beamed through the curtained window of Dragonfly. He could feel an aching pain building at his left temple and realized he didn't have any aspirin to relieve what was the beginning of a headache. The combination of the night air and the pressure of the day had worn him down and made him so very tired, but he had to watch her. He had made it his business to protect her whether she wanted protection or not. The chiming bells of his cell phone glistened on the bench seat next to him and he lifted it to see if he recognized the number of the person who was distracting him.

"Macie?" he was surprised at her number appearing in the view window of the phone. He pressed the button decorated with a green phone receiver and answered, "Hey, Macie."

"I heard what happened tonight. I was worried about you, and Trey wanted me to call and check up on you," the anxiety in her voice led him to see through to her genuine heart. "Is everything all right? He said that you weren't at home."

"I'm not," he didn't take his eyes off of the house.

"Where are you, Jason?"

He might as well tell her. She probably had a good idea anyway, "I'm parked a little ways from her house. I can't let her be alone. I still have a feeling that all of this is not over. Gina never confessed to sending the guy into her house and we still don't know what happened to Jake Warren. There are just too many questions with no answers and I can't leave her alone."

"I understand," he could almost hear her smile through the phone. "You don't have to convince me."

"I don't know what happened, Macie," he confided in her. "I thought I was finally getting through to her, showing her what we could be together, earning her trust. It all shattered again in a matter of minutes. I don't know if it was something I said or Gina said, but she put that wall right back up. I'm just not sure if I have the strength to ever get through it."

"She is a hard woman. She only knows how to be tough and protect herself," she explained. "Maybe she saw herself falling in love and needed to run before she got hurt."

He didn't accept that excuse, "I would never do that to her. This whole thing is driving me crazy. She is all I think about, all I dream about. I can feel her when she enters a room even before I see her there. I know her pain before she tells anyone about it. I have a deep connection to her now and I can't give that up. I sound like a blubbering idiot. I think I'm tired and delirious."

She giggled, "No, you're not. You're in love."

In love, he couldn't have fallen for her that hard that quickly, or could he? He knew he cared very much for her. She made his heart leap when she walked into a room. It skipped a beat at her touch. It was a feeling he had never had before, for any woman. Could he have crossed that line with Aubrey? Had she become the reason he woke up in the morning and the last thing he thought about at night because he had fallen so deeply for her? Had the harshness of their relationship become a faded memory to him, replaced by the hope of a future with her? He realized that he didn't just want her to stay in Walker, but he wanted her to stay...with him in Walker. It had become so much more, "Macie, I am in love with her. Madly, deeply in love with her."

The air had cooled tremendously since the rain had come through and the night was filled with the sounds of the owls in the trees and the gentle sloshing of the lake water against the bank of the slough. The weather would begin to shift now making its final descent into winter. It was hurricane season in the South and after some minor bouts already there was a tropical storm brewing in the Gulf that would make a serious punch along the southern coastline. It would cross through the islands building steam and then reach the shore with power. Once it hit dry land, probably along the Texas bend and as far up as southeast Mississippi, it would encircle the southeast like a pack of wolves ready to devour. It would leave rain, damage, and death in its path, and then settle into calming showers in a matter of days. After the trauma was over, the coastline would begin to rebuild what they needed, but inland Walker would begin to reap the beauty of the destruction. The cool air would signal the animals to settle down for winter or fly south for warmth. Hunters would clean their guns and prepare their camouflage costumes for the killing season. The last of the fiery leaves would loosen their hold on the limbs of the trees and fall to a blanket of bright color on the ground. For all of the rapturous beauty, he would be without her.

For ten years now he had been without her. He continued to sit in his truck quietly as his eyes opened and closed slowly with the drowsiness of sleep. But he couldn't go to sleep. He needed to watch out for her. He couldn't let her be alone, even if he had to do so from such a distance. All he wanted right now was to go stomping up to her door and knock, have her answer and with no words, no restrictions, take her into his arms and protect her, kiss her, love her. But she refused to let that happen. The entangled web that she insisted on having around herself would not let anyone get too close. What was it about tonight and Gina that had made her change her mind so quickly? For days now they had grown closer, gotten to really know each other, and in one night it was gone. He couldn't think clearly enough to figure it out. He was much too tired to find any conclusions, but his mind raced through the interview at the police station and that helped him stay awake.

Maybe tomorrow there would be some answers. He would pick at Trey's brain to see if he could help him piece it together, but he had to admit that he did have one other priority for tomorrow. He still had a murder case of his own that needed to be solved and earlier in the day there had been a lead that demanded his attention. Around two o'clock there had been an anonymous phone call to the station, but the caller had demanded to talk only to Officer McNally. Once Jason was on the phone, the caller had revealed that she had information that might be of interest to him in the Jake Warren case, but she had been both unwilling to discuss it over the phone or come directly to the station. She wanted to meet in a more neutral and familiar territory, so Jason agreed to drive closer to her and meet with her at a coffee house the next morning. Only Trey and Macie knew of this secret meeting. Someone in the department needed to be aware since it concerned an open case, and Macie was his back-up plan to help keep an eye on Aubrey until his return. With any luck, this new information would blow his case wide open, Trey would find evidence to connect Gina to

Aubrey's attacker, and it would all be over.

His eyes became so intensely heavy and as hard as he tried to let them close only for a few seconds, the time drew out longer and longer until finally they would no longer open and Jason fell into a deep sleep.

Chapter Twenty-Seven

Jason walked into the coffee house and glanced around looking for the mysterious woman who had called him the day before. She was somewhat vague about her appearance stating she would be wearing a coral pink top and sporting a short blond crop hairstyle that flipped out on the ends. Just from her voice over the phone he assumed she was maybe in her 50s. As his eyes shifted from the left to right side of the large room laid out with wooden tables covered in glass tops and walls decorated with historical pictures of the county landmarks, he caught the slight wave of a woman seated and noticed her attire. She must be the lady from the call.

He approached the table and asked, "Mrs. Lockhouse?"

"Yes, Mr. McNally. Thank you for agreeing to meet with me," she gestured for him to have a seat across from her. "Would you like some coffee?"

"No thank you. I'm fine. You sounded very urgent on the phone," Jason recalled. "Can I ask what this is concerning?"

"My, my, young man, you have no time to waste it would seem. You like to get right down to the point at hand, don't you," she seemed amused.

"Forgive me, ma'am, but I do have some urgency. I have to get back as quickly as possible," he retorted.

"Ahh, fair enough then. As I mentioned over the phone, I believe I might have information that will help you solve your 'man in the car' case," she began.

"And how did you come across this information?" he questioned.

"I was a close friend of Jane Todd and Jake Warren at one time. My name back when we knew each other was Kathryn Shields and my ex-husband is Johnny Shields. We were very close to Jake and Jane until an incident that tore our friendship apart," she glared at him remembering a time when the four of them had shared their lives together.

"I have heard of Johnny Shields," Jason said, "but he has been gone from town for a long time."

"That was part of the agreement that was made when Jake disappeared and I decided that our marriage was over," she began to wring her hands in a nervous gesture.

"Go ahead and start from the beginning if you don't mind," Jason encouraged her now as he was very intrigued by her words.

"Certainly. See, Jane and I had been friends since she settled in Walker many years ago. We had a lot in common, strong willed women that loved life, and we just hit it off quickly. She was a bridesmaid in my wedding to Johnny. After a few years Jane and Jake crossed paths and began dating. They were a great couple at first, both beautiful people and lots of fun to spend time with, then after a while it began to change. Jane became even more dedicated to her work. She spent a large amount of money on restoring her lake house, and focused her summers on her niece," she lifted her cup to sip her coffee.

"So they began to grow apart?" Jason wondered.

"More than that, they stayed together for all the wrong reasons. It wasn't like they had children or even pets to keep them together, but they didn't want to be tied to anyone else. Then Jake began to make regular visits to Gus's Pub on West and 3rd. He was seen flirting with numerous women, and then he was seen leaving with a couple of those same women at closing time. Rumors began to spread that he was cheating on Jane along with consuming excessive amounts of alcohol," she recalled.

"How did that affect your friendship?"

"At first we simply found ourselves doing fewer things together," she said. "Jane and I still tried to have a girl's lunch every once and a while, and Johnny would meet Jake at the Pub for a beer. Jane thought he would change if she just hung in there with him, but he didn't. She just couldn't see the truth for loving him."

"So, what led up to that night," Jason leaned back into his chair to get more comfortable.

"I have to admit that I've always held the guilt for that one," she raised her hand to nervously play with her earring. "I engaged in behavior that I was not proud of. Before we were married, I was unfaithful to Johnny and had an affair. I thought that since I had chosen Johnny in the end that he would accept it and move on when the truth came out, but he was furious," she leaned back as well. "He became very suspicious any time I went out especially at night. We would fight and he would bring up my past, something that I truly wanted to forget. Then he began to mention it in front of Jane, who was very aware of it, after all she was a close friend. I had told her everything before my wedding. Johnny just couldn't forgive and forget."

"Was Johnny a violent person?" he asked.

"He hadn't been up until then, but he let it eat at him until it became his obsession. Along with his distrust of me he decided to retaliate, and chose Jane. I soon realized that he wanted Jane both for himself and to get back at me. Jane didn't have the least bit of interest in Johnny. She had such deep feelings for Jake and thought that one day he might cross the wrong person who might use force to convince him that what he was doing was wrong. You know, maybe some other lady's man would rough him up a little and teach him a lesson. When that happened he would see his error and come back to her with loving arms."

"And it didn't happen that way?" he leaned back toward Mrs. Lockhouse folding his hands together on the table, resting his elbows on the edge.

"Not exactly, he did cross the wrong person, but it wasn't so simple. That night Jake had gone out to the Pub and left Jane at home, as usual. She called me and we talked for a bit. I told her that Johnny was getting to be more than I could handle and she admitted something that broke my heart. She had managed enough strength the night before to confront Jake about his cheating, and he had grown angry with her and struck her across the face. About that time Johnny walked in and asked who I was talking to. When I told him it was Jane on the phone he asked if Jake was gone for the night. That was when I let it slip that he had hurt her the previous night. Johnny became enraged. He left not long after and I was convinced that if we went to the Pub we could find them both. I went over to Jane's because I had a feeling that would be the first place Johnny went after he saw Jake. After a couple of hours or so with no word from Johnny, Jane and I headed out to find the truth."

"What did you find?" his back stiffened as he listened, enthralled by her account of the past.

"As we came around the corner and approached the pub. We saw Jake and Johnny arguing in the parking lot. They had both been drinking which didn't help the situation. It was hard to understand what they were saying, but then Jake got into his car and left. We hoped it was over and got out of the car to talk to Johnny, but before we could reach him we saw him hop into his truck and take off after Jake. I told Jane to get back in the car and we followed them both."

"Where were they headed?" Jason soaked up each word carefully.

"I think originally Jake was headed home. He just wanted to get away from Johnny, but Johnny ran him off the road out by the lake side on Highway 80 past the bridge. His car went down into the woods a little way. Jane and I pulled over to the side of the road about twenty feet behind Johnny. It was around 1:30 a.m. by that time and there was no one around. When Johnny got out of the truck he had a large crowbar in his hand and blazing fire in his eyes. I knew that Jane was about to get her wish."

"Her wish?" he asked.

"The idea that Jake would cross the wrong person one day and get a beating that might give their relationship another chance. Only there was no second chance. After the third blow to his back, I took Jane to the car. She was screaming and unable to control herself. As I forced her back to the car I saw Jake take the next blow to the back of his head. I was terrified that Johnny might come after Jane and me next. I saw his eyes and they were not the eyes of my husband. They were the eyes of a stranger. He had so much anger in him. We were very scared."

"What did you do then?" his eyes narrowed wondering where the story would turn.

"We were heading back into town, to tell someone, to get someone to help. I stopped once we got to the Pub and thought about the outcome. I didn't want them to take Johnny away. I didn't even know how bad it was, so we went back to Jane's instead. Johnny came looking for me after everything was over. We talked until the sun came up, but Johnny never admitted to what had happened. He said he realized that we were there when he heard Jane, but just couldn't stop himself. He wouldn't say anything beyond that, so we really didn't know the truth of what happened to Jake and the worse thing was that we never questioned it either. We agreed to never speak about it again and to go on with our lives."

Jason took his stare away from her as he let the facts sink in, "You said he is your ex-husband?"

"Yes," she replied. "As hard as I tried I couldn't bring myself to love him like I had before. Although, I didn't know exactly what he had done, but I knew he had done it for Jane, and I could hardly look at him from day to day. He was never the same and Jane had removed herself from both of us. She had found new strength in herself and had begun to start her life anew. I wanted to start over as well, so I filed for divorce and moved to Nashville. He agreed to move as well to let Jane have her life and to find something better for himself. As far as I know he has never set foot in Walker since then."

He drew a conclusion that had his head reeling, "Do you think he might know we found Jake Warren?"

"Mr. McNally, as soon as you pulled that car from the lake it became big time news. He knows and unless he has changed a great deal since we were married, he is nervous that you will discover the truth," she looked at him quizzically wondering where these questions were heading.

"Nervous enough to come back to town?" he continued.

"Maybe. Why do you ask?" she finally turned the tables on him for answers.

"Jane's niece inherited Dragonfly and was attacked in that house a few days ago. The assailant was looking for something, but we aren't sure why?"

Kathryn suddenly became uncomfortable, "What was he looking for? Do you know?"

"He mentioned something in a box with a Dragonfly on it."

"I remember that box," she said as she began to wring her hands again. "She always kept her dearest treasures in it, nothing of any value to anyone else, but they had worlds of value to her. She hid the box in a spare closet that opened into the hallway. She had jewelry, ticket stubs from movies we went to see, sentimental things like that. Oh, and she had this notebook in there. I had given it to her for Christmas one year." Kathryn gave a pleasant smile as she recalled that time in their lives. "Jane was always writing. She would write a phrase that made her laugh, song lyrics, and short stories. She was actually very creative with her writing. She said it was relaxing for her, almost therapeutic after a long day. I think she turned the book I gave her into a type of diary."

Jason began to put the clues together and recalled the book that Aubrey had discovered with passages written by her aunt, "Was the notebook leather with a dragonfly on it?"

Kathryn took in a deep breath, "Oh, no. You think he was after something in that book."

"Perhaps. Aubrey, Jane's niece, has the book and has read a few passages, but hasn't mentioned anything out of the ordinary about Warren or your ex-husband."

"There might not be anything in it, but Johnny doesn't know that," she revealed. "If he remembers the book then he might believe in the possibility that she wrote about Jake's disappearance in it. We all made a pact not to ever tell anything, but nothing was mentioned about writing it down. He knew how she loved to write. Since you found the body and with Jane's recent death, he might fear that something will be found in that book that could point to him."

"Have you heard from him recently or know where he might be?" Jason knew where his search would take him from here.

"No, but I believe my son has kept in touch with him. He

moved to Nashville last year, and I believe he has been in contact with his father. I can give you his number. Maybe he can tell you where to find Johnny. You said this person has already broken in to Dragonfly once? Johnny can be a very determined man, Mr. McNally. If he is behind this he will probably try again until he finds that box with the book."

"Aubrey!" Fear immediately bled through Jason's veins as he pictured Aubrey alone with her attacker on the loose. He no longer felt that Gina was involved. She had been telling the truth about her role in the attack. This person was after Aubrey for a very different reason and Jason had to get to him before he tried to get the book again.

"Where are you going?" Mrs. Lockhouse asked as Jason rose abruptly from the table and struggled to put his jacket on.

"I have had cops watching the house since the attack and I've been there with her until today. There hasn't been any sign of him, and we suspected someone else of hiring the attacker. Now there is no patrol on the house and with me gone, that has left her alone. He might be watching the house and he will know that no one is there with her. I have to get back to her before he does. Please forgive me, Mrs. Lockhouse, but I have to go catch a killer."

She bowed her head to him, understanding the urgency and said, "I'm so sorry, Mr. McNally, for not coming forward years ago with what I knew, but Jane and I felt it best at the time. I truly hope that Ms. Todd is safe. I know Jane loved her very much."

Jason thought of how much she meant to him too, "Thank you. I'll be in touch, Mrs. Lockhouse."

She shook her head knowing that her story would be told again one day.

Jason took out his phone and dialed Trey's number as he quickly started the truck and backed it out of the parking space. Time was now of importance for both him and Aubrey to insure her safety and catch the man he was now hunting.

Trey picked up after only two rings, "Yeah?"

"Hey, man I need you to do me a favor," neither had a need to waste time with greetings. "I need you to check around to all the local hotels and see if anyone has checked in under the name Johnny Shields. If not then see if anyone has noticed someone suspicious hanging around lately."

"A stranger at a hotel, that should be easy enough," Trey said sarcastically.

"I know there are strange people hanging around hotels all the time, but this one would have gotten there around the time we pulled Jake Warren from the lake," Jason informed him while speeding onto the interstate heading back to Walker. "He more than likely is around six feet tall with a good build and has dark hair or maybe even salt and pepper hair. His car should have Davidson county plates."

"So, does this have anything to do with the anonymous caller you met with today?" Trey wondered.

"I think I might have an idea of who we are dealing with now, what he is after and why," Jason gave Trey the condensed version of Kathryn Lockhouse's story. "He and his ex were good friends of Jane and Jake around the time of his death. The caller was the ex and she seems to think that he might know something about how that car ended up in the lake. You should run his name too. I don't think there are any priors, but let's be sure that we have everything we can on him."

"I'll get on it. Have you talked to Aubrey yet?"

"No." Jason said solemnly.

"Don't you think you should?" Trey prodded. "Maybe she has calmed down now."

Jason thought of the night before, "I slept in my truck outside her house last night. I just couldn't leave her there knowing she was by herself."

"Yeah, Macie told me you ended up there last night," Trey wanted to ease his friend's mind, but knew it was a lost cause. "I guess I can understand how she feels being watched over like a little kid. She is the strong independent type. I'm sure she just wants her life back to normal."

"I don't know how to get through to her, man," Jason felt frustrated just thinking about her stubbornness.

"She'll come around."

"I don't think so. Not this time. Look, I don't want to scare her with speculations. I'd rather make sure we are after the right person, but I wish we could have a couple of the guys drive by to check on her. If I call it in and she sees them drive by, I've had it," Jason felt as if his hands were tied and he couldn't get loose. "Let me know what you find out about Shields. Then maybe I'll give her a call."

"Will do. I tell you what. I'll make a drive by there, just to check in. If she sees me, she won't be as likely to get mad and think I'm checking up on her, or she'll think that it was Mac's doing. Will that make you feel a little better?" Trey's concern came through the phone.

"Thanks, just try not to let her know you are there. She might not think Macie first, and she will have my hide if she finds out we are still keeping an eye on her." Jason laughed as he relaxed just a little. He wouldn't trust anyone more than he could trust Trey.

"No problem. I'll talk to you soon."

Jason continued down the interstate praying that he wasn't too late and hoping that he was right about Shields. It was time to put an end to all of this. He turned his radio up and sped down the road with blue lights glaring and her face fresh in his mind.

Chapter Twenty-Eight

Aubrey stood in the bedroom with a suitcase spread open on the bed. She took out stacks of items from the dresser as the radio played a pop song she had never heard before. Folding each piece into a small package shape, she placed them carefully into the bottom of the bag. She would be bringing extra things back with her and needed to have as much room as she could for them. Macie made her way into the room bringing with her the requested items Aubrey deemed necessary to return with to Memphis.

"You can't be mad at him for anything with Gina. He went out with her before you came back to town," Macie said moving around the room with ease and joining in the packing effort, lending a hand to fold items in the same fashion.

"You don't understand," Aubrey shared with worry in her expression. "Something happened last night. The next time you see Jason," she stopped for a moment holding her favorite t-shirt in her hands, "ask him how his chest is healing."

Macie stopped her efforts and stared, "What are you talking about?"

Aubrey looked up at her friend with glazed eyes, "When he came here last night, I wasn't expecting him. I had the music playing loud so I didn't hear him come in. He simply placed a hand on my shoulder and immediately I turned a knife on him. I gashed him and he was bleeding badly."

She swung around and plopped down on the bed beside the suitcase. She still had a hard time admitting that she had cut him. Just to say the words aloud make her chest grow tight and her shoulders ache. Flashes of the look on his face as the knife sliced through his flesh were etched in her mind and she wanted to break down, but knew she would have to be strong, strong enough to let him go.

"Oh, Aubrey," Macie's concern broke into her thoughts.

"I was defending myself against someone who I know would never do anything to hurt me."

"It was just an accident," Macie came to sit down next to her. She wrapped her comforting arms around her friend in support.

Aubrey smiled, "He said the same thing, but accident or not, I couldn't live with myself if something happened to him. All of this started when I came into town, so it would seem that the trouble is with me. I care too much for him now to see him hurt," she lifted her head and turned to look Macie in the eyes, "So you see, it's not just Gina. It's me, and this place, and if I don't go now I might be tempted to change my mind. I have to leave it behind, Macie. It's just not meant to be."

"He cares for you so much," Macie narrowed her eyes letting the wrinkles come in waves across her forehead, "Don't you see that?"

"I've thought about it. In fact it is all I have thought about for days," Aubrey rose to continue her packing. She finally tossed the still wadded up t-shirt into the suitcase and picked up the next item, "and it actually helped to make my decision a little easier. In a few short weeks he has opened my eyes to emotions that I have never felt before. For that I will always be grateful. I care very deeply for him, so much that I'm going to let him go because it's what is best for both of us."

Macie wasn't buying the reason behind her urgent change of heart about Jason. She couldn't help but think that there was something that Aubrey wasn't sharing.

Macie narrowed her eyes accusingly, "You are in love with him."

Aubrey's head came up with a quick jerk, "What? I am not."

"Yes, you are, and it has you frightened, made you afraid enough to run," Macie rose from the bed staring in disbelief as Aubrey shook her head in disagreement.

"No. I've only been in town for a couple of weeks. That is hardly enough time to fall in love with someone."

"But you have, and you are scared to death," Macie felt proud of herself for diving into her friends innermost feelings and coming up with the correct answer for the quick departure.

"I didn't come to Walker for romance. I came with a task and I don't like distractions," Aubrey found the banter with her friend very intrusive.

"I believe you found some past feelings that maybe you never realized you had for him," Macie began to smirk.

Aubrey turned away so her face wouldn't reveal the truth. She knew that her heart had already deceived her.

"I can finish settling the estate from Memphis. That's all there is to the story. I do not want anything more than that," she forced the words out knowing it was a lie.

"I think you are making a big mistake, but then I've always thought that you fit in here."

"That's because you wanted it to be true, but it just isn't."

Macie looked around the room at the furniture, pictures, and treasures, "What are you going to do with the rest of these things?"

"I'll leave some of it here to help sell the house," Aubrey said glancing around. "I'm just going to send a moving truck to pack the rest up and bring it to Memphis. I was hoping you might be available to let them in when they get here, and watch them to make sure it all gets done correctly," she flashed Macie a begging smile.

Macie pursed her lips in disbelief, "I should say no just on principle, but since I have a hard time saying no to you I guess I can help."

Aubrey wrapped her in a grateful embrace. She knew she would be able to count on Macie for help. "Thank you. You know I don't want to hurt you, don't you? This doesn't have anything to do with our friendship. I need that to continue because I've missed being close together over the years."

"I know," Macie said sincerely. "With technology today we should really be able to keep in better touch, well that is if we ever get good cell and internet service around here. We will try harder, and I'll come visit more. Maybe we can meet in Nashville for a few days soon."

"I would love that," Aubrey smiled, straightening out the shirt in her hands and realizing it didn't belong to her. She brought it to her face to take in the fragrance he had left behind in the material and then she tossed it into the box at the edge of the bed as her expression again turned somber.

Dearest Diary,

I stood up to him tonight and it cost me dearly. I admitted to him that I knew about the other women and that I wanted him to change his ways or find the door, but he had other plans. I am writing this in hopes that if anything were to happen it would be found and my story heard. He did something to me that no other man has ever done. Right now I sit on my bed holding a bag of ice to my face. I have learned in a short amount of time that he does not care for ultimatums, and turns violent when he has been given one especially after he has had alcohol. I wasn't aware, but I will try my best not to make that mistake with him again. I had always believed that love could conquer all, if I carefully guided him in the right direction, he would find his way back to me. I cannot live with someone who chooses abuse over love. I do not intend to live with that choice, and I believe it is clear that he is making that choice. We have come to the end of the road for our relationship. If he shows another ounce of violence I believe I will take a trip to visit my brother, sister-in-law, and my precious Aubrey. I wish I could simply spend a few days with Kathryn and her handsome little boy, but I don't feel comfortable in her home right now. That is an entry for another day. For tonight I will try my best to get some sleep and hope for a better tomorrow.

Yours always,

Jane Elizabeth

Chapter Twenty-Nine

The groundskeeper turned the key in the lock to cabin number 12, and turned the knob to reveal a dark room. He pushed back the door and stepped out of the way in order to let the two officers enter with their guns drawn for protection if it were needed.

Trey had his weapon carefully pointed up with the curve of his right arm. Slowly he called inside to assure that there would be no surprises, "Walker police, we are here to ask you a few questions." He heard nothing.

Jason took his turn to enter the room, also sporting his weapon with his badge clearly clipped to his belt. He noticed the man following behind him, "So you say he hasn't been here all day?"

The man focused only on the empty room and searched the wall with his fingers to find the light switch he knew the officers could use, "Don't believe so."

Trey came back through the main living area after a quick glance through the other rooms and shook his head at Jason giving him the all clear, Jason turned to speak directly to the curious worker, "Well, we appreciate you letting us in."

"You say he is a person of interest in a case you're working?" the man let his curiosity slip through his lips. "It wouldn't be that

Warren man's case, is it? The one they found in the lake?"

"I'm sorry," Jason explained, "we really can't discuss the details of the case."

"You think he has something to do with that murder?" his eyes brightened and he sprouted a devious grin as if he wanted the inside scoop and believed the officer might actually give up the secrets.

"We don't really know." Jason was determined to keep his answers vague, and began walking the man back toward the door. "We just need to take a look around. I can only say that he is a person of interest right now."

"Oh, I get it. Hush, hush, until you find proof, right?" he was face-to-face with Jason's broad chest and felt the intimidation. "That's all right, I'll leave you to it. Just lock and close the door when you leave and I'll get out of your way."

Jason all but pushed him on out the door, "Thanks again." He quickly closed the door and turned around to find Trey flipping through papers left behind on the small round dining table that separated the kitchen from the living room. Jason returned his gun back to the holster that laid flat against his left kidney.

"Well, this guy isn't OCD or anything," Trey stated the obvious as he twisted his expression into one of an unpleasant nature and covered his nose to help avoid the neglected stench of spoiled food sitting in the heat of the summer. His stomach quivered while he stepped over empty pizza boxes and other trash left behind on the floor. "This place is a mess. There is garbage left behind everywhere. How does he live in this? He favors fast food hamburgers and fries among a lot of other things it looks like, so he has been here at least a few days now."

"Cleaning must not be on the top of his list of things to take care of while he is in town. Did you get a chance to go by Dragonfly?" Jason walked around the room shifting his glance from tables to walls to the floor looking for anything out of the ordinary. He occasionally picked up wrappers or clothing to get a better view underneath the well-lived in space.

"I talked to Mac. She was there helping her pack, but she said she would be leaving soon."

The two each made their way around opposite sides of the

room joining again close to the short hallway that led to the bedroom and bathroom.

"All this could mean that he isn't a perfectionist like a lot of premeditated murderers. He is more likely to leave behind evidence," Trey said digging through a stack of magazines on the floor and still finding nothing of interest.

"But if he is the one that came after Aubrey, he is clean at a crime scene. We found nothing in the house or the woods. We need to spread out and look around before he decides to come back," Jason said glancing around for the best places to search. He tapped Trey on the shoulder and motioned down the hallway, "I'll take the bedroom area, you check in there. Mrs. Lockhouse said he didn't show signs of violence until his obsession with Jane and even then it was always directed toward Warren."

"So, why has he come back to town now that we have found Warren's body?" Trey asked across the hall to Jason. Then his heart almost stopped beating in his chest as he saw the shrine made by a mentally damaged stalker of the beautiful woman with chestnut golden hair and emerald green eyes. "Jason, you need to see this."

Jason reached for an old cigar box on a shelf in the linen closet, "What is this?" He recognized the brand as being one that his grandfather used to smoke when he would visit. His mother had used the very same type of box to store money from yard sales in the summer time as he was growing up. He lifted the lid and then studied the contents carefully before shouting to Trey, "He has some ammo for a .38 in here. What did you find?" He took the box across the hall and into the bedroom to show Trey. He froze as his eyes make contact with the mirror over the dresser.

"Check out the shrine," Trey whispered.

Pictures in the standard 4x6 prints were posted with clear tape around every edge of the mirror. Her hair was a little darker and her eyes a brighter hue, but the facial features of the woman in the pictures were almost identical to Aubrey. Both men stared at the local beauty in business attire, elegant dresses and summer shorts in numerous locations throughout Walker, "These are pretty old pictures and all of Jane. He must have saved these over the years, but she's gone. Why would he still have these up?" Jason wondered. "He can't go after her."

Trey walked across the room to the other side of the bed and opened the double curtain to reveal another shrine of photos taped to the glass window that looked out over the lake, "Jason, it's not about her anymore. He has another target."

Jason turned around and immediately felt an ache rip through his gut. There she was with her auburn hair blowing in the breeze, one of her sitting in a chair reading, a couple with the sun shining on her glowing tan skin, "Trey, these are all recent pictures of her."

"I know," he agreed, "I remember seeing her in that outfit yesterday."

Jason narrowed his eyes to look closer at the photos and clear his vision. He pointed to one of the photos of her with a book in one hand and a glass of bronze liquid in the other raising it to her lips, "Wait, this is the back deck of Dragonfly. He has been taking them from the woods leading down to the lake. Trey, if he is watching her that closely…"

"Then he knows she is alone right now," they had reached the same conclusion and it made them both jump to action as if a taser had sent a volt of electricity through their bodies.

Trey took out his phone before Jason could get the words out of his mouth and they both started for the door, "I want you to get a call in to the station and have backup meet us out there. Go by the station and request a warrant for his arrest then meet me at the lake house. I'm going to head on out there."

Trey shook his head and they each made their way out of the cabin and back to their vehicle's, speeding off as quickly as legally allowed by officers with sirens blaring.

Once on the main road, Jason pulled his phone out of his pocket and dialed the number he now knew by heart. It rang for more minutes than he had patience for and her voicemail finally activated. He heard her soulful voice say, 'This is Aubrey Todd with Stark Real Estate, I am not currently available but please leave your name, number, and a brief message and I will be glad to return your call at my earliest convenience. Thank you and have a bright and wonderful day.' There was a short pause before the heinous beep made an eerie sound, "Aubrey!" he said with urgency, "Aubrey! Please pick up the phone baby. I believe I know who is after you. You have to be careful. If you get this message, go to

Macie's as quickly as you can." He hung up the phone to focus on driving. He had to make it to Dragonfly before Shields finished his objective.

Chapter Thirty

The phone rang making Aubrey jump startled at the sound. She knew that Gina was being closely watched, but it was becoming a habit when it came to loud sudden noises. She would have to readjust to things like that. She had hoped that Jason could help her overcome those fears, but that was over and she must go back to depending on herself. There he was again, sliding through her thoughts and her heart so easily, just as he had slipped into her house and her life after so long. She had spent most of the day trying not to think about him and she had failed miserably. Picking up the phone she took a breath before sporting a fake smile and softening her voice.

"Hello," she beamed stretching her hand across the counter to retrieve the squash and onions she needed to chop.

"I know it has only been a little while, but I made a promise to Jason and he would have my hide if he knew that I left you there alone," Macie sounded rushed.

"Please stop worrying. Gina has a police detail on her and you don't owe Jason anything."

"I can't help it. The whole thing makes me nervous," Macie wished she could leave the meeting, but it had become mandatory and as it often would, the boss had become long winded. "Is something wrong with your cell? I tried to call it first, but it went to your voicemail," Macie asked her shifting the conversation from the one person she was sure her friend did not want to talk about.

Aubrey shifted the cordless phone from one ear to the other, "Jason has tried to call and I'm not ready to talk to him yet, so I turned the ringer off."

"That explains it."

"Macie, did you cut out of part of your meeting to call me?" Aubrey wondered.

"I excused myself to make a trip to the bathroom," she explained.

"Honestly, it has been very quiet around here," Aubrey shared with Macie over the phone as she threw the vegetables into the sauté pan to cook. The aroma of garlic and butter seeped into the steam that rose up from the pan, "so you can stop check in on me, I'm fine. I thought I would have a nice dinner on my last night here, take a warm bath, and slide into bed early tonight."

"All right, I'll leave you alone. Have a wonderful evening *alone*. If you do need anything just give me a call. I'll keep my phone on vibrate."

"I will. I promise and thank Trey the next time you see him for all of his help with the Gina situation," Aubrey requested.

"Sure. Goodnight."

"Nite." She hung up the phone and went back into the kitchen to check on the chicken baking in the oven. It was time to cut the bread so she could toast up some fresh croutons for the salad. She never seemed to have enough time to cook like this in Memphis. It was nice to be able to act like a gourmet chef. This time would be over very soon. Was she really making the best decision? A slower pace of life would suit her if she would let it. No, she couldn't go back to that way of thinking. She had made her decision and she was going home to the city. It was for the best.

As she brought out the cutting board and sat it on the island in the center of the kitchen, Aubrey heard a noise that made her jolt upright and take notice. She stood very still for a while trying to let her ears adjust to the sounds around her hoping to hear it again, but after a few moments of nothing out of the ordinary, she returned to the task at hand. She lifted a serrated knife from the silverware drawer and crossed back to the island, this time with her back facing the opposite direction so that she could see clearly out the back windows to the lake. She had an eerie feeling that she was being watched. She decided that after the events of the past couple of weeks, it was probably just a normal over reaction to her natural surroundings.

With the radio tuned to a retro station, Aubrey began singing along with Phil Collins hoping it would help her uneasy feeling and get her in a more productive mood. She finished cutting the bread into cubes and tossed them with a little olive oil, salt, and pepper before pouring them on a baking sheet and popping them into the oven. They would spend the remainder of their time basking in the glow of the warm oven as the chicken continued to cook through. Remembering that she had left the new table cloth she had purchased at Alexander's Emporium in the back bedroom, she took time while her dinner was cooking to go get it to use as the base of her tablescape. She might only be here for one more night, but she saw no need for it to be less than an elegant one. Besides, it would remain on the table for display while her realtor showed prospective buyers the benefits of the open floor layout. It was a beautiful layout and the colors in the cloth bounced off of the wall color. She only wished that there were someone there to share it with, a friend and companion to enjoy the peace that she was feeling. He would have shared every moment with her, laughing, eating, kissing, and capturing her heart and soul. His passion had awakened something in her that no one else had ever been able to find. Why couldn't that be enough for her? Why couldn't she keep her word and let him go?

Aubrey returned from the back bedroom to hear a sound that reminded her of someone scurrying across a floor. Her powerful thoughts of Jason floated out of her mind as she became cautious.

"Is someone there?" she asked nonchalantly, thinking that maybe Trey had paid her an unplanned visit or even Jason. With no reply, she continued spreading the table cloth out over the dining table and walked back to the kitchen to fetch a classic white dinner plate and salad plate from the overhead cabinet above the dishwasher. She reached into the cabinet to take out only the things she needed, and as she turned back from the cabinet the two plates fell from her hands and broke into pieces on the tile floor. Aubrey gasped for air as she saw the dark image of a man in her living room, staring at her.

"How did you get in here?" Aubrey's eyes shot beams of terror as she stood frozen unable to move.

"You really shouldn't leave the door to the lake unlocked. If someone really wants to get in they only need to find their way around the side of the house, into the woods and up the path to the porch. I would have thought that your new boyfriend would have you be more careful than that." Every word from his mouth made her skin tingle with fear. She recognized his voice.

"What do you want?" she stuttered to get the words out. She already knew.

"To finish what I started the first time and to leave with the box," his growling voice sang in her ears as he let the words flow from his mouth like a rushing river. "Did you think I wouldn't come back?"

"I…I don't know," Aubrey tried not to let the trembling of her voice come through, but found it difficult to keep it in her throat.

"You know I could have gotten a lot more out of you that night, if you hadn't given me such a low blow. Did some defense class teacher show you that move in college?" he stepped out of the shadows with a crooked grin on his face and she saw him clearly for the first time. She took in his features and recorded them to her memory, even the small scratches she had left on his cheek from her previous encounter.

Aubrey felt a sense of urgency to not let this man terrorize her as he had done before. This time she needed to show him her strength. "I want you out of my house."

"This isn't your house. This is her house," he snapped at her.

"It is my house and I want you out," she took a step forward and stood with her hands by her sides balled into fists. She didn't know where the courage was coming from, but she prayed that it worked and he would decide it wasn't worth the fight. Her heart knew that wasn't going to be the case. If he had the guts to return to try for the box again, then he would not leave this time without it.

She was ready to make her move. Seeing the knife still on the island Aubrey whisked through the kitchen in one fluid motion, took the knife and came across the kitchen to approach where the man was standing. Before she had reached him, he removed his right hand from the small of his back and aimed the Smith and Wesson toward her head. With stunned eyes at the sight of it, she stopped.

"Now what do you think you are going to do with that?" he said with a laugh knowing he had the upper hand this time. He was prepared this time. She would not get away from him, this time. "Do you think you can protect yourself from me? Do you think that I can't take whatever I want from you?"

"It doesn't appear that you have gotten what you want just yet," she said in retaliation.

He took another step closer to her continuing to point the gun at her face, "You are a sassy little thing, aren't you. Well, we'll see how smart that mouth is. I think this might be fun after all." He lifted one corner of his mouth in a devious smile and immediately dropped it to a more serious solemn glare. "What has made you so cocky this time?"

"Jason will be back any minute," she said staring down the barrel of the gun knowing it wasn't the truth. "You should know that."

"What I know is that you told his back up boys to take the night off, and he has been on a wild goose chase trying to find out who I am," he furrowed his brows and pulled the chair out at the island to have a seat. "You have a new found confidence, Aubrey, that I am so impressed with. It's too bad that I'm going to have to shut that down."

She leaned back toward the counter knowing she didn't have an escape route if she wanted to avoid the gun.

"I'm going to try everything I can to keep it from you," she let it slip from her tongue.

His eyes opened wider and his face perked up. A genuine smile graced his lips, "So, you do know what I want. That makes it all very simple. All you have to do is give me the box."

"I don't know what you want with it. There is nothing in the box, but some old costume jewelry and family letters," she told him. "If you want jewelry I can give you my things that are worth more than anything in the box."

"I'm not after jewelry and I don't need money," he frowned and shook his head at her notion that he would be just a simple thief. "There is something in that box that is much more important to me. I want the book."

"The book?" she questioned.

"And since you know where to find it, I think it is time we go dig it up," he flicked the gun toward the hall to motion her in that direction. "Just remember not to try any stunts like you did last time and you won't get hurt. I really do hate violence."

She felt her heart beating out of her chest and with her knees shaking she turned slowly to walk down the hall. He closed the space between them and she felt the tip of the gun touch her side. She led him to the guest bedroom and dropped to her knees to reach under the bed. She fished out the twelve-inch, square wooden box with a dragonfly carved into the lid and handed it to him. He laid the box on the bed and opened the top, still holding the gun facing her and glancing back and forth from Aubrey to the box. As he sifted through the contents, he found that the one item he had hoped to discover was not there. He threw the box against the wall in a sudden fury that made Aubrey jump.

"Where is it?" he yelled at her as his face grew red with anger.

Aubrey fought back tears not knowing what he might do next, "I gave you the box."

"I want the book," he said through clenched teeth bending down to let her feel the force behind his words. He lifted the gun to sit directly on her temple and with his thumb cocked the hammer back.

She closed her eyes. "I don't have any book," she snapped at him with a tremble in her voice.

"He said it would be here. He said it was in the box with the dragonfly," the stranger began to panic and his breath quickened with each word.

"Who are you talking about? Are you working for someone else?" she asked.

"You are hiding it aren't you. You know what is in that book and now you have it protected just waiting for the right moment to give it to your boyfriend," he panted out the words.

"Just tell me who sent you and we can end this right now," she began to negotiate the situation, but he wasn't interested in a quick solution. He had a job to do and he wasn't going to leave this time until it was complete.

"Get up! Let's go," he lifted Aubrey to her feet by her arm and slung her toward the door before she had regained her footing and she fell into the doorway. He came behind her and put the gun to the back of her head. "I told you not to mess with me. That little smack I gave you the first time is nothing compared to what I could do to you."

She felt her bravery begin to waiver and her chest clenched tightly. He took her by the elbow and helped her back to her feet. They made their way down the hall just as they heard a knock at the front door.

"Keep quiet. Whoever it is can go away."

Chapter Thirty-One

"Aubrey," a strong male voice sang from the other side of the door as he continued to knock on the wood. She might not let him in, but she could never resist saying something hateful to him when she was mad at him. If he only heard her voice he would know that she was safe.

She moved a little quicker from her assailant to try to put a slight distance between them as she made the daring decision to answer the calls being made from the front porch, "Jason!"

The stranger quickly wrapped his hand around her mouth from behind and pulling her to him, he whispered, "That was a stupid move. I told you to keep quiet. Now tell him to leave. He knows you are here, convince him you are fine, but can't let him in right now."

"Aubrey, are you all right in there? Open the door," Jason said sternly not caring for the tone she used when she spoke his name. It had sounded a little desperate which made him now want to see her instead of just hear her sweet voice.

"Tell him," the stranger groaned into her ear. He removed his hand from her mouth one finger at a time to assure himself that she wouldn't ignore his request.

"Jason, now is not a good time," she said as calmly as she could under the pressure of his hand on the back of her neck and his gun at her head.

"You need to let me in, we have to talk," Jason tried to convince her to open the door for him as he continued to try to turn the locked doorknob giving it a shake.

"Brush him off or I will shoot a bullet through that door and hit him right in the chest," his words made her stomach twist into knots.

"I'll meet up with you later, OK?" her voice cracked slightly and she did her best to cover it. Would he notice the change in her voice? Would he believe her words or feel the fear in her voice?

"Is something wrong, Aubrey?" Jason asked quietly.

"No," she said very sing-songy. "I'm just in the middle of something and can't come to the door. It's not a good time. We can talk later, I promise," her voice trembled slightly at the end and she felt tears welling up in her eyes. If he did believe her and left, she would be as good as dead, but she needed to protect him.

"All right, come by my house about seven. Will that give you enough time?" he was buying it and soon he would be safe.

"Yes, that will be plenty of time. I'll grab us a bite to eat and bring it with me," she calmed down a little and her voice was finally steady and solid.

"I love you," his words were low and slow and dripped with concern.

She echoed back with all her heart as she closed her eyes, "I love you, too."

They could hear Jason's footsteps as he crossed back over the porch and walked down to his truck. It had worked. He was going to be safe. He cranked the engine and immediately drove off spinning gravel as he sped away. Her hope now was that he had realized something was wrong and had gone for help. When it was all over, she prayed that he could find it in his heart to forgive her.

"Good job. Now, that loverboy has left we can get back to business," her attacker could care less that her throat had just closed with those three words that Jason had spoken. Did she only return his words to give Jason some way of knowing that she was in trouble, or had she let them escape because she felt the ache of the words in her soul and needed him to hear her say them? "Now where were we, oh yes, you are going to tell me where you hid the book." He pushed her back out of the way of the door.

She wanted to buy a little more time, hoping for Jason's return with his gathering of officers, so she challenged him to tell her more about the reason he was there and after her aunt's possession, "What do you think is in the book that is so important?"

"She wrote about everything in that book. He was afraid that she told it all. If it is there and you or your man finds it, then it's all over for him," he said letting her go and spinning her to face him in the process.

"Who is he? Told what?" she asked searching for the reason he was so determined to get the journal.

"That's all you need to know," he said.

Suddenly, with a crack of the front door Jason burst in gun drawn ready for the battle they had all hoped to avoid.

"Jason, No!!!" she screamed and the stranger pushed her to the floor and pointed the gun straight at Jason's chest.

Jason held up his hand as if to calm the now very nervous stranger, "Hey, Brent."

"How do you know my name?" he asked.

"I'm a detective. It's my job to know," Jason answered. "I started putting two and two together. And, I had a nice conversation with your mom this earlier today."

"You leave her out of this," Brent snapped.

"We also found your cabin at the lake. Nice photography work by the way. It should give us plenty of evidence for a stalking charge," Jason continued watching Brent's face turn pink with heat as he took careful steps toward him. "Now, just put the gun down and we can all walk out of here safe and sound."

"I can't do that."

"Why are you doing this? It isn't your fight. You had nothing to do with it," Jason said as Aubrey listened to him coax information from Brent. As he began to open up to Jason and focus more on him, she saw the opportunity to slide into the back ground.

"You are not going to pin this on him," Brent was totally drawn to Jason's words and Aubrey reached back behind her to slowly open the hideaway drawer in the coffee table.

"Why are you defending him? He wasn't there for you," Jason

caught Aubrey's movement out of the corner of his eye. He kept Brent talking, emptying his heart of the trouble he held inside himself.

"That was my mother's fault," his words flew from his mouth like knives piercing through a target. "She took me away from him. She said he was a bad influence and that we were better off without him, so I grew up without my father."

"He was a killer," Jason raised his voice slightly to keep his attention.

"She didn't know that. He was defending himself," he snapped back waving the gun around while keeping it pointed at Jason.

From his peripheral vision, Jason saw that Aubrey had something in her hand and was raising it out in front of her and swaying from side to side nervously.

"Is this what you are looking for?" Aubrey raised the leather bound book to eye level so Brent could get a good look at it in her hands. His eyes glowed with excitement at the reddish-brown case in her hand. His mouth opened slightly and he was distracted enough for Jason to make his move.

"There it is," Brent let the words slip from his lips, "Let me have it."

Jason stepped forward reaching one hand for the gun and the other around Brent's neck to gain control of the situation, "Aubrey run." Brent's arm held the gun raised into the air and a shot went off into the ceiling of Dragonfly.

Aubrey turned to the sliding glass door and with unimaginable strength pushed it open to the point she was afraid the glass would break. She made her way through the door and ran to the back of the porch to the steps leading down to the lake. There was such a commotion behind her that she stopped for a moment wondering if she should return to help Jason. With shouts and bodies scuffling from inside she turned back to the steps and took them two at a time when she heard the sound that made her heart stop. There was nothing more but silence. Her mouth dropped open in astonishment. The gun shot had been so loud and suddenly she couldn't breathe. What had happened? Where was Jason? She first heard the sound of someone dropping to their knees then a body hit the floor of her house. As she dropped her head she could hear footsteps on the porch behind her.

"Stay right there or you'll be next," Brent's voice burned her ears and she felt her heart break inside her chest. She slowly turned around and raised her head to him as large tears fell from her eyes.

Chapter Thirty-Two

His hand was heavy with the weight of the metal pressed against it. He trembled and knew that if he tried to take his shot to stop her, he would surely miss the mark. He needed to be in a closer range to kill her and get the book, but he turned his mind to something else. Her aunt had caused him pain and this woman only added to that hurt. Jane Todd was the reason his mother had left his father, and the reason his father wasn't allowed in his life, but she wasn't here to suffer for her sins. She had died suddenly with no pain. Her niece would not be allowed the same luxury, he would be sure of that. He would make her suffer with the knowledge that she had caused the death of the officer who had cared so deeply for her.

Aubrey thought quickly. She had to tell him something to make him see the seriousness of his actions, that this was not a game. "Don't you realize what you've done? You have shot a police officer. You can't run from that."

"Oh no, you are not going to make this my fault," he shouted in protest.

He was talking, just keep him talking. Buy some time for someone to come. Someone else must have heard the shot, "What are you going to do? They will find you. The police force will hunt

231

a cop killer twice as hard as they would anyone else. You know that."

He shook his head with disgust, "You're right, they didn't look very hard when Jake Warren came up missing, did they? The rules are different in a small town, pretty. But don't worry. I have a plan for you."

"What plan?" she was genuinely interested in what he had come up with to make a double murder plausible.

"When they find his body in the house, they will start looking around for clues. That's when they will find you deep in the woods," her eyes grew large at the thought. "It seems that you took the officer's life and then couldn't bare the shame so you ended your life as well."

"No one would believe that," she almost stuttered the words. "Jason and I were seen all over town together in the past week. Our closest friends know how we feel about each other. They would never believe that I would shoot him."

A coarse grin swept across his face when he saw that his words had her frightened, "Of course not on purpose, but let's just say that you were taking a shower and didn't hear the doorbell. Your precious cop gets worried because he can't get you to answer the door and he becomes concerned that something might have happened to you, maybe your attacker has come back. You hear someone beating on the door and frightened you grab your gun. Just as you are getting to the doorway, he storms through the door and not knowing it is him, you shoot and kill him on the spot. It's so sad really. He had his whole life ahead of him, a great career too."

"No! No one will believe your story."

He continued, "Then heartbroken that you just killed your new lover, you walk into the woods in a daze and do the one thing that can end your suffering and the blame that the town will surely have toward you. You take your own life."

"How can you be so evil?"

"I do what I have to do to be a survivor. My father taught me that," he replied starting to walk toward her, closing the distance between them.

Who was his father? What was his connection to the book and

her aunt, "Your father?"

He inched in her direction with the gun still in clear view and she began to back away slowly. Her steps were careful so she wouldn't slip or cause a sudden movement that might startle his shaking trigger finger. She could see fire burning in his gray eyes as he spoke, "I guess you should understand why you will have to die. It is only fair that you know the reason behind it. Jake Warren's death was no accident, but I'm sure you have that part figured out. What you may not know is that my father killed him to protect your filthy trash aunt."

Aubrey's eyes darkened at the thought of him calling her aunt an untrue name. Her heart began to beat faster and she worked to keep her emotions under control. She could not tip her hand to him and let him be aware that he had aroused her feelings. It was best to try to be calm and keep him talking. Where was help?

"Jake and Jane had been in a terrible relationship for a long time," he continued, "but instead of breaking it off with him and finding someone else, she spent her spare time flirting with my father and coming on to him when my mother wasn't around. She was such a whore, strutting herself in front of him, in front of my mother. She didn't care if it broke up their marriage. Everything she did worked too because my dad fell for her and it tore him up when she would act so hurt when Jake would show up drunk or he had beat her. He hated to see her in pain even when she deserved it."

"But what does all of this have to do with me," she eased back a little more.

"It really isn't about you, but about the book. We couldn't take a chance that she wrote about any of it in the book. As long as he was at the bottom of the lake and Jane was alive no one would know, but when you got her place and then they found Warren, well, I just couldn't risk it. You should have let me have the book the night of the carnival. Although, I did enjoy my time with you. The way your body felt under my fingers was amazing. I could have had you so easily until you found your courage."

His smug grin made her belly twist into knots. She felt a thousand tiny prickles run across her skin when she thought of the night he had attacked her and how close he had been to her, whispering in her ear and touching her. She swallowed hard and forced the visions from her mind. She needed to stay focused.

"Now that you know the whole story, I can't let you live," he shifted his weight to his front foot and raised his outstretched arm in front of him.

Staring down the deep dark barrel of the gun, Aubrey took one last breath and closed her eyes. She muttered a final short prayer. The loud pop from the gun rang through her head and made her ears burn. She braced herself for the shock, for the pain, but it had not come. As she opened her eyes, she saw her enemy doubled over and viewed the rushes of red coming from his right hand. His terrorized voice bellowed in anguish and he fell to the ground. With surprise and relief that she still had her life, Aubrey took a few unsteady steps back from the man. Confusion setting in, she first looked to her right then turned her head slowly to her left to see Jason standing only twenty feet away with his Springfield .40 caliber semi-automatic still raised in defense at eye level. He was alive. She felt herself begin to sway and the blackness close in around her. Like the water swaying in the lake, her legs became weak and fluid. She could no longer see and the ground was cold and hard when it met with her suddenly limp body.

Chapter Thirty-Three

Her eyes fluttered as she struggled to awaken. She heard a muffled voice calling her name. Who was it? What had happened? Where was she? She had so many questions, but found it hard to get a clear picture of her surroundings. Why was her head spinning so? She once again attempted to open her eyes, and saw his handsome face. He was there and seeing him had not been a dream.

"Jason?" her voice was raspy and her throat prickled with soreness.

"Hey, Sweeney. How are you feeling?" his smile was a beautiful and a welcome sight.

"You're alive...but I heard the shot. I heard you fall," she told him as she reached up to touch his cheek. She wanted to be sure he was truly there in front of her. She needed to feel him not just see him to know that he wasn't a dream.

"Shhhh! It's all over," he brushed his hand across her forehead to sooth her fear.

"What happened?" she asked, still in awe that he was leaning over her alive.

"Bullet proof vest, babe!" he said with a wicked grin.

"And you're all right?" her eyebrows dipped with concern.

"I'll have a nasty bruise on my stomach tomorrow, but yeah, I'll be fine," he shook his head and helped her as she sat upright on the couch.

She couldn't take her eyes off of the miracle she found before her, "What made you put that on?"

"Are you kidding?" he gave a small chuckle. "All of us small town cops love to wear those things. It makes us feel important. Shoot, when I was a rookie I would sport my vest and a pair of tighty whities just to go get the mail out of the mailbox."

She couldn't help but laugh at his remark, "Don't make jokes right now."

"I'm sorry," he retorted.

"How did you know that someone was in the house with me?" she continued.

"You gave me a good clue," he placed his arm around her shoulders and let her fall against his chest.

"A clue? What was that?" she questioned as she leaned her head and let it rest just under his chin.

"You told me you loved me. I know you wouldn't say something that desperate unless you were in trouble," he said as his expression went blank. He hoped that she would give him a different reason for the words, but she remained quiet not arguing with his theory.

She rose up to look at him with a similar blank stare. She didn't know whether to admit the truth, or if she should keep it to herself. She had said the words afraid that something may happen to her, and she did not want to die without him hearing it from her. Now she tucked it all away in her heart.

"I guess not," she replied sadness filling her eyes.

"One of these days maybe I'll get the courage to ask you how you came up with that idea," he said as if reading her mind, "but for now I just need to know that you are safe."

She lowered her guilty gaze and returned her head to his chest, "My head is still spinning, but I think I'm going to make it. What happened to Brent?"

"We called for a bus to come get him and take him to the hospital. I believe he is in surgery now. He lost a lot of blood, but should be fine. We have officers at the hospital ready to talk with him as soon as he comes out of recovery and they get the OK from his doctor," Jason answered.

"That's right, he was shot," she recalled hearing the gun fire and seeing the surprised look on Brent's face before he fell to the ground. She had put it to the back of her mind after she saw Jason. It was all so vivid in her thoughts now.

"I only hit him in the hand. As much as I wanted to kill him for the hell he had put you through, I knew better so I aimed for his hand to relieve him of his weapon," Jason's voice twitched as he relived the brief moment that saved her.

"Why did he do it? If his father was the one involved in Jake's death, why did he come after me?" she rose again and twisted to face Jason. She was ready for the truth and needed to know what had made Brent so desperate. What made him risk so much for her aunt's journal.

"After we pulled up Warren's body, Johnny told him what had happened with Jake. Johnny, his wife, and Jane had all made a pact never to reveal what they knew. He always felt that Jane might have written about it in her journal though, so when we discovered the body, Johnny and Brent knew it would only be a matter of time before we found the journal since Jane was no longer alive and you had inherited all of her possessions in the house. If the secret had died with her it would all be over, but they couldn't risk something being in that journal. Johnny is sick and Brent didn't want his father to spend the rest of what could be a shortened life in prison. To prove his loyalty to his dad, Brent decided he would come after the book and had been stalking you for the past couple of weeks."

"How did you know it was Brent?" she asked.

"I didn't at first. The informant that I spoke with today was his mother and she told me what happened all those years ago, or at least what she knew about it. She was never sure that her husband actually killed Jake, but she suspected it. She said Johnny became obsessed with Jane, but Jane was never interested in an affair. As time went on he began to change and became possessive and violent at times. Kathryn grew weary of his obsession for Jane. She divorced him and took Brent with her, telling him that his father was a terrible person and had become someone other than the man she had married," he revealed.

"She was the 'Kathryn' that Aunt Jane spoke of," Aubrey discovered.

"Yes."

"How did you know Brent was the one who had broken in to Dragonfly?" she wondered.

"On a hunch, I had Trey call around to all the local hotels and lake cabins to see if any strange guests had been living there for the past couple of weeks. We were searching for an older man originally thinking Johnny might be the one we were looking for, but as it turns out a younger man fit the bill. Trey and I went over to the cabin to visit with the stranger, but he wasn't around. The manager said he came and went often, so after some coaxing we convinced him to let us take a peek inside the cabin. What the stranger left behind spoke volumes for our case."

"What was that?" she found herself getting nervous at his response to her questions.

"It was obvious it had something to do with you. There were pictures tacked all over the bedroom window of you. He had been stalking you and photographing you since the day after we pulled Jake's body from the water. There were also some old photos of Jane too, probably given to him by his father, as a reference since your features are so much like hers. Just like his father he became obsessed with a Todd woman at Dragonfly."

"Pictures, of me?" she was in shock. He had been watching her, following where she went, witnessing her private moments. He had invaded her life. Had he seen her with Jason, in their more intimate moments?

"Once Brent was old enough and decided to find his father, he heard a very different side of the story than his mother had shared growing up. He felt she had stolen time from them and he didn't want the remainder of that time to be spent on a Sunday afternoon visitation from behind prison walls. He didn't want anyone to ever know the person his father had been or what he had done. The only people who stood in his way were Jane... and you."

"She kept her end of the pact as far as I know. She didn't tell anyone what she had witnessed, and always seemed to believe that Jake simply went away," Aubrey confessed.

"Well, at some point in a last ditch effort to win her love,

Johnny admitted to Jane what had happened that night. According to Brent he tried to convince her that he did it out of love for her. When she stayed true to her friend and refused him yet another time, Johnny finally gave in to the divorce from Kathryn and left town never to be heard from again."

"So Kathryn kept her end of the deal as well?" Jason could see that it was all beginning to make sense to Aubrey.

"He never truly confessed to Kathryn, so she just put it out of her mind and moved on with her life," Jason had found relief in that. Kathryn was not directly involved in any of it.

"The only solid evidence, he believed, was in the book," she realized.

"Depending on what Jane wrote, it could be enough to open a case against him," he agreed.

Aubrey shook her head, "That's just it Jason, she didn't write anything in the journal. There were no details connecting Johnny to any crime, not even a mention of Jake's murder or anything that happened that night."

"I guess Brent didn't think he could take that chance, so he decided he would do whatever he needed to get his hands on it."

"So, what do we do now?" Aubrey asked.

A smile slipped across his face, "Brent, will be arrested and charged with crimes against you and me. His dad may be arrested too, but more than likely we won't find the hard evidence we would need to convict him in Jake's murder. We were only able to get a partial fingerprint from the car and any blood evidence is inconclusive."

"We go on with our lives as if it all never happened," she turned away from him and Jason quickly reached for her and drew her back around to face him.

She fell deep into his rich blue green eyes, "We let the past be the past, and move on to the future. This is only the end of a chapter, Aubrey. There is still the rest of the story to experience."

Is that the way he moved on from each case he investigated? He would simply close that chapter and wait to begin another one. It seemed so easy when the words escaped his lips, but there were so many twists and turns on the road to a happy ending and then again not every situation ended happy.

Dearest Journal,

My soul is crushed. I have reason to believe that Jake has made his choice and he has chosen to move on to another life. I have not heard from him in days and although I worry that something could have happened to him, I believe the truth will lie in the fact that he has moved on from me as many in town told me he would do.

It has been three days. Three days since I have seen Jake, three days since I have talked to Jake, three days since I lived through what may be the worst night of my life. I without a doubt believe something tragic has happened in this town, but I dare not accuse anyone. I can only state the facts and I refuse to cast stones or feed blame. Three nights ago was indeed the last time I saw my love, the man I pledged myself to, the man who continues to disappoint me by being false in our relationship. Three nights ago as he had so many times before, he took himself to the local tavern and drank to improve his mood. Three nights ago I followed him there and then watched him leave. Three nights ago I saw another man stand up for my honor, and three nights ago I turned my head and walked away. I can't say for certain which road he took, or if he was forced, so I won't say anything at all. Three nights ago I lost my love, forever and I will have to move on with my life.

I was always afraid that his infidelity and alcoholism might be the end of him, and I can't say that he didn't deserve to have his world torn apart as he had done to mine so many times. Fear drove me to understanding the dire situation I was involved in and courage brought me to the conclusion that he might one day get what he had so foolishly avoided until now. That's not to say that he isn't just fine, shacked up with some pretty little blond thing a few towns over, but I will say there are benefits living in a small community where friends are family and family are important. They will always take care of their family.

With that said, I wish him nothing but the worst for the rest of his deceitful life. May his next stop be one that will show him the type of person he has been to others, and may it force him to want to repent instead of repeat his sins.

Until my dying day, I will have nothing else to say about Jake Warren.

Sincerely,

Jane Elizabeth

Chapter Thirty-Four

Silverware clanged together and the background noise of the diners talking left a low hum in Jason's ears as if a bee were buzzing around his head. He could almost make out the conversations from the tables both to his left and right. One couple carried on about how they were going to spend the rest of the day in the warm glow of the fall sunshine. Coming to a final decision, they wondered how the lake would look from the state park trail that they would hike in mid-afternoon.

From the other direction two ladies sat reminiscing about old high school classmates and the upcoming alumni tailgate party before the local high school homecoming game. They discussed the pros and cons of the years past and wondered if this parking lot party would be different since there was a new alumni president this year.

Jason tried hard to focus on the words coming from the man across the table from him, but noticed that there were also some stares and whispers in their direction, certainly curious onlookers questioning the rumors of what had actually transpired last night at Dragonfly.

"Did you hear me?" Trey raised his voice to his friend to demand his attention.

Jason's head snapped back around, "Sorry, what did you say?"

"It's nice to have a day off, man," he repeated.

Jason let the corner of his lip curl up in a half smile, "You aren't kidding. I still can't believe how it all unfolded. So, what are you going to do today?"

"Thought I might go out on the lake and do a little fishing," Trey answered plunging his fork into his scrambled eggs.

"Thought about that myself," Jason followed suit and dug into the sweet syrup and pancakes.

"Something else seems to be on your mind though," Trey chewed and let his eyes narrow in concern.

"It's nothing," Jason shook it off. He wasn't sure he wanted to get into a conversation about what was truly eating at him.

Trey put his fork down in his plate and leaned back in his chair. He was not getting out of an explanation that easily, "It's something, spill it."

Jason fumbled with his food, not looking up because he didn't want to face his companion and give him a chance to read his expression. He was sure it was clear as a bright azure blue sky on his face. He missed her and desperately wanted to see her, talk to her about what might be in their future. Trey was his best friend, had been since grade school. He already knew what was on Jason's mind without even looking at him, so a confession wasn't really necessary when it came down to it.

Jason drew back in his chair and took in a deep breath then released it out of his chest along with his resistance for the truth, "I thought about going by and seeing Aubrey for a little while. I realized this morning that we haven't actually spent any quality time together since this whole thing started. It has been laced with a murder case or her break in case and there hasn't been a time that we weren't talking about one of them. We could actually be together without any pressure from what is going on around us."

Trey slowly let a sinister grin emerge, "Sounds like you have another type of fishing in mind. Why don't you head on out that way. I think you will be a lot happier spending your day off with her than pinned up in a bass boat with me."

Jason grinned and shook his head in disbelief, "Who would have ever thought, me and Sweeney Todd. She is really something else. I can't get her out of my head."

"You don't have to get her out of your head, as long as you can keep her in your life," Trey advised him.

"Well, if it isn't the town heroes, or maybe the town's biggest idiots. I haven't decided yet," they both turned and lifted their heads in the direction of the female voice dripping with sarcasm and love. Macie stood over them happy to know they were both safe and sound after the second hand stories she had picked up around town and the immediate account from Aubrey. She leaned over placed a gentle kiss on each of their cheeks as a silent "thank you" for their bravery.

"Hey, we have done our 'Protect and Serve' duty. They actually gave us the day off," Jason told her as he gave her arm a playful pat.

She beamed with gladness at them and her voice became solemn, "I'm glad you are both all right. I was scared to death just listening to Aubrey tell me the story late last night. I offered to come out and spend the night with her at Dragonfly because I knew there was no way she would be able to sleep, but she insisted that she would be fine. "

Jason went back to forking his fluffy pancakes, "I thought I might take a drive out there to check on her later."

Macie's smile dropped from her lips and confusion filled her eyes causing a frown line to form across her forehead, "You might want to go this morning if you plan to see her. Haven't you talked to her?"

Jason looked up suddenly concerned, "Not since I left last night. Why?"

"You really don't know do you?"

He put his fork back down on his plate and scooted his chair from the table to angle it toward Macie, "Don't know what?" he asked.

"She's leaving in a little while to go back to Memphis," Macie told him quietly bracing herself for his reaction.

"What?"

She shook her head hoping his broken feelings wouldn't release themselves to her, "I'm sorry. I assumed she told you. She has given her statement and they said she was free to leave if she needed to."

"She can't leave, not with everything that has happened," the volume of his voice gathered the attention of the other diners as they began to turn their heads toward the commotion.

"Her plans haven't changed. She had her bags packed ready to leave today," Macie added.

"And she wasn't going to tell me," he was hurt beyond what he could explain in words. His heart ached that she wanted to leave him now. He didn't understand how she could simply walk away. He arose from his chair because he felt that he needed to do something. As much as he wanted to rush after her, he wasn't sure that it would even matter. He couldn't stay here though. He could barely even think straight anymore. How was she doing this to him? His head started spinning like the carnival ride they had enjoyed together only a short time ago, when they had found each other's hearts and shared each other's passion, before all of the fear had set in. He was finding it harder to catch his breath and heard the noise of a familiar voice.

"I'm sorry, Jason. I really thought you knew," Macie said again.

He regained his composure and not able to look at either of them quietly whispered, "I have to go stop her. She can't leave me now, not now."

"I'll take care of the bill here," Trey stepped in. "You go see if you can change her mind."

Jason turned and looked down at Trey who understood without explanation that she had seeped into not only his life, but his heart and his soul, "Thanks, man. I'll owe you."

Jason took Macie by the shoulders and gave her a quick smacking kiss on the cheek. Before she could respond he was running out the door of the diner and fishing his keys out of his pocket to make the drive to Dragonfly before he was too late.

Chapter Thirty-Five

With the last of her suitcases in her hands, she walked out the front door of Dragonfly. She sat them down and turned around to close the door behind her. She would miss the beauty of the pewter insect attached to the navy blue paint. She ran her fingers over the wings carefully so she could remember the feel of the metal beneath her fingertips. She slowly swept back around with a pleasant beam on her face and her eyes met Jason's as he stood like a cement stone at the bottom of the steps.

He fumbled to find words and wasn't sure he had actually spoken them as the rumble of the syllables rang in his ears, "What are you doing?"

Aubrey stiffened her gaze and raised her head, "What does it look like I'm doing? I'm loading my car."

"Why?"

"I have to go back to Memphis."

His eyes narrowed in disbelief, "You are going to leave just like that."

"I need to go back to…"

"After everything that has happened," he interrupted, "you know, I'm not going to let you go that easily this time."

"But, Jason…"

"I didn't believe you the last time you left when you told me you weren't coming back, so I'm not letting you go this time without a fight," the frustration began to build in his voice.

She could barely look at him and let her eyes wander from the ground, across the porch, to the crystal blue sky and back to her hands that she was beginning to fidget with in front of her, "It's different this time. I don't have that anger."

"I spent ten years of my life with an ache in my heart and I'm not going to do it again. I should have come after you and not let those years go by without seeing you. Look at me, Aubrey," she regretfully raised her face to connect with his, "I am sorry, but this time I'm not letting you go without saying what I need to say."

"Jason, please don't…"

"I love you, Aubrey," she took in a quick breath as she felt her chest tighten, "I have always loved you. I just didn't know it until you came back. Macie was right about my other relationships. I couldn't find the right person because none of them were you and I see that now. You are what I've been missing in my life. I know it is hard to believe because of our past, but it is the only thing that makes sense to me."

"Can I say something, please?" she begged.

"As long as you tell me you won't go," he pleaded.

She shook her head and began down the few steps that felt like a mile long walkway, "I can't tell you that."

"Why?"

It was time to find her courage, "I haven't changed my mind. I don't belong here. What do you want me to tell you?"

"You could tell me that you love me."

She wanted to say those words so badly, but knew if she did it would change nothing and complicate everything, "You are making this so hard for me."

He became furious with her choice, and felt his hands ball into fists next to his sides. She was not going to let him in, no matter how much he cared for her and he knew she cared for him, "Go ahead and run then, you have always been good at that."

"That's not fair."

"Oh, isn't it," he began to raise his voice to her as he took a step back. "That's what you have been doing for years, running from anything that could make you happy. When are you going to live your own life and do what is best for you?"

Her voice trembled as she shouted at him, "And you think you are what is right and what is best."

"I don't think I could be wrong," he retaliated throwing up his hands in a surrendering gesture.

"What did you think?" Aubrey became defensive against Jason's assertiveness. "Did you think that I would come back to town and you would turn on that sweet country boy charm and sweep me off my feet? That would be all it would take, right? I would fall head over heels."

"I thought you would stay because you wanted to. The past couple of weeks, what has happened between us, wasn't a scheme. I didn't plan any of this," he verbally struck back at her taking a few steps to stand directly in front of her.

"No, but you are taking advantage of the situation."

"Oh," he threw his head back letting the sun beat down on his face before glaring directly into her hazel eyes, "Do you think I am putting a guilt trip on you? Stop fighting me," Jason took her face in his hands and pulled her closer until they were only inches from each other, "I am in love with you."

He embraced her mouth with his desperate lips, breathing life into her heart and feeling her melt into his essence. The warmth of his lips seared through her body torturing her from the inside out. He released her mouth and stood still gripping her in his hands. His forehead was pressed against hers as if he wanted to share his thoughts telepathically so she would see his visions of their life together. He closed his eyes to more deeply feel her breath as the cool air swept around them. This was his last chance to change her mind, to make her understand his passion for her.

"Tell me to stop. If I mean nothing to you, then tell me to stop and I'll walk away."

She took his wrists in each hand and clung tightly to him. She closed her eyes to collect her thoughts. Her heart was beating at such an alarming pace that her feelings were barely able to keep up. Finally, she pressed the words from her mouth like whispers from the trees blowing in the autumn wind.

"I can't do this, Jason. I can't...stay." She regained her

composure and pulled away from him releasing his hands from her face and sliding them back to his sides. "Please, just let me go," tears began to stream down her already flushed cheeks. "You are breaking me apart. Don't you see that?"

She turned away from him and took her luggage into her hands, lifting it as if to prove to him that she had enough strength to walk away. She attempted to stroll around him and stopped even with him and looked to the side to try to catch his gaze, but he only stared down at the ground directly in front of him. All of the sudden the silence between them had become deafening and she was barely able to handle it. She faced forward once again and continued, determined not to look back.

He stood facing Dragonfly, afraid to turn around to watch her leave. He knew the ache in his chest wouldn't be able to bear watching her get into her car and go. He listened as she opened the passenger side door to her BMW, threw her suitcases in the back seat, and slammed it shut. Her feet shuffled as she moved around to the driver's side of the charcoal colored vehicle. She opened the driver's door and took one last look at his back, then quickly got into the leather seat. Not taking the time to buckle her seatbelt or adjust the mirrors, she simply put the car in drive and sped out of the driveway, back to her old life in Memphis.

After he was sure she was gone, he walked to the porch, turned around to see the remaining dust she had stirred, and sat down on the top step. Then with a release of his fears and feeling, he let his face drop into his hands unable to believe she was gone.

Chapter Thirty-Six

The bustle of waiters and waitresses made her head spin. Of all places to come for dinner after the exhausting day she had faced, she had chosen Beale Street. Normally Aubrey drew strength from the activity at the Rockin' Blues Café, as the smell of tender juicy barbeque ribs whiffed by her leaving her salivating in the wake of the fellow diner's plate. The atmosphere was always alive with the music of the fathers of blues and the caroling of round, African American women dressed to impress their audience as they belted out strong voices that demanded attention. The rustle of a diverse group of onlookers and chiming of silverware made it difficult to concentrate, but you didn't come to Rockin' Blues to think clearly. You were there to partake of delicious concoctions and to find freedom. Aubrey needed both.

She heard a mumble in front of her as her eyes scanned the room to settle on the vintage Gibson Les Paul guitar hanging on the wall in a glass case. The waitress finally snapped her fingers to get Aubrey's attention and she shook it off as she cleared her head.

"What can I get you?" the blond haired gangly twenty something asked.

"Just water for now, please. I need a moment with the menu," Aubrey answered.

She sat and stared as person after person walked through the door. A handsome man in his late twenties swept in barely picking up his feet as he walked. Jason did that when he strolled across the police station floor so confident the first day she went to see him. She had been so angry with him that day, but that was the day...

She brushed her fingers gently over her lips. She could suddenly recall the heat of his lips pressed to hers. Her eyes drifted closed and she could see his face, his dark eyes burning with passion. Her heart skipped and she had to catch her breath. The quiet peace that she had felt as she saw him was immediately interrupted with the loud bustle of music and another group of people entering. Her eyes skimmed first one side of the restaurant and then the other taking in her surroundings and remembering where she was. She was alone. She was always alone.

***

The sun came through her office window violently making her forehead draw and increasing the lines in her face. She had grasped at sleep relentlessly the night before, just as she did most nights. Weeks had passed since she had left, but her dreams were filled with Walker both when she was asleep and awake. She could feel his strong arms around her, hear that Lady A song playing over and over when the radio wasn't on, then she would see the blood on his chest and hear the gun shot. More than once she had woken screaming frightened that it had not been a dream and he was dead. Then she would relive the dream during the day, trying her best to determine why the memories were haunting her.

"Ms. Todd," she jumped at the voice coming from the black box, "Mr. and Mrs. Doubthitt are here for their appointment," the cheer in the voice of the receptionist was apparent even through the speaker of the multi-line phone.

"Thank you, Heather. I'll be right out," Aubrey pushed the red key to end the call and spun her leather chair around to pull out the file of George and Cheryl Doubthitt. It was time for her to put on her business look and do what she did best. The couple had called Aubrey to enquire about selling their home. It was a beautiful brick four bedroom house in the suburban area of Collierville which was known for winding two lane roads and wealthy lifestyles. The couple had made the choice to move to Georgia to be closer to their hometown and grandchildren. It would be a nice commission for Aubrey, but first she had to convince them that she was the right agent for the job.

Aubrey walked down the hallway from her office and turned the corner to see the couple sitting comfortably on the couch holding hands. She approached them with her outstretched fingers and Mr. Doubthitt shook her hand vigorously as polite introductions were made. Aubrey led them into the conference room and asked them to have a seat at the rather large table that could easily seat twelve to sixteen people while she closed the door for privacy.

She began her presentation with the research she had produced leading into her pricing strategy and ending with the ideas she had developed for her marketing plan. The onscreen charts were bold and she knew she had made an impression by the expressions on their faces. Aubrey was pleased with her work and confident in her ability. It was time to close the deal.

"And as you can see, Mr. and Mrs. Doubthitt, by using our latest resources in social media we can extend the outreach to potential buyers by 20%. Our publications reach thousands of homes each week and we will actively have your house on the market in time for the next issue the middle of next week. Through our numerous organizations in which we hold memberships, we will be able to publicize your residence throughout the western region of the state as well as Northern Mississippi and Eastern Arkansas. It would stand to reason that we should be able to sell your home in an estimated three to six months. I believe our statistics will lead you to conclude that this prediction is very obtainable. Our background at selling homes in this area, certainly those homes that are priced as well as our suggested price for you, will prove this task to be very much in our reach. I feel we can accomplish this while demanding the top dollar amount that you deserve making it a success for all parties involved," she paused waiting for an astounding agreement from the seller's, but there was only silence for what seemed to be a lifetime.

The couple took a moment to look at each other and without words they reached a combined conclusion, "That all sounds very comforting, Ms. Todd," George Doubthitt began, "but I have a question for you."

Surprise swept over Aubrey, but she tried her best not to let it show, "Yes, sir, Mr. Doubthitt," she gave him a willing smile. "Would you like for me to go over something again for you."

The gentleman shook his head as he leaned forward on the table placing both elbows on the glossy wood and threading his fingers together, "No, no, just answer me this. Do you have any family, Ms. Todd? Any children to speak of?"

A strange question she thought, "No sir, I'm afraid I don't. Some would say that I am married to my career, but I hardly understand what that has to do with selling your house."

"Oh, that's too bad, you see because there are some things in life that are much more important than money," he looked over at his wife, smiled and then turned back to Aubrey. "I certainly hope you will not take this the wrong way, Ms. Todd, but although you have nice charts, graphs, and fine speaking skills with your social media and all, we are looking for someone who in invested in us as much as they are invested in finding someone to buy our house. See, we are hoping for someone who understands what it means to fit into a home, to have that feeling that it is the right place for them to not only live, but grow as a person, as a family, as a unit. We believe a person should be able to see themselves in a house, know what it will be like to have the kids running around the living room or friends and family gathering and chatting in the kitchen. We just feel that this is too much of a business for you, Ms. Todd. You need to find that feeling yourself before you can understand the feeling someone gets for a home. It is more than just a house, you know. It is home."

She was losing them. Because she didn't have a husband or children she was going to lose them as clients. But she was a determined person, business oriented and good at what she did. Did she have to have a family to prove that she was Wonder Woman? She had devoted years to growth as an agent, and sacrificed friendships and relationships to be a success. Now, this man who didn't know the first thing about her was telling her that she wasn't good enough to represent him because she didn't have a home, because she didn't feel at home in her own apartment, because she didn't feel at home in her own life anymore?

"I see. Mr. Doubthitt, I will be glad to tell you a little bit about my home. This is a business to me, it is my job, my career and I love my work," she stopped and gazed past the gentle man realizing the very place he had mentioned was only seconds from her grasp and hours from her life, "but I do have a place that feels like home. My dear aunt gave it to me when she departed this life. It is a lake house about six hours away in a small town called Walker." She began to smile as the memories poured back into her mind, racing through her like a tidal wave. "My best friend watches over it while I'm here. It is beautiful with a fireplace in stone and a solid wood deck. There is an old plank path down to the dock where the neighbor leaves his canoe. The crickets chirp and the trees blow in the night air. The leaves change to such wonderful colors in the fall. There is peace at that home and my aunt named it Dragonfly because no matter where you go in life, just like a dragonfly, you will always fly back home. So, you see, I believe I do understand, Mr. Doubthitt. I've just had a hard time finding my way back home."

Chapter Thirty-Seven

"They got a trial date set for Brent Shields today," Trey shot the words out to Jason as he passed by him in the main lobby of the police station. It was the end of the day, but Jason had been busy with a vandalism case and Trey with paperwork from a car wreck from earlier in the week.

"Yeah?" Jason replied laying a small stack of papers on the desk of an overweight jolly lady whose fingers moved so quickly across the keyboard it was astounding.

"It is supposed to start a month from Tuesday," Trey looked for any spark of interest in his friend of who might be involved with the trial.

"That's good," Jason said blankly. "It should be over pretty quick unless they try for some type of crazy defense."

"I guess Aubrey will come back for it." Trey decided to be blunt instead of dancing around it.

"I don't think she has to," Jason kept his emotions in check. He thought about her often, but didn't need to let on to anyone.

"What are you waiting for man? Just call her," Trey had made the statement so many times over the past month that Jason had almost grown tired of hearing it. "It's not right. You were meant for each other."

"I appreciate what you are trying to do, man, but she made her choice, and it wasn't me," he breathed a sigh. "Anyway, that's all in the past now. It's been over a month. She isn't going to come back now, not ever."

Trey was getting used to the rejection of his suggestions to Jason. He had given up on Aubrey, and although he loved her he was going to abide by her rules and let her go. "You want to go grab a bite to eat?"

"I think I'll just head home," Jason lowered his head as if in defeat. "Maybe I can get to bed early."

Trey pursed his lips and shook his head in agreement, "All right, I'll catch you later then."

"Yeah," Jason's voice was solemn. There she was in his mind again, fighting to escape, but he just couldn't let her memory be and it would haunt him another night.

"Hey, McNally!" the gravel voice came from across the room as Sergeant Mason was hanging up the phone on his desk. "We just got a call in from old man Carter out at Cedar Grove. He said that he heard some noise and saw lights at the Todd place."

"Dragonfly?" Jason said with confusion. "There's no one out there. Aubrey went back to Memphis weeks ago and Macie hasn't found a renter for it yet."

Mason rubbed his hand down his face, "That's what Carter thought too, so he called it in. Are you heading that way?"

"Yeah, I'll go by and check it out. Maybe one of the realtors is showing it or something, but it doesn't hurt to make sure," Jason tilted his head toward Trey in a gesture to the door. "Later?"

"Call if you need me."

He agreed with a shake of his head. The meaning behind the simple comment spoke volumes between the friends.

Jason pulled into the driveway and saw the front door of the Dragonfly standing open. The light of the living room shone through the fading night sky and began to attract the insects that had managed to make it through the first cold snap of the season. He stepped out of his truck quietly as not to arouse the suspicion of whoever might be inside. If it were someone as simple as a real estate agent showing the rental, he wanted to be able to explain himself quickly and refrain from terrorizing them. However, if this were an intruder, he needed to be prepared. He walked up the steps slowly with his gun drawn. Stepping to the side of the door he only let his eyes breeze through the doorway to see if there were anyone in plain sight of him. Then seeing no one, he turned and walked in through the doorway sweeping the area with his weapon as he searched for the visitor.

"Walker police," he shouted as he took a few more steps from the foyer to the living room. "Is anyone here?"

Suddenly her ears tuned to the rambling noises coming from the walkway just inside the front door. She could hear his footsteps stop and she knew his stare was brutal and ready to pierce through her like a knife. She slowly turned to face him. He lowered his drawn weapon.

"Aubrey?" she caught her breath so tightly that she was afraid to move. She couldn't release it. She felt as if she were choking. He immediately put his weapon away and went to her to take her into his arms before she fell to the floor. "I was ready to shoot. I thought someone had broken in. Is something wrong?" he said brushing ringlets of auburn hair from across her forehead. His questions came so quickly. She still had not been able to release her breath and could only stare at him with fright in her eyes. Once she regained her focus and her heart began to beat normally again he asked her, "What are you doing here?"

She raised her head drawing her hazel eyes up to see his handsome face full of stubble and worry, "I came here to see you."

"You made it clear the day you left that I didn't mean the same to you as you meant to me," he released her from his grip. His words were daggers to her heart, but she knew he would harbor hard feelings. She had expected the resistance. She reached out to take his hands, but he tucked them quickly into his pockets.

"It wasn't like that Jason. I couldn't explain it to you because you were so upset and hurt. I didn't really understand my feelings myself. I couldn't uproot my life just because you came to my rescue or because a wind of change blew through our lives that made us see each other as grown-ups and not children. I had to know if what I felt for you was real," she pleaded her case with sincere enthusiasm.

"And?" his eyes narrowed.

She walked over to the middle of the kitchen counter, opened the drawer to the right, and took out a piece of paper. She unfolded it and handed it to him, "See for yourself."

He took it with hesitation, not taking his eyes off of her. He straightened it in his hands then looked down and read.

"What is this?" he asked seeing the words but not ready to comprehend them.

"It's the paperwork to complete the transfer of my real estate license to an agency in Walker."

He lowered the paper then turned his blue green eyes back to her, "Are you saying…?"

"I bought out the lease on my apartment," she told him with great freedom in her heart and a smile on her face.

"You what?" he removed his other hand from his pocket and tilted his head in disbelief.

"There is a moving van coming with my things tomorrow," she continued.

"But you and the city…"

"I went back to Memphis," she lowered her head as if she was a child caught with her hand in the cookie jar, "and you were all I could think about. I missed you." Shrugging her shoulders, she raised her head to face him, to let her words bore into his soul. "I can't stay there. I can't stay away from you. I shouldn't have even tried. I'm going to move to Walker, and live at Dragonfly."

"Then why did you leave," he had to have the whole story.

She looked past him to gather her thoughts and with pouting lips and a deep sigh she focused again on him, "I have built my whole life around being successful. I deliberately pushed away anyone that could interfere with that. I refused to let a man take control of my emotions because I didn't want him to be able to control my life. I didn't want to ever be hurt. But as hard as I tried to keep you away, you always came back. I didn't want to have any type of feelings for you, but I did and I didn't know how to stop them except to leave. You were right. I was running away, again."

"Aubrey…"

"No, let me finish. When I heard the gun shot that night I felt like my heart had been ripped from my chest. The only thing that ran through my head was how was I supposed to live if you were dead. So, I decided the day I left that it would be safer to find a way to live without you. I wasn't giving you a clue through the door that night when I told you that I loved you. Thinking he was going to kill me, I had to tell you the truth before it was too late.

Jason, I have spent so long trying to be just like my Aunt Jane, a strong and independent woman that didn't need a man to take care of me. All this time the only thing she wanted for me was to find the happiness that she had found here. She was in love with this place and I can see why. I want to be close to Macie and I want to get to know the people of Walker. I want to be happy and in love. No more trying to be like someone else, I need to find what I am looking for and right now I am looking for you."

He scooped her into his embrace and into a hard kiss that encircled them with warmth and fed their obsession for one another.

"Aubrey Elizabeth Todd, I can live with that. I am so in love with you."

She returned the kiss wholeheartedly as she wrapped her arms around him and fell deeply into his embrace. They could almost touch the future they would build together in this quiet little town, where friends were there to offer a helping hand and love was overflowing.

Aubrey drew herself back to stare into the eyes of this often challenging, always incredible man.

"Now, what are we going to do about Macie and Trey?"

He simply laughed.

Epilogue

My dearest Jane,

Today I give my love, my heart, my soul and my life to one man. He is enthusiastic, passionate, creative, breathtaking and most of all everything my heart could desire. We never believed we would ever be destined for this day. If anything, we should be as far from each other as humanly possible, but your thoughtfulness and love brought a new world to me at a time that I needed it the most. In turn that new life brought me to him. I can't be without him, in my darkest days and brightest hours he is in my thoughts and my prayers. His physical beauty is only intensified by his inner strength and compassion. My future is finally stable and glorious and I hope you know how much a part of that you have been, not only now, but always. I will be grateful to you for the rest of my life. I love you and miss you every day, but I know that your blood surges through my soul and your spirit moves freely through Dragonfly.

Yours always,

Aubrey Elizabeth Todd

Photo by Erin Cassell

ABOUT THE AUTHOR

A Tennessee native, Carrie Sparks McClain always saw herself as a writer spending her younger years penning songs, essays, short plays, and newspaper articles. Using her writing skills to earn a bachelor's degree in public relations from Middle Tennessee State University, she returned to her hometown to marry her college sweetheart and work in undergraduate admissions at Sewanee: The University of the South. Carrie's love for writing continued through creative music sessions with her husband and friends until she met the challenge of a New Year's resolution and began her first novel. She has found a passion for writing fiction with the completion of her first book *Dragonfly*. Carrie also enjoys cooking for her family and friends, entertaining and spending time on the lake with her husband and daughter during the warm seasons of the South.

Made in the USA
San Bernardino, CA
06 July 2014